Michael

A novel by Gerald Jones

OTHER NOVELS IN THIS TRILOGY:

The Consequence

Sam

ISBNs:
Paperback: 978-1-80541-476-6
eBook: 978-1-80541-475-9

For my great grandson, Sterling Pryce Alksne

"If tears are the substance of emotion could
handkerchiefs hold the meaning of life?"

Gerald Jones 2023

Acknowledgements

Kevin Wilson
Shan Lewis-Hobbs
Wyndham Ward (retired RAF 'Red Arrows' pilot)
Ian Williams
Eric Praton
Newtown Library, Powys
and Beryl for coming up with the last two words of this book

1

Michael adjusted his goggles and peered over the side of the Tiger Moth, the rush of air filled his lungs as the methodical purring of the gypsy engine filled his senses. Flying amongst the clouds gave him the feeling of freedom he had expected. The only thing to compare with it, was when he went skinny dipping in the Irish Sea off the Welsh coast the previous summer and even that was a poor comparison. The plane dipped its starboard wing and banked, slipping into a steep decline that stirred his stomach. At eight thousand feet, the plane levelled off. Michael glanced at the altimeter in front of him. He'd got to know every dial on the instrument panel and the reason for it being there. The instructor, sitting up front, had told him when he got into his seat to place his hands on his lap and not to touch anything, his job, he had added, was to observe. The joystick between his legs was a temptation hard to resist but resist he did.

Michael's interest in flying started at the age of fourteen when he saw a yellow by-plane flying over his home in Llandyssil, a village in mid Wales, five miles from the English border. The Tiger Moth intrigued him. He wanted to know how it stayed in the air. Michael would ask his father questions he couldn't answer. Michael's questions were constant and so when his mother was next in the local town, she called at the newsagents and bought a magazine, "Popular Flying" by W. E. Johnson. This was the start of Michael's obsession and many more magazines and publications regarding the principles of flying followed, all of which he had been eager to read.

Michael had left school at the age of fourteen and, like those who had left with him, had started work in the surrounding area. For the first six months he flitted from job to job, too young to be taken seriously and not old enough for the same reason. Farm work was not what he wanted and to work in the timber industry, he wanted even less. He was meant for better things. His dream was still to fly, to become a pilot but the reality of this happening was slim, due to his background and his limited education. Nothing short of a miracle would get him where he wanted to be. However, aircraft engines had to be serviced and put right when things went wrong, as they invariably did. Michael realised that the only way he had any chance to fly was to become a mechanic and join the support crew at an RAF base, to join those people that were invaluable in keeping aircraft flying. He would start as a mechanic and somehow worm his way into the cockpit of whatever machine had wings.

Six months before his fifteenth birthday, Michael began working weekends at Corfield's garage in

Abermule, a small village a two mile bike ride from his home in Llandyssil. There he learned about the things that intrigued him most, engines. Car engines, motorbike engines, stationary engines, those that drove belts that made things work, any block of steel that had pistons in its belly would one way or another become instrumental to his future.

Walter Corfield, whose father owned the garage, was a few years older than Michael. The previous year he'd taken his Velocette motorcycle to the Isle of Man to compete in the Tourist Trophy races. His endeavour's that year had not amounted to much, in fact he didn't finish the race. However, undeterred, the twenty five year old pursued his obsession and for the next three years entered the same competition.

In June of 1934, Michael started work full time at the garage. A month later, Walter tried his luck at the TT races again. This time he fared a little better and finished twenty third in the senior MGP race.

During this period at the garage, Michael was busy learning his trade and Walter's fascination with the Isle of Man TT races was an added excitement.

"Now that's one hell of a motorbike," Walter announced as he tossed The Daily Sketch onto the table where the boys were having their dinner break. Michael read the headlines.

"Too Big for Wealth and Glory
Lawrence the soldier dies to live forever"

"Did your Dad ever see Lawrence, Michael? I mean when he was in Egypt during the war?"

"I believe so," answered Michael, still reading the report of the death of T.E. Lawrence.

"I think he saw him drive past in his Rolls Royce on the way to Damascus."

"What happened?" Walter queried, pointing his finger at the newspaper.

"He crashed while riding his motorcycle."

"A Brough Superior, like I said, one hell of a bike. Apparently, it was given to him by a fellow by the name of Bernard Shaw, George Bernard Shaw, the playwright?" Michael looked up smiling.

"What's one of those?" Walter smiled back.

"Someone who writes plays."

"Like Shakespeare?"

"Something like that." Michael looked again at the pictures of Laurence, one was of him in full Arab kit, as Lawrence called it, and the other in military uniform sitting astride his motorcycle. Michael looked at the date of the newspaper. Monday May 20th 1935.

Three weeks later, Walter was sending his Excelsior around the winding roads of the Isle of Man. Again, he wasn't able to finish. A year later he entered one last time. His motorcycle stood the course and he finished in 6th position, not bad for a local lad.

One Saturday morning in the first week of April 1938 when Michael, had just removed a front wheel from an Austin Seven, he heard a car pull up on the garage forecourt. Taking an oily rag from his back trouser pocket, he wiped his hands. The car door of a Wolseley opened and out stepped a rather flustered man, he looked over Michael's shoulder into the garage.

"Can I help you sir?" Michael asked smiling.

"Well, I hope so," answered the man with a look of concern.

"The car isn't running as it should; do you have a mechanic that can have a look to see what's wrong?"

"Well, the boss is in town and the other mechanic is having a day off," said Michael, still smiling.

"What seems to be the problem?" Michael noticed an attractive looking lady in the front seat, flipping through the pages of a magazine. The man was quite tall, in his mid-thirties. He wore a dark blue blazer with silver buttons and cream trousers, he spoke with an undefined accent. His handlebar moustache and slick combed, black hair were typical of a 'privileged' man.

"It doesn't seem to be firing on all cylinders."

"A fuel problem," said Michael, still holding the rag in his hand, "would you like me to have a look?"

"Have you worked on one of these before?"

"No, not one of these, but I believe it's got a six cylinder Morris commercial derived 3.5 overhead valve engine." Michael paused, then stated the obvious and determined to make an impression, "as you will be well aware, Wing Commander, all combustion engines, whether in a car or an aeroplane, work on the same principle? By the way, I'm Michael." Michael couldn't help but smile as the man he'd just referred to as Wing Commander stood open-mouthed and then, with an equally broad grin, asked how the young man standing in front of him knew that he was a Wing Commander.

"Is that not your RAF uniform coat on the back seat of your car sir? If so, then your ranking insignia is on the sleeve." Michael glanced through the passenger window, and the gentleman's gaze followed.

"Very observant of you Michael," the Wing Commander said. "You seem to know your engines. Do you think you can fix it?" Michael didn't answer as he opened the side panel of the car bonnet.

"Not firing on all cylinders, you say? It could be a number of things so let's start with the obvious. Fuel line, spark plugs, maybe the fuel mix."

"How long will it take?" the man, now sounding anxious, spoke as he would to a mechanic and not to a young kid who would hardly know what he was about.

"A half hour, maybe a bit longer should do it," said Michael, not looking up. "Perhaps you'd like to pop next door for a cup of tea, the pub is open and they cater for people passing through, I presume you're going up to the coast?"

"Your presumption is correct, Michael. I have five days leave so I thought we would visit Aberystwyth." Without a thought, Michael went around to the passenger side of the car and opened the door. A shapely leg, followed by another, swung over the edge of the tanned leather seat. A lady emerged from the warm interior. The cream clutch bag she held matched the cream suit she wore. Her wavy blonde hair, free of any adornments, fell to her shoulders and, for the want of a better word, she smelt exciting.

"Thank you," she said and smiled as Michael closed the door behind her.

"Not at all," answered Michael, noticing a wedding ring on the hand that firmly held the clutch bag. The scarlet lipstick she wore reminded Michael of his Aunt Megan when, on the odd occasion, she got all dolled up to go somewhere special.

"I'm Sorry," said the Wing Commander, "I didn't introduce myself; I'm Simon Fairweather and this is my wife, Jennifer. We were married just yesterday."

"Congratulations," said Michael as he watched them turn and walk over to the pub. Mrs Fairweather's heeled shoes of cream and brown leather supported the fine legs he'd seen exiting the Wolseley and he couldn't help noticing the perfect line of her seamed stocking. "An attractive lady," he thought.

Simon had left the keys in the ignition but Michael didn't need to know how the car engine sounded, and after taking it into the garage he went straight to the spark plugs. The first one he looked at had a slight furring, the second and third the same. The fourth was in a state that couldn't possibly produce a spark, that's the one he said to himself. He didn't bother looking at the other two, he just replaced the lot. Next came the carburettor, checking the fuel line as he removed it. The carburettor he cleaned with a toothbrush in a dish of petrol, before replacing it and making sure the float was free and working properly. Feeling that he'd done what was necessary, he lowered the side panel of the bonnet and went to get a dust sheet to place over the driver's seat. The moment he turned the key, the engine came to life running like new. He let it idle for a minute, then put his foot down on the accelerator. The engine responded as it should. He switched the car off, took out the key and removed the sheet covering from the seat. Michael was quite pleased with himself as he sat in the office to make out the Wing Commander's bill. Ten minutes later Mr Fairweather poked his head around the office door.

"Have you finished?" he asked with a bounce in his voice. Michael looked up and rose from his seat. He had already taken the car out of the garage and parked it on the forecourt. Michael smiled but didn't reply. He walked to the car and opened the driver's door and handed the Wing Commander the keys. Fairweather turned the key and the engine sprang to life.

"What was the problem?"

"I've replaced all the spark plugs and given the carburettor a good clean, all seems fine now."

"How much do I owe you?" Fairweather reached into his jacket pocket.

"If you follow me," Michael said, walking to the garage office. Mr Fairweather paid the bill that Michael had already written out, after which the two men spent a short time discussing Michael's work and his future plans. Michael explained his dream of flying and his hope that working as a mechanic was a step in the right direction. Wing Commander Fairweather listened intently. He was already impressed by Michael's ability to fix his car and his astute observation skills. During their discussion, Michael had managed to refer to his knowledge of the De-Havilland Tiger Moth and the gypsy engine that kept it in the air; all the while, trying to show that he knew what he was talking about without sounding like a 'clever sod'.

Wing Commander Fairweather was intrigued.

"How old are you, Michael and how do you come to know so much about the Tiger Moth?"

"I read a lot," smiled Michael "and I turned eighteen on the 1st of January, sir." Simon paused and stroked his chin.

"At the moment I'm stationed at Shawbury, you know of it?"

"I do, it's a few miles the other side of Shrewsbury."

"I don't know how long I'll be there, as things are starting to hot up in Europe, so I may not be there when you arrive."

"When I arrive?"

"It seems, young Michael, that you are dead set on joining the RAF, so I suggest you give me your details and I will see what I can do."

"Will you be able to get me in as a mechanical technician?"

"I have no doubt about it, getting you in the air is another matter, but I have a feeling you will get there eventually. I'll make enquiries as soon as I'm back." He smiled. "Pack your bags, Michael, you'll be going on the ride of your life."

Above him, Michael watched wispy clouds float by, their damp vapour mysteriously suspended by heaven knows what. Below, green fields passed by. Michael was amused by the fact that everything looked flat; the scene giving no indication of any rise and fall of the land. He was now higher than any tree he had ever climbed and thus a damned sight higher to fall from. In front of him, every now and again, the pilot, with gloved hand, pointed down and then banked the plane for a better view of what he wanted Michael to see. The smoke from the Cambrian Coast Express train rose into the air leaving its trail way behind. For a mile they flew parallel with it, then veering to port, they climbed and headed back to the airfield. The sounds and vibrations, sky and land, the rise and dips, moments when he would catch his breath and the exhilaration of being in the domain of the birds. "This," he thought, "was just the beginning."

2

Within three months of Michael shaking hands and giving Wing Commander Fairweather a stunted salute on the forecourt of the garage in Abermule. he had joined the RAF, as a mechanic at Shawbury air base in Shropshire. To what degree of influence Commander Fairweather had in getting Michael a position in the hangars of Shawbury he didn't know, but his first objective was realised.

Politics, a subject Michael was not remotely interested in, soon became a subject on everyone's mind. On the 17th June 1939, Michael was taken up on his first flight. The reason, he gathered, was to show what he and his co-workers were capable of doing with just an array of screwdrivers, spanners, nuts, bolts and the knowledge needed to get planes to fly. Without them nothing would get off the ground. On that same day Hitler's Brownshirts had attacked hundreds of Jews in Berlin, pursuing the antisemitic stance of the Nazi regime. Five days later a British ship was bombed and sunk in the waters off Valencia, bringing about a marked increase of activity at his and all RAF bases. German aggression was rife in all of the British newspapers, resulting in more personnel walking through the gates of the base, increasing the numbers in all sections. Older men, along with some senior officials, feared war imminent, but it didn't happen. Over the coming months other incidents took place, with Germany being the instigator of aggression. Again, nothing happened, except of course for a steady increase in sabre rattling speeches in the House of Commons. The crying out for revenge and the threats of war now becoming a common topic of people's conversations.

It was only a matter of time when the question of Britain entering the war became one of when and not if. That question was answered on the 3rd of September 1939 when Prime Minister Neville Chamberlain, in a radio broadcast announced on behalf of the government and its people, declared war on Germany.

Michael was four months short of his twentieth birthday and two months after the declaration of war, when he stood with eight other trainee pilots in the cold November operations room at his RAF base at Tern Hill, seventeen miles from his first base at Shawbury. His presence there, he had learned later, was in part due to the recommendations of the Wing Commander whose Wolseley he had fixed on Abermule garage forecourt eighteen months earlier. Other reasons being that Britain needed pilots and lots of them. Plus, his own dogmatic belief that he could succeed in the profession, if that's what it was, to become a pilot. Michael wasn't the first and wouldn't be the last ground crew mechanic to put down a spanner and pick up a RAF flying helmet. He had studied, reading through his textbooks dozens of times and never missed an opportunity to be up there with the birds. It was they and they alone who were the masters of the sky. On hot days, in the summer months he often watched them from outside the hangars in Shawbury, buzzards soaring on the warm thermals, that rose from the corn and wheat fields surrounding his base. Seeing them, seemingly in slow motion, dip and raise their tail and wing feathers, adjust, and trim their bodies, functions needed to be done before they could accomplish a determined flight path. If only I could do that he would say, if only, but there was no answer to these creatures' ability to fly.

The realisation that flying could also be the cause of his demise, was, at this time, just a passing thought. If taken seriously he would have abandoned the idea of becoming a pilot a long time ago.

3

Five years had passed since Sam and Grace had left Liverpool docks for New York. In that time Sam's perception of the little Welsh village where he had spent his early years hadn't changed. For him, it was, and always would be, a place to leave from and a sanctuary. Whether in body or mind, it was a place to come home to. His recollection of leaving eleven years earlier to follow in the footsteps of Michael Gill, a man whose tales of adventure were relayed to him by his Aunt Megan, had become a distant memory, but not too distant as to diminish his memory of wanting to go in the first place.

Sam had collected his mail from the lime green mailbox that stood outside his home on Hudson Street. He stood for a moment sifting through the letters and flyers, placing them in order of importance. Business correspondence went to his office workshop and personal letters were delivered to the house. With the flyers placed on the bottom, Sam looked at the topmost letter. He knew who it was from and what it contained. It was an invitation to Billie Fleming's seventeenth birthday party.

The Fleming's had become like family to Sam and Grace. Sam first met Joe, Pageant and Billie in a railway carriage travelling to Liverpool docks en route to America. At the time, Billie was six years of age. Joe had a position awaiting him as a newspaper reporter for the New York Times and Pageant, as Sam recalled, had sat smiling, looking demure and altogether charming. Sam slipped Billie's invitation into his pocket as he carried the rest of the mail to his front door. Inside, he placed the bundle onto a small table and picked out another letter. It was from Michael, a close family friend. He was in the habit of writing two or three times a year, telling of how things were in his life. He had forbidden his mother Megan to mention him in her letters, much preferring to tell Sam about his life in his own words. Michael had mentioned about becoming a garage mechanic in previous letters and always asked after Grace and the children, before going on at some length about what particular car he was currently working on. Michael used mechanical jargon like 'overhead cams', 'rocker arms' and 'crankshafts', words that were not in Sam's vocabulary. This letter dated the 11th September 1938 started off in much the same vein, but unlike the others, it detailed a significant step forward in Michael's life. He told of his first flying experience in a Tiger Moth. "You remember Sam, exactly like the one that flew over our house when you were home last?" Yes, Sam did remember the aeroplane flying over. How could he forget the visit and saying goodbye to everyone? His father had seemed broken, just saying the words, "see you next time you're home." His mother had cried, and his Aunt Megan had shed a tear.

Michael wrote of the chaos in Europe, a fact Sam was well aware of. Michael had intimated the importance of the RAF if conflict with Germany was to happen. For a moment Sam stopped reading. He looked blankly at the page. Don't wish for something that may not occur. Michael: already feared that the prospect of war seemed more probable than not. Sam crossed the hall and entered the kitchen. Willena was at the sink humming a gospel song. He placed Michael's letter on the kitchen table and said, "Hello."

"Jesus Lord Sam! You frightened the life out of me, you do that one day and I's drop dead." She turned and gave Sam a big smile.

"Before use ask, Henry is upstairs and the rest have gone for a walk; Miss Mary came over and she gone with 'em."

Willena had lived in this house since she was a child and Sam sometimes forgot that Willena actually owned the home that they lived in, since it was left to her in the Will of its late owner, Mrs Margaret Doyle. Willena was well into her seventies and was at first reluctant to give way on what she called 'her duties' in the kitchen, but give way she eventually did and now, as she got older and with young children in the house, her presence in the kitchen became visibly less, instead she chose to spend time at her church and knitting clothes for Sam and Grace's children.

Sam's business, manufacturing coffins, had now grown to a point that he could spend a day away from the workshop. Since he had arrived home, following his trip to Wales and marriage to Grace, Sam had read the conflicting reports of the American economy. Domestic affairs were still the number one concern. With the depression not really being over, but in a better state than it was five years earlier. Even now in September the need to look after your own was still the priority. The outlook on world events differed from those in Europe. Their main concern was the expansion of Germany into neighbouring countries, but Europe was still a long way from the shores of America. President Franklin Roosevelt, although concerned with the goings on across the water, was too preoccupied with the state of his own country, to get involved with matters that didn't concern them.

Grace had settled in surprisingly well, and after the birth of Henry, her health and that of their son were what mattered most to Sam. Henry was six months old when Grace's parents finally arrived. They stayed in the house for four months before moving into a small apartment that Sam had bought for them, a five minute walk away. Sara was born two years later and Mary, named after Grace's mother, eighteen months after that. Jimmy came along sixteen months later. Willena and Mary were a godsend in looking after the children, giving Grace the time to do the book work for Sam's business. She wasn't for, as she put it, hanging around waiting for her children to dirty their diapers and change them every half hour or so.

Diapers being a word she had got used to saying. Nappies, as Willena would remind her, was a British word and not used in America.

George, Grace's father, worked twenty hours a week at Sam's workshop, sweeping floors and generally being a dog's body to the carpenters at their work benches. With little responsibility and a lot of free time, his interest in American history grew.

<h1 style="text-align:center">4</h1>

Four days after Sam had received Michael's letter, Willena went to Long Island to stay with friends. Sam drove her up on the Friday morning and had arranged to collect her the following Friday. Five days later, a tropical hurricane made landfall. It hit Long Island, New York, and New England. It was a ferocious storm. Sam and his employees battened down the workshop as best they could, then he told them to go home and look after their own. Debris was flying across the roads, and the rain was such that Sam found it difficult to drive and was running over all manner of things that had blown onto the road. He made it home and parked his car on the forecourt. An uprooted lime tree lay across his lawn, the branches of which hampered his access to the front door. The door opened on the lee side of the wind which at least meant that it opened easily. He rushed through the house shouting Grace's name.

"We're in the cellar!"

He could hear Grace's voice. Sam got to the cellar meeting George on the top step.

"Jesus, George, all hell is breaking loose out there, is everything all right?"

"Yes, how about you?"

"I'm fine."

In the cellar the children were sitting on a mattress that George had brought down from the spare bedroom. Sam hugged everyone, thankful that they were safe. Outside the wind blew and the rain fell.

"There was no way to get in touch with you, and the phone is out," Grace cried.

"Wipe your tears Grace, it looks like it's going to be a long night," said Sam, his voice was calm, not showing any of the anxiety he felt.

"I'll go and get some candles and the torch." Mary rose from a chair she had brought from the kitchen.

"I'll come with you." George held out his hand, a reassuring gesture that Mary needed at that moment.

"And I'll bring down some blankets from our bed, it may get cold down here later on."

"Bring Henry's mattress with you, Sam," Grace said, having gathered herself a little.

In the bedroom, Sam stood for a moment and listened to the storm. The sash windows rattled, as did the roof above his head. "This isn't good," he thought as he gathered blankets. In Henry's room, he looked out of the window. The rain fell unabated, lashing the windows unmercifully. He looked at his watch. It was ten past one. It had been raining since morning. With the wind gathering strength by the minute and the daylight subdued by grey skies, his thoughts of the night ahead were one of fear. Within half an hour back in the cellar everyone had settled down. Grace had opened a bottle of red wine. Henry was sharing a picture book with Sarah, Mary, at two years of age, was playing with her doll and Jimmy, aged four months, clung to his mother's breast, not missing out on a drink himself. The night passed without incident. In fact, the sound of the storm could hardly be heard, and by two o'clock, all were asleep.

At five in the morning Sam awoke with a start.

"Willena!" he said. "Jesus Christ, I hope she is alright!"

He rose, and climbed the brick steps out of the cellar, all the while listening for any sound of the storm. In the darkness, he shone the torch, finding his way to the kitchen and looked out of the window. Although it was pitch black, his senses told him that the worst was over, but he could still hear the wind. He made his way to the front door and opened it, shining his torch into the darkness. The branches of the fallen tree were waving about as if wanting to be free of whatever held them. He was right in thinking that the main thrust of the storm had passed, but still not enough to venture out. The rain still fell, but again not as heavy as it did six hours earlier.

"How are things out there Sam?" said George, Sam turned.

"Well, it's not as bad as it was, but still not fit for a dog to be out. Give it another few hours and we should be able to go outside."

By ten o'clock, Sam and George stepped outside, the eye of the storm having passed during the night, the worst was over but the tail end was still with them, with the wind now blowing in the opposite direction. By two o'clock in the afternoon the rain had ceased and the wind had dropped to a level that meant people were now emerging into the street. The following day, reports were coming through that the storm had caused considerable damage. Lives were lost as houses were demolished by the strong winds, electricity and telephone lines were down and there was no way Sam could drive the twenty miles to where Willena was staying, but he was determined to go. The following morning, he and George got in the car and drove as far as they could. He was surprised to see the main roads had been cleared to a point where it was open to single line traffic. Municipal workers and even the general public were busy with shovels, clearing a way through. Sam was stopped a couple of times by the police wanting to know if his journey was essential. He drove to within two miles of where Willena was staying but could get no further. Sam parked the car and he and George walked the rest of the way.

The shock of seeing houses that had been flattened in the storm was unimaginable. People were sifting through rubble, searching from house to house. When they got to where Sam thought the house Willena was staying in was, his heart sank. The house roof timbers and sheets were lying on the ground and all the walls had collapsed. Sam looked at George and shook his head.

"No one could live through that."

People had searched and were still lifting timbers and roofing sheets.

"You are looking for someone?" a burly man with an Irish accent asked, and without stopping, he pointed to a church. "You'll find the dead in there. The living…," he shrugged, "are all over the place."

Sam followed his pointed finger.

"We've searched all these houses and there's not even a dead cat here." Sam looked at the man but said nothing. The church, with part of its roof missing, was some three hundred yards away. As they approached, a flatbed truck passed by. Laid out upon it was the unmistakable form of bodies, covered over with white sheets. Without speaking, Sam and George entered the church. Inside, people were anxiously milling around and like on the back of the truck, corpses lay in two rows. Some people stood staring, as others knelt holding back the white sheets to expose the closed eyes of people that were known, or unknown to them.

"Can I be of any help to you sir?" a priest asked.

"I don't know," stammered Sam. "We're looking for a lady, Willena."

"I'm afraid that here names have no significance, I suggest you start at the end of the row and work your way along."

"She's a black lady," said Sam, not really knowing what to say.

"We are all the same here," the man said, before moving away.

The first four corpses were white people, the next three, black. Sam had seen many dead people but this was grim, the cyclone was indiscriminate in its choice of victims. There were the old and the young, one clearly the body of a young child whose shroud Sam wouldn't' touch. Halfway up the second row, Sam stood transfixed, staring at an elbow that was proud of the sheet that covered a body. He knew that it was Willena. He recognised the blue jumper. It was the one she had worn the day he dropped her off. He didn't even lift the sheet to check it was her.

"We must take her home," his voice was breaking as he spoke.

"How?" said George softly.

"In the back of the fucking car if we have to."

"It's a two mile walk back to the car."

"Then I'll carry her." Sam was visibly upset, and angry.

"Hang on for a few minutes, Sam. I'll be back."

George went outside. People were anxiously looking for loved ones, seemingly not knowing what to do. George noticed a bread van; its back doors open and inside were two bodies covered with a sheet. A man was closing the doors. Five minutes later the man followed George into the church.

"This gentleman will take Willena to your car, Sam."

"How much?" asked Sam, reaching into the inside pocket of his jacket.

"Five dollars," the man said, clearing his throat. Willena's body was placed in the back of the bread van and, before being driven away, Sam signed a paper given to him by the priest claiming responsibility for the body.

"They will also require notification of her final resting place etc. and a note from the relevant authorities regarding the death certificate. Some people think they can take them home and bury them in the back garden." He shrugged. "Maybe they can, I don't know, in any case, I have your name and address."

A short time later they drove a sad and still hazardous drive to Sam's workshop. Sam had decided to stop off and put Willena's body into one of his coffins and from there he would take her to Willena's church on his own flatbed truck. As it happened, Ian and Tom had called at the workshop to check the building. George sat in the car as Sam went in to see the boys. The news of Willena's death was better coming from him. Her coffin was placed onto Sam's truck with a tarpaulin sheet thrown over the top, after the coffin had been strapped down. Sam with Ian in the passenger seat, then drove the truck to the church Willena used to attend. Following in Sam's car, George thought of the events leading up to Willena's death and placed them in his box of life's trials. You expect things to happen in your life, but what you don't know is when, where and to what extent these happenings will affect you. As he drove through the rubble strewn streets, he thought of his own life. From his childhood, in the backstreets near Liverpool docks, to this moment driving down a road he didn't know in a country over 3,000 miles from the country of his birth. It might as well be, he thought, three thousand years away from the squalor and rat runs of life that had been his introduction to the world. Oh yes, he had seen people with nothing, he had seen people hurting other people and taking from them what they wanted. George knew about thieving, as a kid he was good at it. He remembered once being told to be as honest as he could afford to be.

Before the Great War, George's father had worked at the docks, unloading cargo ships for the British market, and loading the same with goods for export. Between 1880 and 1881 he spoke of his contemporaries in army uniform setting sail for the Transvaal in South Africa to fight the Boers and was glad he didn't count in their numbers.

George was the eldest of three brothers and at the age of fourteen had started work at the docks himself. Many times, he had seen his father beat his mother and take what little money she had saved. George, on a number of occasions, had tried to intervene but was beaten away. Many times, he swore that he would avenge his mother's tears. George had just turned fifteen when he came home from work and found his mother, again cowering under the stairs with his younger brothers. His father had come home early, beaten her, and taken back money he had given her to buy food. After putting her in her bed, George had told his brothers to stay with her. Then bending down, he whispered into her ear, "I won't let this happen again Ma."

At nine o'clock George left the house; he knew the route his father would take on his way home from the Jolly Roger, where he would have spent the food money.

At twenty to ten, in the darkness of an ebony sky, lit by a waxing moon, George lay in wait. In an alleyway between the store sheds of the docks, George caught sight of the man who had sired him, and thereafter had been the blight of his life. He sank back into the shadows of a doorway waiting for his father. Reaching into his overcoat pocket, he brought out the carving knife he had taken from the kitchen drawer. As the man he had come to hate, came nearer he tightened his grip on the knife's handle, then the silhouette stopped. A spark from a flint and a flicker of flame lit up an unshaven face and moustache that covered his upper lip. George watched his da walk forward the tip of his cigarette glowed more brightly each time he took a drag. George wasn't going to confront him, he was going to stab the good for nothing man in the back. The only problem with that was his father would never know who hated him enough to end his life, so George changed his mind. He stepped out from the shadows, his father stopped and raised his head. "Da" was the last word his father would ever hear. George thrust the knife forward into his chest. There was a slight resistance before the knife went fully in. He gave it a twist, then pulled it out. George heard an intake of breath, followed by a long drawn out wheeze. His father went to his knees and with shoulders hunched and his head slumping forward he gave a shudder and fell to the ground with a thud. George didn't see him fall. He was gone.

From that day on, George never again lifted his hand in anger. In the aftermath of his father's death, the police had called at George's home a few times asking his mother if she knew of anyone who would want to do him in. They made enquiries at the docks and at the pub where he drank. Unsurprisingly, no real motive for his murder was found, eventually it was passed off by the police as a robbery that went wrong. There was a whip-round at the pub and at the docks. A large amount of money was collected for George's family. The funeral was paid for by donations.

As they stood over the hole that George's father was put into, he looked at his mother. She glanced up, having caught his eye and George smiled, just a little smile and winked at her. He didn't give a shit if anyone saw him. Besides, they were all too busy looking into a hole his father wasn't likely to get out of. George thought that not a male hand with the intent of hurting her, would ever be laid on his mother again.

Many years later, on her death bed in the Admiral Rodney, George's mother had held her son's hand and thanked him, not for doing away with her husband, but for the life her son had given her since. George had done what he had to do, and his father's name was never mentioned again. He hadn't dwelt on the rights and wrongs of his actions and was content to let time erase all knowledge of the man's existence.

It was ironic that George and Mary had made a living from a business that many people would regard as being responsible for the breakdown of many families. But their public house was, in part and from their point of view, a haven for men with troubled minds, especially after the war years. The Admiral Rodney was not a place you go drinking in, after beating your wife. That seemed a long time ago now, George and Mary had done their bit to try and support those who needed a helping hand out of whatever gutter they had fallen into.

George looked ahead; Sam had pulled over into a clearing by the side of Willena's church; there were already a number of people gathered as George parked alongside the works truck. He got out of Sam's car; Ian, one of Sam's workmen, was in the process of taking the straps off Willena's coffin and shouted to George to give him a hand to fold the tarp. Sam was talking to the pastor; George saw him cross himself when he was told that Willena had perished in the storm. The pastor walked slowly to the truck and laid his hand on the now uncovered coffin. After uttering words that could not be heard, he called for assistance. Four black men stepped forward and lifted the coffin. Then, with a dignified and synchronised step they entered the church. On exiting, Sam was approached by a gentleman who introduced himself as working on behalf of the local council. The gentleman had called at Sam's workshop in anticipation that someone would be there and had been sent on to the church. The man in question had the authority to request the acquisition of all the cheaper coffins that Sam had in stock, plus a request for fifty more with the option of supplying extra units in the next two weeks. This request was sanctioned by the state government. Payment of said coffins would be paid for in due course.

For Sam and the boys at work, it was going to be a long few weeks.

"There are winners and losers in disasters like this," said George as he stacked pine boards in the centre of the workshop. "And I have concluded that life is a rollercoaster of happy times and sad times. Life owes us nothing at all. The penalties we pay and the rewards we receive. Just so long as the swings don't outnumber the roundabouts. When life offers you a gift, take it with both hands; as you don't know when the next one will come along."

"What's that all about," said Tom looking rather confused, not altogether understanding what George was saying.

"It's just the way I see life Tom, maybe you see it differently."

"I do," said Tom with a cocky reply of youthfulness. "I wake up in the morning, go to work, get paid and spend my money. Isn't that what it's all about?"

"It is until the shit hits the fan, as it does from time to time."

"And if that were to happen," answered Tom laughing.

"I simply switch the fan off," George smiled and shook his head.

"Well, that's fine if you know where the switch is," smiled Tom.

On Wednesday Willena was buried. There was little formality or ceremony about the whole business, as soon as her coffin came out of the church, another poor sod in a coffin went in. This was a testimony to the destructive force of the hurricane, the dead were being incinerated or buried all across the state. Willena was laid to rest in the Marble Cemetery next to her mother and not far from the graves of Gordon and Margaret Doyle to whom Sam owed so much. There was a gathering at Sam's house. The home he had first entered eleven years earlier, now belonged to him by virtue of Willena's passing. The mood of this gathering was in no way sombre. On the contrary, there was laughter, with mourners reflecting the joy that Willena had brought them. Willena's world was not of theirs, but her hunger to know that world was endearing. Sam's close friends, ones that had known Willena for almost as long as he had and some for much longer, raised a glass to the memory of a lady who, in her own way, had touched all of their lives. One young lady that had shed tears over Willena was Billie. Billie, whose birthday invitation still lay on Sam's office desk. Sam, like Willena, had seen Billie grow up. From the age of six, when Sam had first met her, she had been an inquisitive and independent child. As she got older, she would sometimes stay for a sleepover when her parents wanted to see a show on Broadway, or for no other reason than to have Willena read her bedtime stories. And when discussing what Billie wanted to do after she had finished her schooling, Willena had suggested that Billie, with her temperament and caring nature, would make a good nurse. So, Billie, from the age of sixteen, had decided that nursing was what she was destined to do.

"Yes," thought Sam, Billie would miss Willena.

5

Since the declaration of war, the atmosphere at RAF Shawbury had changed. There was now an urgency creeping through the base. From the operation rooms to the kitchens, from men in the hangers, to the gangs upgrading the runways. Everyone from Major Generals to administrators had things to do especially with winter around the corner. Even the postmen making deliveries to the base looked worried. It seemed that Armageddon was about to happen. All knew that things would change, but to what extent, that was the biggy.

Aeroplanes of all descriptions were flying in and flying out. Manpower was needed in all departments. The RAF were short of pilots and the time in training them, though necessary, had to be reduced from eighteen months and 150 hours flying time, to six months and 50 hours flying time. This was a big turn of events and doubts were raised as to the wisdom of the decision. To do his training, Michael, along with six others were posted to RAF Tern Hill's No. 10 Flying Training School. His time had come. Michael's confidence had soared during his first few weeks of training. His peers were no better and no worse than he, including two individuals who wondered what a mechanic was doing in their midst. In the following months he was to prove their doubts were misplaced.

Michael looked to his right. Dixie Dixon, like himself, sat in Examination Room A2 as the test papers were handed out. Dickie twiddled with his pen, his face expressionless. To his left, Archie Winchester looked up, his nervous grin and furrowed brow embodied the thoughts of all eight that were to take the test. Michael took deep breaths and, with fountain pen in hand, looked at the paper in front of him and read the heading.

'Central Examinations Royal Air Force'

Airmanship and Maintenance

There were eight questions, with two hours to answer. Michael quickly read through the paper and smiled.

"Question (1) What precautions should be taken by a pilot when taking off or landing at aerodromes situated at high altitude.?"

After an hour and forty minutes Michael placed his pen in the top pocket of his tunic and looked up. Five minutes earlier, Dixie Dixon had left the room. The examiner rose from his seat when Michael acknowledged that he had finished his paper.

"Finished Michael?" he said cheerfully.

"Yes Sir."

"Have you checked it?"

"Twice Sir."

"Then you are free to go."

Michael, being the second to finish, stood and left the room.

Dixie Dixon, the son of a wine merchant from Wolverhampton, had joined Michael's group a month earlier, along with Tony Martin. All eight were a motley crew, coming from various backgrounds and from all parts. of the UK. It was a two month elementary ground training course, where pupils learned the basics of how to fly. They were instructed in navigation, mathematics and the principle of flying an aircraft. One such aircraft was the DH 82 Havilland Tiger Moth, that Michael knew a lot about and in which they were to fly their first solo. Flying solo, for Michael and the rest of the group became a natural progression in his quest to master the sky. After landing, and with the adrenalin rush having passed, he sat in the cockpit of the 'yellow flying machine.

"I got the bugger up ..." he said to himself, and to savour the moment he thought of how far he had come, since standing in the garden with Sam watching the plane fly overhead and against the odds, he had done it.

There were other tests and exams to follow and in the six months of his training Michael became increasingly more relaxed in the company of his fellow trainee pilots. Some had been to boarding school and talked awfully posh and their presence would have seemed out of place in Michael's village pub. Then there were others with no pretence of being any different, but all in all they were a grand bunch of lads. It was when they were socially gathered that Michael noticed their true selves. Their strengths their weakness, the joker, singer, piano player and the 'Don Juan', the lover of anything in a skirt in fact there were two of those. Then there was the drinker and the smart ass; there is always one of those in a gathering of young men, who after having had too much to drink, thought they would all live forever. All eight of them were behaving in a way, exaggerated now to a point that would have raised eyebrows in their home environment.

Michael noticed it, was it a fear of the unknown? A fear of failure? A fear of not stepping up to a line that was expected of them, indeed a line that they expected of themselves.? Sometimes their guard would drop, but on those occasions and there were many, they didn't give a shit as to their language or behaviour. Subconsciously, they knew and knew all too well, that their future was not in front of a bar supping ale and doing the Hokey bloody Cokey, but in the air doing barrel rolls and aerobatics that would amaze the Billie Smarts of this world, with the chance of dying while doing it.

Michael spent Christmas at home, on a nine day pass. He arrived late on the day before Christmas Eve and was the only one of his group to step over the English border into Wales. The others were from Shropshire, bordering counties and beyond. As proud parents, Bill and Megan were always happy to see Michael home on leave. Especially his mother who, in the past, would have fussed over him almost to the point of annoyance. Now, to the great relief of Michael and his two sisters and brother, she had tempered her enthusiastic greetings. Holding in her joy of having him home, and in doing so, everyone began to feel more at ease. In the village, Megan would have once, with pride, spoken of her son's progress in the RAF, but now she would wait until she was asked. Bill had told her, on more than one occasion, not to be overprotective of him when he came home, reminding her of the women who had seen their son's leave home twenty five years earlier to fight in another war.

"With some never to return," she answered back. Bill could see her anguish and she understood his reasoning, but it was hard for her, having lived through it all before. Many times, in her teens she had seen her mother in law cry for her son. And many times, Megan had knelt at her own bed, with hands clasped tight praying for Bill's safe return. She knew in her heart that history was about to repeat itself and her hands would again be drawn together, this time not to pray for her love in Egypt but to pray for Michael, her own son.

Overnight, it had snowed. It had fallen silently, disturbing nothing but the air it had fallen through. Michael breathed on one of the twelve little panes that had brought the morning light into the bedroom he shared with his disgruntled brother. Dan, at fifteen, had already gone to work, a little unhappy about having to accommodate his older brother's presence yet again. With his warm breath melting the ice crystals that had formed on the inside of the pane, Michael wiped away the wet surface and looked out. It was eight thirty. The snow always reminded him of the white down that covered the belly of a goose except that the down that covered the land was cold and uninviting. Of course, it was always pleasing to the eye, in a poetic sense, but that's where the resemblance ended. Michael remembered the cold winter days inside the hangars at RAF Shawbury and the garage in Abermule, where the bitter wind would whip at his hands, making them numb. Thank God he was finished with that line of work, but at the same time he was thankful, as it had been a means to an end.

As the war raged in northern Europe, Christmas in Michael's village was much as it had always been. The church bells rang for the morning service and everyone dressed in their Sunday best, although Christmas Day happened to be on a Monday. Michael put on his suit, white shirt, and tie, only then to be told to put on his RAF uniform instead. Without question, he did as he was told. As his mother explained, he was representing the British Air Force and other members of the armed forces on leave would be attending church in their uniforms. Apart from anything else, it was the right thing to do. So, Michael, with his two sisters, one on each arm, like everyone else, kicked off the snow that had gathered on their boots before entering the church. He sat and looked around. There were a few in army uniform. One lad he knew well. Then his mind started to wonder, this is the church where he went to Sunday School, where he was christened. The church his parents were married in. He glanced at his sisters. Esther and Sally were different now, they weren't little girls anymore. They had changed in mind and body. From being dependent to becoming independent. Their thoughts no longer the thoughts of children, but of adult responsibility. From pinafore to lace, they had become of age. In fact, they were the same age now as when, a long time ago, their mother was writing letters to another man in uniform - their father! Michael's brother didn't attend the service, he was busy milking. Like the church bells, the cows were unaware that it was Christmas morning and Dan thought it pointless telling them that it was. He didn't do church, preferring the company of dogs, cows and sheep, who he said were much less complicated than people.

Outside, with snow underfoot, the congregation gathered, huddled in small groups. They talked of the war and of the children evacuated from cities in England who were now in their midst, some of whom had attended the service in the company of their guardians. Young men gathered around young women, Esther and Sally being amongst them. They were attracted by the fact that the girls were available in the livestock market, as jokingly described by one farming lad.

"You couldn't afford me or my sister," replied Sally, giving the lad a friendly clip to the head.

"I hear you'll be getting your wings shortly, Michael?"

Michael turned and recognised the girl speaking.

"Hello Jenny," he smiled, "It's nice to see you. Hopefully, but it will take a few months yet."

"I had heard," she said, looking him up and down.

"You look awfully smart in your uniform, when do you go back?"

"On my birthday." Michael replied immediately wishing he hadn't mentioned his birthday.

"You go back next week?" she said, almost laughing.

Michael was surprised that she had remembered his birthday, but why shouldn't she? She was the same age, only her birthday was the following day.

The smell of roast goose drifted through the house as Michael opened the door and walked in. Sally didn't like the smell, so she stayed outside until the odour of it had gone. She had done the same on each occasion roast goose was on the menu. Dan, for the last three years, had been responsible for acquiring the feathered creature. He killed it, feathered, and gutted it and oversaw the cooking of it. And, with the grace of a ballerina he would, with pomp and ceremony, place it on the table. Then, and only then, when the aroma of the roasted bird had subsided, would Sally come back into the house. This had now become a ritual and was always a reason for a good laugh. Party hats were placed on heads as Dan carved the goose. The saying of grace was dispensed with, before everyone helped themselves to veg, stuffing, roast, mashed potatoes, and gravy. Rhubarb wine was drunk, toasting the health and wellbeing of all.

After dinner, the whole family called in to see Sam's mother and father, Michael's Uncle Jim, and Aunt Violet. They talked of Sam and Grace and the chances of America joining the allies in the war.

"Mark my words, sooner or later America will fight, they won't have an option, like before, with Australia and New Zealand, we will fight as one". Jim smiled as he looked at Bill, both momentarily remembering unspoken deeds of their past.

Instinctively, Michael gave the bird a three foot lead and pulled the trigger, then he swung his shotgun slightly left and, giving the second pigeon a bit more lead, another shot rang out. The two pigeons fell, hitting the snow one before - the other. He looked at his brother.

"You haven't lost your touch," said Dan, grinning. Michael picked up the birds and placed them in the bag he had slung over his shoulder. Going shooting with their father on Boxing Day was something they had done since childhood. Then it was their father that carried the gun. Now all three walked with a shotgun, counting off missed shots like they would at a clay pigeon competition. They walked the snow covered land, looking for tracks that would heighten their anticipation of further kills. They strolled open fields and skirted the gorse covered hill sides that went on and on. Wood pigeons, partridge, wild duck, woodcock, rabbit and maybe a pheasant were their quarry. Not to be confused with poachers of the area, permission had been granted to Michael's father by local farmers, in return for a brace of whatever was shot. The acquisition of meat from wild game in the hamlets and villages of Mid Wales had never been an issue, as it was for the people living in large towns and cities. In the second week of January 1940 bacon, butter and sugar were government rationed. The first two items caused little hardship for local people, but sugar was something that was hardly likely to be shot or pulled out of the ground. Country folk had to be thankful, like everyone else, for the amount of sugar that was rationed to them.

When the boys arrived home, Megan was preparing dinner, Sally had finished loading the wood basket and Esther was darning her father's socks. With the shot game hanging up on nails in the outhouse, they took off their dirty wellingtons and had replaced them with their slippers, before walking into the house.

"I see farm workers are to get a two shilling a week pay rise?" said Michael.

"Proposed pay rise," corrected Dan, raising his head from a farming magazine, "and what you're reading won't apply to me."

"But you will get a raise?"

"Maybe," he said, burying his head back into his magazine.

Michael had spread the Express on the dinner table and was reading the local news. He read various articles, with pictures and reports of children evacuated from Birkenhead arriving at Newtown Railway Station. Results of whist drives played in village halls were listed and there was an interesting tale of a young man, who did not attend court proceedings, charged with fishing without a licence. He was fined five shillings, his joining the army accounting for his absence in court. He read a story of a family of five boys and one girl, the eldest aged eleven, who lived in an isolated part of the parish. The local rector had heard that not one of them had been christened. He made arrangements for all five to attend church to be blessed and welcomed into the Christian faith. Then in conversation one boy declared that he had never seen a train. There was a story of a Welshpool RAF pilot who had bombed a submarine but had pulled out too low and crashed into the sea. His observer was killed instantly and the pilot had been taken prisoner. He had been reported as 'missing in action' until his father received a letter from him written from some prisoner of war camp.

Three nights later, Michael, his sisters and two of their friends had piled into the back of a butcher's van. The driver, a friend of Sally's, suggested that Sally sit in the front with him. He had offered to take them all into Newtown for a night out before Michael returned to camp. John, the driver, an amiable chap, was the kind of guy that if smacked in the face would apologise for something he didn't do. Now, having been egged on by Jenny, he sang all the way to Newtown. He didn't disappoint, in fact his rendition of 'If I Had My Way' sounded not unlike Bing Crosby's. His voice drifted through the grill that separated the two seats in the front from the carcass that usually swung from hooks in the back.

"Jesus John, we're going to get out of here smelling like dead sheep!" Esther shouted, as they bounced about in the back, John stopped singing.

"Hardly surprising," he laughed. "At least we'll all smell the same."

Then he carried on crooning. With the van moving from side to side every time John went around a corner on the winding country roads contact with Jenny was unavoidable. She had sat by Michael when they got into the back of the van and he sensed that she didn't mind the number of times they were thrown together. John parked in the main street, taking a spot just vacated by another vehicle whose lights disappeared up the road.

The town was busy. The young, and not so young, walked the streets. Some soberly contemplating the future, others drunkenly fearing it. But most, just for tonight anyway, couldn't give a damn, they were living in the moment. Couples walked arm in arm, the women dressed in winter coats, knitted hats, scarves, and woollen gloves - some, no doubt, given as Christmas gifts. There were men wearing army overcoats, whose brass buttons stood out against the darkness of the early evening. The pavement under foot, wet and slushy with melted snow, was beginning to freeze again and breath, like vapour, rose from the mouths of people talking. With Jenny's arm threaded through his, Michael felt a warm feeling of contentment. Groups of people gathered beneath streetlights, dimmed because of the blackout laws that had been imposed since September. Young men in forces uniform walked from pub to pub, the glow of their cigarette ends and muffled chatter in the darkness announcing their presence. Inside, the pubs were alive with singing and laughter. The atmosphere was boisterous but hospitable, making it difficult to hear any normal conversation. Placing his empty pint mug on the table, John suggested they leave the Buck and go around the corner to the Bear Hotel. Esther looked at her glass of port and lemon on a table in front of her. It was the first port and lemon she had ever had in any snug room, in any public house. She felt uneasy, as she was underage. If a copper had walked in to see her drinking, she would have been in trouble. But while the drink was on the table and not in her hand, then it didn't belong to Esther. "They won't let me in there," she said.

"Yes, they will," said John.

He looked at Michael. "With your brother in his RAF uniform. I'll wager there won't be many in there dressed like him. You will be fine."

Esther smiled. They finished their drinks and walked to the Bear Hotel, where it was a little quieter. The barman looked at Michael, standing behind a chap with some tinsel wrapped around his trilby. He smiled.

"Hi Michael," he grinned. "You home for Christmas?"

"Hello Tim," Michael said, surprised to see the man who used to deliver engine parts to the garage in Abermule.

"Yes, on leave for a few days."

"What can I get you? I see you have your sisters with you?" he glanced over Michael's shoulder. "Hi ladies."

"Hi Tim, I didn't know you worked here." Sally said.

"Part time," he answered, giving Sally a wink. Michael ordered the drinks, remembering to ask for a lemonade for Esther.

"Take them through to the snug, Michael; there's a nice fire in there. It may be a bit crowded but you should get some seats."

"So, what's on at the Regent tonight?" asked John.

"The 39 Steps, an Alfred Hitchcock film, it's a spy film, about this guy who…"

"Don't tell us anymore, Wendy," said Sally, speaking to a friend who had ridden with them in the back of the butcher's van.

"She hates it when I tell her about a film we're going to see, but I love winding her up."

"And what's the second film," asked Jenny, placing her third empty port and lemon glass on the table.

"Now I don't know anything about that one", Wendy sighed, "other than what I've read in the paper. It's called 'Sergeant Murphy' and stars Ronald Regan, whoever he is."

The 39 Steps was, as Wendy had stated, a spy film about a Canadian civilian in London, who gets caught up in preventing enemy spies from stealing British military secrets. There were some anxious moments where Jenny had grabbed hold of Michael's hand and whispered her thoughts concerning the complex issues involved in the film. He, in return had reminded her that it was only a film and not to get too serious about it. After the Patha news, the second feature, Sergeant Murphy was just that, a second feature, a poor film.

John sang quietly all the way home, his soothing voice a perfect backdrop to the conversation taking place in the back of the van. Sally, sitting in the front seat, closed her eyes and drifted away to Nat King Cole's *'Ramblin' Rose'*. She concentrated on the words. *"Wild and wind-blown, that's how you've grown, who can cling to a ramblin' rose."* When the song was over, Sally begged John to sing it again. She sat back in the uncomfortable seat and looked at him. Was he singing about her, she wondered. She had guessed he had a soft spot for her, but until this moment she hadn't really taken much notice. John was five years older than her and worked as a driver for a local abattoir. The pair had gone out together but usually or always with others. Sally had noticed that on each occasion, John had insisted that she sit next to him in the front of the van. John dropped Wendy off at the crossroads. The group said their farewells with Wendy wishing Michael good luck for the future. Further up the road, they entered the village. Pulling over, John got out and opened the back doors of the van.

"I'll walk Jenny home," said Michael.

"I'll be fine Michael, it's only ten minutes."

"Well then, it will only take me ten minutes to walk back, won't it?"

"Thank you, John, for the evening out. No doubt I'll see you again when I'm next home and by the way, thanks for the entertainment, you're not a bad singer either."

John laughed.

"You flatter me," he said as he shook Michael's hand. He turned and gave Sally a cwtch, one that was five seconds longer than what a normal hug would last, giving her a kiss on the cheek at the same time. "Get in touch," he said. He gave Esther the kind of hug you give your granny. As the back lights on John's van disappeared around a corner, Sally and Esther started to walk the five hundred yards home. In the frosty darkness, ice crystals that had formed on the wet road and in the ditches, sparkled as the beam of light from Sally's torch moved over them. To the right, another beam of light was showing the way ahead. Michael and Jenny walked the narrow road in silence, both thinking of the company they had found themselves in. They had known each other for a long time but, for whatever reason, their paths had not crossed in recent years. Tonight, in the back of John's van, Jenny had felt the closeness of Michael, a reassuring closeness that had surprised her. In town she had linked his arm and she had reached for his hand sitting beside him in the cinema. Now alone, the two of them walked side by side. They turned left. A little further and they were outside Jenny's farmhouse. A dog barked in the yard. Michael drew Jenny close and, in a whisper, as formal as it was, thanked her for her company.

"Will you write to me, Michael? I need you to write."

"I will," he promised. Still holding her, savouring the moment before kissing her softly on her forehead. "Now I need to ask you something," he hesitated. "Can I borrow your torch, or I may end up in the ditch walking home?"

6

During the first four months of the year, the boys continued their flight training and when, for the first time, Michael sat himself in a Hurricane fighter, he knew this was what he wanted. Nothing came close to the nervous excitement he felt when the Rolls Royce Merlin engine fired up and the propeller blades started to rotate. He eased the controls and the wheels lifted clear of the runway and locked into place under the wings. This was the moment, when the feeling of freedom entered his very being. Nothing had changed since his first flight in the Tiger Moth, but that now seemed such a long time ago. With the runway slipping away behind him and the crop fields stretching far in front, Michael glanced at the instrument panel. His objective was to fly at its service ceiling height of 34,500 feet for a period of fifteen minutes, 900 feet below its absolute ceiling. From this vantage point, in a clear, blue late March afternoon sky, Michael gazed below. The sight never ceased to amaze him. The landmass moved very slowly. It looked like a quilted bedspread with fields and woods sectioned off by hedges and fences. And colours, such colours of brown and forty shades of green. Yes, this sight was a privilege to behold and something that he had so desperately sought.

At lower altitudes of 500 feet, he could see people walking in fields and on footpaths, dogs chasing rabbits, children flying kites and men sitting fishing on riverbanks. All looked up as he passed overhead. A group of children waved, and Michael waved back, it's what people do. He wondered why they would wave in the first place. Train passengers do the same. He concluded that people do it just to say hello.

Michael found the Hurricane a responsive machine to fly. Its Rolls Royce Merlin engine made light of powering the three and a half ton plane across the sky. He and his fellow pilots often practise manoeuvres. Flying in formation, then peeling away to attack an imagined enemy, or to avoid such an enemy by using cloud cover. At other times, they came from behind such cover, having anticipated the flight path of an enemy plane, thereby using all the advantages of an attack. The sun also played an important part in the tactics being played out. Of course, these manoeuvres and anticipated enemy flight paths were all well and good, but it would only take one to outsmart you and your flying career would be over, and in a lot of cases so would your life. This, for the moment, was how they lived with death so close you could almost touch it.

They would be in the air for a period of one and a half hours or so, then would land and go to a classroom to debrief the morning's flight. This pattern was repeated day after day until flying became instinctive to them all. When flying there was always so much to think of and seemingly little time to act. Being enclosed in such a small space gave rise to a claustrophobic feeling, where the senses of all pilots came to the fore. The smell of high octane fuel and oil, the vibration of everything made them sensitive to their surroundings. Sometimes Michael's feet would tingle, his legs would feel heavy. He would catch his breath with every dip and surge of vicious down draughts. There was no getting out. The air outside became a wind that played by its own rules. The currents, eddies, ripples, and flows, when all the time, it seemed to him, he was sitting in a saddle mounted on a Rolls Royce engine, an animal let loose in the sky, turning propellers that he was ultimately responsible for.

On Wednesday the 1st May 1940, with little ceremony, Pilot Officer Michael Barry Jones, along with seven of his group, were presented with the accolade they had sought, namely the silver embroidered wings of an RAF Pilot. As Michael stood to attention, with arms to his sides, he turned his fingers in on both hands making a fist. He was tense, proud and grateful. With thoughts of his family running through his mind, he silently exhaled the words "thank you" to his parents. They had been with him every step of the way, with words of encouragement and had never once doubted his ability to achieve his dream. Some of the seven with him had lived a life of privilege, never knowing what it was like to have very little and to have worked hard for even that. But he would defend them all for their character, integrity and flying ability. They had been where he had been and all deserved the wings being placed in their hands.

Even so, it wasn't over yet, there would be another four weeks of operational training before being sent, hopefully, to airfields in southern England. There they would patrol the skies, warding off enemy aircraft that were already testing the British defences and attacking shipping convoys in the English Channel.

The landlady at the Stormy Petrel public house, in Tern Hill awaited the arrival of the young airmen, she had been notified earlier in the week of the expected celebrations. Doris had seen it all before and understood the importance of these young men gaining the swift like wings as their predecessors had done before them. Many times, she had thought of their youthful exuberance, and many times she had witnessed their impetuous need for something beyond what they had and their desire for all what they dreamed. Which, in truth, she smiled, amounted to much the same thing. She often dwelt on the fact that she was old enough to have lived through those moments; that she was old enough to be those boys' grandmother, and old enough to then realise that her future, or what was left of it, would probably equal her past. She pondered that she hadn't really done a lot in her life. Doris put her melancholy mood to one side, when at 6:30pm the boys entered the bar.

"Let the celebrations begin," said Tim, his suggestion being echoed by the fifteen or so lads that followed him into the bar room. The landlord, Doris's brother, had already started on Tim's pint, steadily putting pressure on the white porcelain beer pump handle, his hand covering part of a hunting scene depicted on it.

"And you?" Doris said, smiling at Glyn. She liked Glyn, he was the shortest of the group. He had a curly mop of unruly auburn hair, a round face and dimpled cheeks. He was just tall enough to pull out a set of darts, grouped around the bull's eye of a dart board. Doris handed him a pint of dark mild and he smiled broadly.

"It's on the house," she said "every time you boys get your wings, we buy the first drink. God knows, you've spent a lot of money in here. I see you've brought a few extra lads to help you celebrate?"

"Thank you, Doris, that's very kind of you."

It was not in Glyn's nature to call elderly people by their Christian name, but she insisted everyone call her Doris, she's said it made her feel more connected with the person she was speaking to and so Glyn went along with her request. Glyn was the butt of many jokes, but his ability to laugh at his own shortcomings, in the leg department, was an endearing touch to his overall character. He would often have the last laugh though, saying such things as, he had a lot more room to move about in the cockpit of a Hurricane and had less of a body area to shoot at than his peers. Michael sat with three of his fellow officers. It seemed surreal that he was amongst people who he would never have met but for his determination to fly.

The young lad to his right had come in with another group. This was going to be some party. Michael glanced at him, he looked a lot younger than he obviously was, he seemed unsettled and nervous. He noticed Michael and smiled.

"I believe you're from Wales"? he hesitated, "I really didn't want any of this."

Michael looked at him not quite understanding what he was saying.

"My father", he said, "he wanted this, he wanted me to fly. My mother couldn't give a shit, but what father wants, father gets." He shrugged, stood up and carried his pint to the bar. He stood next to a tall chap with a ginger handlebar moustache, the visual epitome of an officer one would find in a gathering such as this.

Michael stopped thinking and looked around. Groups of men were seated at tables and others, casually standing, were all deep in conversation. Piano music came through an open door at the rear of the bar. He smiled as he recognised the tune, a sonnet by Mozart. He stood and walked to the door taking his drink. In the background he heard the muffled talk of men, but the dominant sound of piano notes being played made him more aware of his own presence. He lingered in the doorway. Troy could never pass a piano stool without sitting on it and letting his fingers flow over the smooth ivory keys of a piano that usually accompanied such a stool. Troy was away in his own world, his eyes closed, as his body moved in time and symmetry to the music he played. Smoke from a cigarette, resting in an ashtray on the top of the highly polished piano, rose lazily upwards, slightly veering from left to right. For about two feet the smoke climbed, then curling in on itself, finally ending its rise in disarray and disappeared in a faint haze.

As the early evening drew on and the rate of beer being consumed declined, a photograph of the eight, newly appointed, flying officers was taken. It depicted eight smiling faces, in various poses, around Troy's piano. The men eventually received a copy each of this photograph. A photograph that ended up behind glass in a frame on someone or other's mantlepiece or dressing table. Some no doubt, and in time, ended up in a drawer along with other photographs taken at a moment in time for posterity or vanity. But for now, each of the eight men basked in their well-deserved self-importance. The banter and the raising of glasses went on. Some of the lads did their party piece. Some watched on as others told exaggerated stories of their sexual adventures when last home, while those disbelievers questioned their exploits.

There was a moment when Troy was ridiculed by Jimmy Harris, a bit of a loudmouth when drunk, but otherwise a nice guy. He questioned Troy's love of classical music, saying it elevated his standing in society. Troy wasn't having any of it.

"Do you really think classical music is a class thing? Classical music is for everyone to enjoy and as far as my standing in society, Jesus Jimmy, I don't have a society to stand in. You are far better educated than me, so for you to say that classical music is for a certain section of people is ridiculous. How come you sing along when I play?"

"That's different", says Jimmy. Then from out of nowhere Troy asked him if he knew how many white notes there were on a piano.

"How the fuck should I know," Jimmy said in a jovial manner.

"Well, have a guess."

"Sixty three."

"No," said Troy. "And how many black notes are there?"

"Forty three."

"No again," answered Troy. Then he asked, "what are those brown pats you see in a field with cows in?"

"Well, I know that one." Jimmy smiled. "It's cow muck, and I suppose you're going to tell me I'm wrong?"

"On the contrary," Troy declared. "You're absolutely right, which is as I suspected…." he paused, "you know more about shit than you do about music." Everyone laughed and to his credit, Jimmy saw the funny side and, taking no offence, laughed too.

Michael's group were given seven days leave after their last week of operational training. It was, in Michael's view, a bit like the calm before the storm, as after the seven days, they would be let loose to live or die in the skies above England's green and pleasant land. As it was, RAF pilots were losing their lives at an increasing rate.

Unsurprisingly, there had been a few close calls during their time at Tern Hill. Michael himself had one scary moment when his Hurricane, nearing the end of the runway on landing, suddenly gave a jolt as the stays to his right hand undercarriage wheel gave way. His machine slew to port, doing a full one hundred and eighty degree turn to end up facing the way he had just come into land. The plane's starboard wing was on the runway with the tail some six feet off the ground. Stories of crash landings involving all types of machines were not uncommon amongst the hundreds of RAF bases throughout the country. But it was a sadder story when the deaths of individuals accompanied such tales. There, but for the grace of God, his mother would say no such fatal misadventure befell any individual during the time Michael was at Tern Hill.

To complete their operational training, the boys were sent to RAF Sutton Bridge in southeast Lincolnshire, where they underwent live target practice, drills for formation flying and various tactical flying evasive manoeuvres, including light spiral dives, hard rolls and loops of varying degrees. This was serious stuff. The four week training programme, they were informed, was now reduced to two because things were heating up in Europe, and their allotted time for home leave was also reduced from seven to four days.

In the two weeks of operational training the boys came under increased pressure to maintain a required standard of flying. On the day they arrived at Sutton Bridge, four Hawker Hurricanes had been flown in from Tern Hill to join another four that had arrived the day before. By mid-afternoon all eight men and planes were in the air. The activity at Sutton Bridge reminded Michael of a disturbed ant's nest. As an observer, it seemed that everyone was busy doing their own thing, with no apparent sign that anything was being done to benefit the colony as a whole. But all was not as it seemed and everyone played their part in making this RAF base run with seamless efficiency. Michael's group were not the only officers doing operational training. There were others who, on finishing their training, had be sent, like Michael, to RAF bases across the UK to join squadrons, where new cockpits of new planes awaited them.

The four days Michael spent at home felt like he had moved on. It wasn't a feeling he'd had four months earlier, and maybe it was an exaggerated feeling that had crept up on him. It was as though he didn't belong anymore. Not to his family, as nothing could ever come between his love and respect for them. As it was, they were all very proud of the fact that he had achieved his dream and his sisters wanted to show him off to all their friends, much to Michael's dismay. His letter writing to Jenny had been sporadic during his training, as was hers to him, but they did manage to see each other during his leave.

Michael called at the farmhouse. where Jenny's mother invited him in for a cup of tea. Jenny was in the dairy turning a milk churn of cream.

"Making some butter?" he asked.

Jenny smiled as she followed him into the kitchen.

"Pilot Michael Jones," she beamed. He kissed her on the cheek. They exchanged formal greetings in the company of her mother, who asked much the same questions of Michael as everyone else did, before Jenny suggested they go for a walk. The sun was shining and the birds were singing, the daffodils had seen their best and wildflowers had made their presence known. The warmth of the sun had stirred the souls of both young and old. It was a typical day, one of those you read of in romantic novels, where boy meets girl. They walk hand in hand, with a soft breeze blowing in their hair, through fields of long grass before they lay down and make mad passionate love, before he kisses her goodbye and goes off to war. But this was no romantic novel and Jenny and Michael's walk was not like that. Somewhere between the time he had borrowed her torch to see his way home and the letters they wrote, the passion that could have unfolded had ebbed away without really knowing why. After their walk, they bid each other farewell. Michael again, kissed Jenny on the forehead and she asked him to write if he had a mind to. On the way home Michael wondered what had happened, why hadn't he pursued the thought he'd had to, at least, fool around in the long grass for a while?

7

Billie's seventeenth birthday party was postponed for two weeks after the devastation of the hurricane that had taken Willena. Her passing was a great loss to Billie. She had been a source of stability in Billie's young life and Billie had thought the world of her. There had been times when Billie had argued with her mother and had wanted to run away, as sometimes children do. She would pack her bags and get her father to take her to Willena's house. It was usually on a Saturday when Billie had wanted to run away. This would happen maybe once a month. The reason is probably explained by the fact that Uncle Sam, Aunty Grace, and their growing family shared the house with Willena and Billie so enjoyed their company.

Up until the time of Britain declaring war on Germany, Billie, from the age of sixteen and with Willena's encouragement, started the long journey that was the nursing profession. In the 1930's, most larger hospitals operated a school of nursing. One, the Lenox Hill Hospital on Park Avenue, was a hospital Billie was familiar with, in that years earlier, two of Sam's female nursing friends had worked there. Sam had met them on board ship as they too had emigrated to start a new life in America. Billie's schedule was one of study and practical work on the wards. The menial and thankless tasks she and her fellow student nurses were required to do were demeaning to a point where the dropout rate was alarming and a cause for concern. Billie had been in the nursing profession for two years when the National League of Nursing Education and the American Hospitals published a manual of the essentials of good hospital nursing service. Although the manual was published in conjunction with the American Hospital Association, hospitals had no obligation to follow it. It seemed strange that recommendations having been made by a national body were at the whim of each state, as each had its own rules and regulations.

Although the work was tedious, Billie enjoyed the study, and found it all very satisfying. Billie loved her job and for a time had worked alongside Sister Sandy Armstrong, one of the nurses who had befriended her Uncle Sam and had often frequented Sam's home on Hudson Street while Billie was visiting. In recent years Sam had lost touch with Sandy, so, it was nice when Sister Armstrong had recognised Billie when meeting her again at the nursing school.

Guidelines regarding nursing training were changing constantly, but Billie, not wanting to pass judgement on a profession she was just getting to grips with, had her own views on why there was a shortage of 'feet walking the wards, and even on how improvements in nurse training could increase those numbers. But she kept her views to herself. At nursing school, Billie's class consisted of twelve training students and as the youngest trainee, Billie was by no means the one to struggle in the classroom. On the contrary, her ability to grasp the fundamentals of nursing was above average. But by far, her best quality had nothing to do with recording patients' vital signs or administering medications, but her ability to communicate. Sandy had said in one of her lectures that communication had as much to do with nursing as the changing of bandages. Sadly, communication skills were a natural thing and very difficult to learn. Sandy was surprised at Billie's soft approach and her gentle way with words plus the fact that she herself had met Willena a number of years earlier and the answer to Billie's maturity, was there in the house where she would run away to as a child.

On the third of September 1939 Neville Chamberlin, the British Prime Minister, declared that the country was at war with Germany. This was now a time of uncertainty for everyone, but Europe was a long way from America and only time would tell what would happen. The subject of Winston Churchill, a British member of parliament, came up when Sandy had finished her closing remarks to a lecture she had just given. A student had asked about America's involvement in the conflict in Europe.

Sandy, who wasn't politically motivated, suggested to the class that international politics are best left to politicians. She did, however, mention that she had actually met the gentleman in December 1931.

"He wasn't the British Prime Minister then," she explained, "he was in America on a lecturing tour and whilst crossing Fifth Avenue one night, he was hit by a car." Sandy's audience of nurses were hushed, anticipating what was coming next as she recalled the incident.

"He arrived at the Lenox in a taxi. Apparently, he was looking for a friend whose address he had left in his hotel room. The friend, a Mr Bernard Beruch, someone you may or may not have heard of, was a financier and a statesman. Needless to say, a very rich and powerful man with influence."

"Mr Churchill," Sandy scanned the room, "was in a wheeled chair and bleeding from a wound to his head. Although in some pain, he was surprisingly relaxed and coherent, asking questions about his injury and enquiring as to who we were. I was assisting the house surgeon at the time. Your name?" I asked. The Right Honourable Winston Churchill, he answered, age, fifty seven. There were more questions and more answers. We spoke for a few minutes, then he asked me where I came from. Coventry, I told him, but added that I'd spent my childhood in mid Wales. He smiled and looked up at me. Anywhere near Abermule? He asked with a curious grin. Abermule, ladies, is a little village that I knew well. In the summer months my friends and I would go there to swim in the River Severn.

I asked Mr Churchill if he'd been there. He told me he had not, but that a cousin of his had been killed, along with sixteen others, in a horrific train crash there ten years earlier. I told him that I recalled the incident of the

Abermule train crash. His cousin's name was Herbert Van-Tempest. Now how could you forget a name like that!? Mr Van-Tempest just happened to be a director of the Cambrian Railway Company, the very company that, in effect, had caused his demise. Mr Churchill was put under sedation, his head cleaned up and stitched and I never saw him again. One could say, she smiled, that I have had the blood of a British member of Parliament on my hands. I will hazard a guess that you ladies will, at some point or other, have experiences in your career that will border on historic. There will most certainly be experiences that seem futile and others that are exhilarating. All, may I add, will be memorable, and some for all the wrong reasons."

8

The circumstances of how Billie got to be in Hawaii in mid November of 1941 was all rather sudden and not altogether planned. Her father, who worked for the New York Times as a reporter, was in line for promotion, but before that was to happen, he was sent on a two week assignment, courtesy of the New York Times and the American government, to do a report on the growth of the tourist industry in the territory of Hawaii. In reality, this engagement was a 'working holiday' as he was allowed to take along his family. The question of Billie having time off from the hospital wasn't a problem, as she was given permission to be absent for three weeks. She could have stayed at home and had the house to herself, but two weeks in paradise island was too good an offer to refuse. As it turned out, Pageant, after going through all the trials that would be encountered travelling to Hawaii with Billie's seven year old brother in tow, concluded that it would be a pain in the backside and all too much. However, she insisted that Joe take Billie with him. With due credit to Pageant, her foresight of the trials and the bother of it all, were well founded. The trip there was, indeed, arduous. Billie found the flight to San Francisco and its connecting flight to Hawaii exciting and sometimes scary. Even though the island was part of the US, the distance was just short of 5,000 miles and the journey would take some thirty five hours.

Billie threw her raffia woven beach bag onto her bed. She wanted to sleep but she also wanted to walk barefoot over white sandy beaches and drink in the atmosphere. Kicking off her shoes, she glided into the lounge of their hotel room. Her father was pouring a scotch from a bottle he had picked up from a table, decorated with shells in the middle of the room.

"How do you feel," he asked with a grin.

Billie rolled her eyes. "I feel tired and excited at the same time, so I really don't know. I'm glad to be here though."

It was early evening when Billie got to walk on the beach. The sun was setting behind her, creating long shadows of palm trees that rose, arching forward toward the ocean. She could hear music; it came from some adobe type buildings a hundred yards or so beyond the high tide driftwood that lay on the beach. Billie closed her eyes. The music, unmistakably Hawaiian, played its part in the overall magic that was the island. Pink and red bougainvillaea, various colours of hibiscus and bird of paradise flowers grew in perfusion against a tall picket fence. They were as much a part of the island as the coconuts that fell on its beaches. In town, Billie walked past street vendors and little shops where people chatted in a language that she had never heard before. Their smiles and gestures and their determination to please was infectious. Billie wondered, if other lands and cultures had this same desire to be courteous and agreeable. She walked past a little harbour, where men in small fishing boats were busy folding nets, as they bobbed up and down like seabirds on the incoming tide. In the setting sun, Billie saw the beach again. Here and there groups of people were gathered, children were playing ball, their laughter a reminder of bygone days of her childhood that really were not that long ago for her.

She stopped and read a sign, 'Tripler General Hospital'. She smiled and walked on. She saw men in military uniform, some good looking and some not so. They were all young Navy and Air Force men. On seeing her, some showed their immaturity by being brash, trying to impress their friends. A few times she overheard comments being made of her looks and other aspects of her appearance. All were flattering. She smiled to herself. At nineteen Billie hadn't thought much about men or boys, naked or otherwise and as for the love side of it all, she could only imagine. She chuckled, as she thought of grabbing one of those lads she had seen and running off into the wind, not returning until she had satisfied a desire. Whatever that was.

"And where have you been?" Joe asked, clinking ice cubes in another glass of whiskey.

"Down to the beach and a walk into town. How about you?"

"Just sat on the balcony admiring the view," he paused. "And what about tomorrow?"

"Another walk into town. I like to see how the locals live," Billie smiled. "And you?"

"I have a few names of people in local government departments and hotel managers that I need to chase up and people in the tourist industry to talk to. Then there is the airline business." Joe raised his eyebrows. "We have had some first-hand experience at that and, to say the least, I wasn't too impressed. Still," he raised his shoulders, "they can only improve."

Billie slept soundly and was up, dressed and out walking at seven thirty the following morning It was a beautiful morning, a warm sea breeze, like a whisper, caressed her face as she, again, headed into town.

Joe rose at eight, went for breakfast at eight thirty and drank the last of his orange juice at eight fifty. The first interview he had in mind would be the manager of the hotel that he and his daughter were staying in, but he had decided to leave him until last. He thought that if he were to let it be known that he was about to question the manager on the running, and future predictions of his hotel, Joe would run the risk that his answers would be more favourable than they would have otherwise been.

The subtle sweet smell of morning breakfast lingered in the streets, as food sellers touted for business. Billie's father had suggested she should read a little about Hawaii before going, thereby getting some knowledge of what she may encounter. Although it had sounded a prudent thing to do, Billie had decided that, apart from what she already knew of the place, which was very little, she would rather go unprepared and form her own, unbiased, opinion of her visit. That morning she wore a white cotton dress, printed with red roses, a wide gold belt around her waist and a single string of pearls borrowed from her mother. She also wore, what her mother would call, a pair of sensible walking shoes. She went from little shops to market stalls, tasting local foods and found that she delighted in anything that tasted of pineapple. She walked in the park and happened upon a wedding feast.

The sound of a conch shell being blown could be heard. A man in native dress stood, military-like, as people gathered around him. Billie stopped, curious to see young women in traditional grass skirts, bare feet, headbands of flowers and leis around their necks that fell to their naked waists. The flowers, a mixture of orchids, frangipani, kika and jasmine blossoms added to the sensual way that the women swayed their hips in time to the, wave-like, movements of their arms. They danced in unison to the music of ukuleles, drums, split bamboo sticks and steel guitars played by older women in long tropical printed dresses. These women wore head bands of shells, threaded with raffia and leis of shells and flowers around their necks. Billie smiled at the sight and sound of this spectacle; it warmed her heart. The swaying motion of the young women, like palms in a tropical breeze, was mesmerising, and something special. She looked around, a man was tending what looked like a fire in the ground. He shifted soil, uncovering a steaming hessian cloth. Beneath the cloth were layers of banana leaves. The man was joined by others who helped clear away the leaves to reveal hot stones, on top of which was placed the butchered carcass of a hog wrapped in leaves. Heat was rising as the men lifted the grill with the cooked hog clear of the stones and onto a nearby table. An array of food and tropical fruits were laid out and guests gathered around the feast. Leis of flowers were placed over the heads of guests, and those who had simply stopped to witness the occasion. An old lady approached Billie and beckoned her to lower her head. She smiled as the woman placed three leis around her neck. Not yet satisfied, the woman asked Billie if she was married. Billie shook her head, whereupon the woman, whose smile never left her face, tucked a yellow hibiscus flower behind Billie's right ear, signalling to all that this young lady was available for marriage. Billie felt like a little girl again. She wished that all who knew her could see her now and felt it was one of those moments in life that she would never forget. But she wanted more, and it was only Billie Fleming that could tread the path of her life. Emotion was a tear away as Billie witnessed such joy.

It was two o'clock when she walked back into the hotel room. Her father was at the table typing up comments from interviews that morning. He stopped and looked up.

"Have you been crying, Billie?" He rose from his chair.

"Only tears of happiness," she said.

She told him all about her day, saying this holiday was going to be special. Joe looked at his daughter standing in front of him. This beautiful creature that came into his life. He used the words, 'his life', knowing that Pageant would be justified in saying the same thing. Yes, Billie was very much his wife's daughter. He had seen them hold hands, laughing at each other's misfortunes and knew that they would always be there for each other.

With the leis around her neck and the yellow hibiscus flower in her hair, Joe hadn't seen her in this light before, she was beautiful beyond words and clever with it, but then he was her father and so likely a little biased. For the next four days Billie and her father spent more time in each other's company. It was like getting to know each other again, only this time as adults. There were things that they had differing opinions about, both putting valid points across but neither conceding defeat.

On Sunday Billie was up early, again. She liked to take an early morning walk on the beach before her feet would take her elsewhere. The sky was blue, puffs of white cloud drifted slowly by and brightly coloured birds tree hopped as Billie walked nearby. She carried her sandals as she walked ankle deep in the warm sea. The sound of an aeroplane approached and Billie looked up. She could see it coming low in the sky, then it roared over her head. Behind this first plane were others. They flew low enough that she could see the pilots. One even waved, so she waved back. Then, in the direction they flew, she saw a cloud of black smoke and heard the muffled sound of explosions. Within seconds, there was the sound, 'ack, ack, ack' of gunfire and within a very short time, dozens of aeroplanes were in the air, like hornets going every which way. Billie noticed the red circle painted on their wings. The Japanese were dropping bombs on Pearl Harbour. The sight, sound and the smell of cordite made her go cold; she stood frozen for a moment before running from the beach towards the palm trees. There, small birds flew in panic and an albatross glided past heading out to sea. Black smoke rose high above the harbour as the sound of gunfire and bombs went on. As Billie ran, she thought that if all they were bombing was the harbour, as at the moment, that was what it looked like, then the civilian population were not in the line of fire and her hotel would be safe. It took barely fifteen minutes to get to the hotel. Her father was waiting at the entrance. People were screaming and there was a lot of panic with no one knowing what to do or where to go.

"I must help these people!" Billie shouted. "I must do something!"

"Stay well away from it, Billie!"

"I'm going to change my clothes, Dad. I want you to take me to the hospital. They will need all the help they can get."

Within minutes Billie was back. Smoke in various shades of black rose above the harbour, as bomb after bomb, explosion after explosion could be heard. Billie and her father ran to the car.

"The Tripler Hospital, Dad, I'll tell you where it is. It isn't far." Joe drove with twenty or so Japanese planes above their heads and, seemingly, little resistance from the ground. A fleeting thought crossed Joe's mind that he would have more to report than he would ever have dreamed of. The sight that greeted them at the entrance to the hospital was one of complete mayhem. People were wandering around in shock. The injured being brought in were screaming in pain. Immediately Billie went into 'work mode'. She moved through the confusion, shouting that she was a nurse and to be directed to wherever she was needed. An orderly of some description grabbed her by the arm and she swung around.

"Look after that one," he said pointing to a young lad with his arm showing bone and very little else. "I'll get you a hat and an apron, just to show them you're one of us."

"Dad," Billie barked, as she took the man's shirt off his back and started to rip it into strips. "I need a stick six inches long and as thick as your finger, try that bush," she looked up and nodded toward one growing on the lawn in front of the hospital, "and hurry; if I don't get a tourniquet on this man in a few moments he'll die." The man was young, eighteen or nineteen. His screaming was no more than an irritant to Billie. She had come to terms with the fact that screaming and pain were secondary to the job in hand. The orderly was back. He gave Billie an apron and plonked a cap on her head.

"I don't know where you came from lady, but welcome to the Tripler General Hospital. When you're done with him, come inside, others will see to him. You look young," he said as a passing comment before hurrying through the double doors and into the nightmare beyond them.

Billie tied a strip of the man's shirt to his upper arm and reached out for the drumstick-like piece of wood her father handed to her. The lad had passed out as Billie tightened the tourniquet, stopping the flow of blood from his arm.

"Will he live?" Joe asked.

"Well, he's alive at the moment," she shrugged, "luck of the draw I guess, luck of the draw, Dad. I'm going inside. The next empty stretcher that comes out, stick him on it. Christ knows where he'll go."

Just then there was an explosion in the gardens of the hospital and Billie looked up.

"Stick around if you want to Dad, but I've got to go in. I'll see you when I see you," she stood and gave him a kiss on the cheek, "love you dad, must go."

Joe looked at his daughter, amazed at how she had handled the last fifteen minutes, how capable and mature, acting on an impulse that was not remotely like anything he had to contend with in his own line of work. There was blood on her hands, on her apron and a smear of the young man's blood on her forehead. Joe stood and watched Billie weave through the panic stricken crowd and realised that for the first time in her life, he couldn't help her.

The bombing of Pearl Harbour went on for two hours and in that time, Billie had seen a lot and learned a lot. She watched men come in that were already dead and others go out the same way. She was directed to triage and given a tube of lipstick.

"Mark their forehead," she was told, "Wendy will put you right."

Wendy looked up from a kneeling position, having just marked the forehead of a man with a mortal wound, the letter F in bright red lipstick printed on his forehead. It all looked rather macabre.

"M for morphine, C for critical and in need and F for those who will not survive. I'm Wendy, it's a fucking slaughterhouse in here, so don't you go throwing up on me or start crying."

There were two, no three, distinctive features regarding Wendy. She had a shock of red hair tied up in a bun and breasts that could fill a picnic hamper, and her age. Somewhere between thirty and forty Billie guessed.

"I, I haven't been trained in..." Wendy cut her off.

"I don't give a fuck if you're not even house trained; you must know something or you wouldn't be here," she smiled, "am I right?"

For the next four hours Wendy and Billie applied their lipstick on what seemed like dozens of unfortunates that lay on litters at their feet. The Fs went one way, the Cs and Ms another. Burns and shrapnel wounds accounted for most of the injuries. The dead were taken out the back. Billie did what she did without question, sometimes making decisions that she would not have taken under normal circumstances, but these were far from normal circumstances. The place was buzzing, nurses, doctors, surgeons and everyone that was needed to make the hospital function worked tirelessly, there was no choice. Morphine was administered, along with tannic acid jelly dressings for flash burns and plasma brought in from the blood bank at Queen's Hospital as a weapon against shock. Sulpha drugs were given orally to prevent infection.

In the hospital's operating theatres, amputations and operations of all descriptions were performed on the living. And for the dying… a prayer. It was said that some had resigned themselves to what was going to happen and died with dignity, which Billie questioned. How can you possibly 'die with dignity', without uttering a word condemning the people that killed you, dying with dignity? Is accepting your death, even when it's taken from you in such a way, dying with dignity? Billie wasn't having any of that talk. For her, life was precious, even to the end and she advocated that there was nothing wrong with entering the gates of heaven or hell kicking and screaming.

For twenty hours, Billie didn't sleep and when she stopped, she walked with Wendy and laid down on the beach, out of reach of the pain that was still to be heard in the wards. Other hospitals in Hawaii had their share of dead and wounded, and the hospital ship, the Solace, was overrun with casualties, but Billie didn't want to know.

Joe concentrated on his report on the bombing, telegraphing up to the minute reports every couple of hours. The number of battleships sunk in the harbour, the preliminary count of the dead and missing, the number of Japanese planes shot down and so on. Four days later, Billie was still at the Tripler. By then, most of the young men that were going to die had died and martial law had been invoked. Japanese people living on the island had been interned for national security and Joe had filed his last report. The following day, young men were being buried at Oahu Cemetery in Honolulu.

Billie left Tripler General Hospital with a letter of recommendation, starting with the words " To whom it may concern" and ending with "Yours sincerely." It was signed by the administrator of The Tripler Hospital, whose name was illegible.

One day later, Joe managed to get a flight out of Hawaii. Billie spent her last afternoon on the beach sitting under a coconut palm reflecting on the last six days. She sifted sand through her fingers as she recalled the moment her life changed. "Jesus Christ," she thought to herself," my father still thinks of me as a little girl. Maybe I will always be his little girl and maybe that's how it should be." But she had made Joe promise that he would never tell her mother how it had really been these last few days. She would always remember that magical moment when an old woman in a grass skirt had placed flowers around her neck. The hibiscus flower that had been tucked behind her ear, she had placed between the pages of The Grapes of Wrath, a book her mother had given her to read while in Hawaii. In spite of everything, Billie would always remember the happy times, but there was something else she would always remember. One of the young lads that had made a remark about her that first day while she was out walking. She had seen him again. She had watched John from Ohio die in front of her; never again to run into the wind as he undoubtedly would have done. That was hard, really hard. She looked out of the aeroplane window as they crossed the New York State line and recalled Sister Sandy talking about having met Winston Churchill and her words about some of her students having experiences in the future that would border on historical, futile, or moments of exhilaration. She sighed. You would never guess Sister Sandy, you would never guess what happened to me.

9

On the 4th July, the wheels of Michael's Hurricane came to a stop. He, along with six of his group, had been transferred to Croydon RAF Base in southern England. His group was attached to 111 Squadron under Squadron Leader, Walter S. Harman. The eighth member of the group, Stanley Wallace, had broken his leg during a game of football at Sutton Bridge and would be out of action for months. All were in good spirits as they were introduced to the rest of the squadron. Some of the squadron had already tasted air combat, while others had yet to face the realities of the situation they were to encounter. The presence of these pilots was unnerving. Their talk of pilots being lost to enemy fighters was, to say the least, sobering. With the rise of aerial attacks over Britain, squadrons, with increasing regularity, were being flown out of Croydon to intercept German bombers. Shipping convoys were the main recipient of indiscriminate bombing in the English Channel and vital supplies of food and raw materials were vulnerable to attack by submarines and German aircraft.

At 5 past one in the afternoon on Wednesday the 10th July, 111 Squadron was scrambled. Michael had mixed feelings as he ran to his plane. He was excited, with an adrenaline rush that put him in a state of mind that shut out everything but the job in hand.

"This is it," he said, as he strapped himself into the cockpit. With his engine fired up and the chocks removed from the wheels, he taxied to his position for take-off. He, like his friends, had been waiting some time for things to happen and his sometime was now. Behind them, Spitfires of the 74th Squadron, along with other squadrons of Hurricanes and Spitfires flew out of Croydon. Then squadrons from North Weald, Biggin Hill and Kenley joined the fray.

After the evacuation of Dunkirk and the fall of France, the next step for Germany was to invade Britain. What stood in their way was the British air defences, the R.A.F. German aircraft began attacking coastal targets, ports and shipping centres. A shipping convoy in the English Channel off the coast of Folkestone had come under attack. The German formation of aircraft that were met by 111 Squadron consisted of Dornier DO 17s with an escort of Messerschmitt's 110 and 109s. Michael's squadron was the first to engage, breaking formation and descending from above. With this, the Dornier, a twin engine light bomber fighter, broke from their own formation, giving rise to a scattering of planes at differing distances and altitudes.

Michael guessed their number to be sixty, seventy, maybe more. He was also conscious of their fighter escorts, well above him. These were now in dog fights with the Spitfires, whose job it was to protect the Hurricanes. Michael picked his target. Looking around there were planes flying every which way. He dove to meet his target, banking left then right. He felt, simultaneously, nervous, anxious, eager and afraid. Breathing deeply, he leaned forward and looked through his gun sight. Having the Dornier where he wanted him, he pressed the brass button on his joystick. A three second burst sent 500 bullets from the 8 Browning machine guns in the Hurricane's wings into the side of the German bomber. As it turned out, not one bullet hit it. Everything seemed to be happening in seconds. A Hurricane flashed below him, his guns ablaze, hitting the fuselage of the bomber he'd missed. The Dornier tilted and slipped to port as Michael turned in the opposite direction and put his plane into a steep climb. The sound and vibration of the Merlin engine at full throttle dominated everything, as it hurled his machine around the sky like a champagne cork in rough water. A 109 sped past, its guns spitting bullets, hitting a Spitfire whose engine burst into flame. Michael had gained around 3,000 feet and was on the periphery of the fight when, to his right, a twin engine Dornier on a straight flight path a thousand feet below him had its port engine trailing black smoke. To its right, was another Dornier. Michael would engage this one from the rear. In front, at roughly the same altitude, a 110 was on the tail of a Hurricane, Michael decided to forget the Dornier and give chase. The 110 turned sharply to starboard. Knowing that a Hurricane was behind him and although the 110 was a little faster than the Hurricane, its turn was not as tight. Because of this, Michael was able to get him in his sights at an angle of forty five degrees. Michael saw his tracers strike the fuselage of the fighter side on. It immediately pitched to the side and, as Michael skimmed over the top of him, he rolled sideways and glanced back. The plane was in a spiral fall. Again, Michael put his plane into a climb, he levelled off, making sure nothing was behind him.

He looked down, away to his right and 2,000 feet below, he, noticed another Dornier. It was twisting its way to earth after having a wing ripped off. Two of its pilots had jumped clear, their parachutes opening up and drifting down to the sea. Amongst the carnage in the sky, it was refreshing to see that not all planes shot down resulted in the men that flew them dying, at least these two would have a chance, but then again, they were still the enemy. Michael, with beads of sweat on his forehead, wriggled in his seat and whispered, "There for the grace of God go I," and flew on.

The weather that morning had been dull and grey with a lot of cloud, but in the last few hours it had changed. There was still cloud, just not as much, in fact the sun now showed itself between them. This proved to be a two edged sword for the hunted and hunter alike, to fly into the sun could be fatal. Impaired vision at any time was dangerous and it didn't matter how smart a fancy flyer was, sometime or other, the sun could be his undoing and instead of being back at base slaking his thirst and discussing the day's events, he'd be in another place…. God forbid!

And so, the afternoon went on. Michael was ducking and diving, twisting his way through the Dorniers and 109s, entering clouds and coming out of them, shooting at the flying frames of his enemy, who likewise shot back.

Time spent in the air depended mainly on two things, the amount of fuel in your tank and how long you held your thumb on the brass button that operated the firing of the machine guns. In all, it would take around fourteen seconds to exhaust the 2,600 bullets that travelled down the eight barrels of the Browning machine guns. After that, it was pointless to hang around. So, home young man. Fill up your tanks and re-arm. There's no time to lose.

On his way back to base, Michael fell into a melancholy mood. How many men would have died in the short time they were in the air? And this, for him, was only the beginning. Now, he understood. Now he had been blooded. Now he had crossed that line and there was no going back. From this point on, he was one of them. He would either follow those that had their names chiselled onto a block of granite, made into a monument that would then be stuck on a hill somewhere, or placed in a pleasant little town or village square, to be read by the visiting populace, with heads bowed, uttering words of gratitude and at the same time thanking God that it was not their sons or fathers name they read. Some young men would forgo a lot of things in life, forsaking everything to press a fucking brass button for fourteen seconds. A lot to ask of any man… alternatively, he would live.

Back at base, the ground crew were anxiously waiting, counting the planes as they came in, one, two, three, four, so far three were missing. Michael undid his harness, slid back the cockpit canopy and dropped the exit side panel. Having composed himself, he stepped out. A warm breeze greeted him as he stood on the wing of his trusty steed and he smiled.

"Are you well sir," asked Henry looking up. Henry was one of the ground crew Michael had met on a number of occasions.

"Everything's tickety- boo. Is everyone back?" Michael asked as he jumped down.

"Waiting for four. I see you've copped a few bullets," Henry said pointing to four holes in the fuselage.

Michael shrugged, nonchalantly. "Nothing you boys can't fix."

"If he'd got you in the fuel tank, you would've known about it. Go and get yourself a cuppa and leave the patching up to us. By the way, how did you fair?"

"Bagged me a 110 and shot up two Dornier."

As Michael walked to the canteen, he thought of Henry's greeting, "are you well Sir?" The first three words, an inquiry as to his well-being, but it was the last word that had caused him to smile. Henry had called him 'Sir'. It wasn't the first time he'd been referred to as 'Sir', but other times it had been tongue in cheek but this time he'd felt this reference was deserving and that it was said with respect.

One and a half hours later, they were scrambled again. This time 111 Squadron were three Hurricanes short. Michael didn't dwell on these losses as he prepared himself, mentally, for what was to come. Michael's group had gathered at eighteen thousand feet with the Spitfires above, watching out for them. To his port side, at a distance of three hundred feet, he saw Shorty raise his gloved hand.

Shorty had landed in front of Michael on their return and, over a cup of tea, had told him he had seen squadron leader Higgs go down. Higgs had crashed into a 109, with both planes falling apart and heading for the sea. One of the other two missing was flown by Jimmy Harris, the other, by one of the pilots not of their group.

This second engagement with the enemy, went much like the first in that their contact with them was in roughly the same area, but this time, Michael thought, there seemed to be less of them.

The fighting was already in progress when they arrived at the scene. Their formation broke away, with Michael diving steeply and swerving to his starboard, having already missed an opportunity to intercept one Dornier as a Hurricane flashed past, letting loose on his intended target. This skirmish lasted until Michael, again, ran out of ammunition and, once more, headed for home.

Sleep that night didn't come easily for Michael, his mind was in an abyss, thinking of what he'd experienced.

He turned over and lay on his back, he lifted his hands and, in the darkness, looked at them. They trembled as sweat ran from his forehead onto his pillow. That afternoon he'd seen men leave this earth in ways that he could never have imagined, or could he? He knew that men would die and had been doing so for some time, but in his heart of hearts, the things he had seen he knew would happen again. But he didn't want to know and brushed those thoughts aside. Like closing a book whose stories were contained between hard covers and placed on a shelf, where its contents would not be revealed until, once more, the reader turned its pages. But unlike a book, the reality of life is that it goes on and cannot be closed merely because the reader encounters things not to his or her liking.

Two men of Michael's group were missing, Jimmy Harris went down with his Hurricane on fire in their first encounter with the enemy and Archie Winchester didn't arrive back at day's end. His body was washed up somewhere on the Dutch coast two weeks later. In the meantime, more pilots took their place, with some having spent less time in the air than it would take to build a garden shed. For Michael, those two weeks and the two weeks after became a learning curve that saved his life, in that he got wise to how the German pilots flew. There were things one didn't do when engaging the enemy and things one did do, learning fast was the key to survival.

All of July and the first fourteen days of August, Michael flew his Hurricane above the towns, villages and fields of southern England, including the English Channel where the Germans were still bombing naval shipyards and ports. Then, on the 17th of August at ten minutes to six in the evening 111 Squadron were scrambled to meet a large number of German Bf 110s Messerschmitt fighter bombers whose objective was to bomb British RAF bases and who were now heading for Croydon. The resulting attack saw multiple substantive hits on the airfield, airport terminal, surrounding factories and a direct hit on the armoury. The factories surrounding the airfield took the lion's share of the bombs, as did a housing estate. A total of sixty two civilians were killed as well as five airmen. The following day saw further attacks. Michael, Troy and Shorty took part in the defence of numerous RAF bases, along with other squadrons. For the German squadrons, the exercise was somewhat a failure, as, due to severe losses the day before, their ability to sustain such attacks were diminishing.

On the nineteenth of August, the boys left Croydon and were transferred to Debden. There was no let-up, they were exhausted and except for a few days here and there when they were allowed time off would head to the coast. There, out of harm's way, they would find a little pub overlooking the sea, get terribly drunk, then sit or lie on a stony beach and gather their thoughts. Michael would reminisce of past summer days, even to the point of penning a few lines in his notebook, as he looked to the horizon for inspiration.

From time to time, I recall the days.
I walked on water and rode on sleighs.
Where the sun always shone, the snow always deep.
Cause even little cowboys need dreams to keep.
We made dens in the fern and climbed trees in the wood.
Lord take me back to those days if you could.
Let me linger a while in that bygone time.
Where a day was a week and that week was all mine.
To a place of laughter in a land of never
Where a child of seven, would live forever.

In a depressed mood the boys talked of the short time they had known each other, spilling out their innermost feelings with the intensity of men about to die. They talked of their last requests if they didn't make it to the end of the runway, meaning if they should get killed during the fighting. Troy was philosophical about the subject, not that he wanted to part this earth, more the point of being that he knew he could do sod all about it if it were to happen. Shorty was more nonchalant and suggested that if he were to fly into the sunset, he wanted the boys to remember this day and raise a glass in his memory. And Michael, he was adamant that there was only one person that was going to get any part of his body and it wouldn't be the Devil or God, it would be a fine lady who would possess him, and he wouldn't be dead when that happened either.

On the eighth September another transfer was in the offing, this time to RAF Drem, a base in East Lothian

Scotland. But although 111 Squadron left, the boys did not. They stayed and became part of the 32nd Squadron for three weeks.

Two weeks before this was to happen, Michael, now a seasoned fighter pilot, if there was such a thing, given the high death toll, became aware of his own failings. It was late afternoon on a hot day in late August. He was tired, anxious and, having just seen two of his fellow pilots succumb to the enemy, all he wanted to do was to get back to base and sit for a while with a cold beer in his hand. With his concentration relaxed and the runway ahead he dropped out of the sky at a half mile to commence his run. At 300 feet he lowered his undercarriage. At 200, he reduced power, but to his amazement his plane didn't descend as it should and he didn't have time to adjust, or even to think of anything. So at 100 feet he gave the plane full power and cleared the end of the runway climbing. Giving the base a wide berth, he retracted his wheels and wondered what the hell was going on. The control tower contacted him, enquiring as to any problems he may be having in landing. He confirmed that there were no visible signs of anything wrong from where they were.

"Just a practice landing," he reported back, lying, but still not knowing why his plane wasn't responding as it should and beginning to feel rather foolish. He circled in a wide arc, thinking, thinking and as he banked, he looked through the perspex canopy of the Hurricane and below him… Jesus Christ! There was his answer, staring him in the face, acres and acres of golden corn, waiving to him in the fields. It grew all around the base, even up to the fence on both ends of the runway. The thermals, the hot air rising from the corn fields. He remembered the buzzards used it to gain height when he was stationed at Shawbury and now it was stopping him from landing. His response to this situation should have come automatically but it didn't. Now with the thermals in mind, he reduced his altitude by a hundred feet on approaching the runway, minimising the effect the rising hot air would have between the ground and his plane. His second attempt went as planned and he landed without incident.

"A practice landing was it?" said a fellow emerging from the control tower, he couldn't hide the grin he gave. "That's the second we've had today", he added.

Michael smiled, knowing full well he knew what Michael was about, but he said nothing, not wishing to add to his embarrassment.

10

The bombing of London went on from September 1941 to the following May and it was in April that 111 Squadron, at the time, based at Debden, replaced its Hurricanes for the Super Marine Spitfire. Michael took the transition in his stride, taking into account the advantages and disadvantages of both planes. The Hurricanes being the sturdiest, the workhorse of the sky as far as fighter bombers were concerned. As for the Spitfires, they were sleek, fast, and already earning a reputation that was worthy of any fighter pilot to associate himself with. For a couple of weeks, they trained and practised manoeuvres well suited to the overall design of the plane. Michael, although used to flying the Hurricane, quickly adapted to his new toy. At this time, the squadrons of Spitfires and Hurricanes criss-crossed the sky, sending a message of unwavering defiance to the German invaders.

The loss of pilots had become a fact and as unpalatable as it was, more young men would step forward and fill the void. Many nationalities flew alongside the British pilots, Polish, New Zealanders, Canadians, Australians, South

Africans and many more. The respect these men had for each other was forged in the sky, etched in the minds of those who were there. From time to time, when exhaustion got the better of them, the boys would spend a few days in the city they were protecting.

Michael's expectations of how the people of London lived was a culture shock. Having been brought up in the country, he was used to a much slower pace of life. He found London exciting, yet a little unnerving. Troy, originally from Kensington, took them on a tour, walking amongst the rubble and demolished buildings that had become part of the London street scene. But this devastation didn't stop young boys in their short trousers and scraped knees from kicking a football about, using their jumpers as goal posts. Their 'goings on' being observed by little girls pushing prams and dragging dolls along the road by their hair, chattering away like the mothers they would one day become.

Michael found it strange, but far from uncommon to see women in gingham and floral pinafores kneeling, scrubbing the stone steps of their homes, or rummaging through bombed houses looking for a frying pan or other items worthy of keeping. Every now and then, air raid sirens could be heard, their eerie mournful sound clearing the streets of people, all rushing to wherever they could find shelter.

"This way," Troy shouted, the tube station is just up the road."

London now became the objective of the German bombers. Day and night the bombs fell, but life went on.

Above them the theatre of aerial activity, almost like a written script, produced scenes of courage and daring on both sides. Life was lived underground until the 'all clear' sounded. Then the curtains would fall as the actors departed the stage, the crowds would stand and exit the sanctuary of the tube stations. But they'd be back when the heavens opened their curtains again to the sound of drums, fire and aeroplane engines. In the Elephant and Castle tube station, the boys picked their way through the crowd, stepping over the inert bodies of the young and old alike. People talked in hushed whispers, some staring at the ceiling no doubt wondering if they would have a home to go back to this time. Michael sat with his back against the tunnel wall making small talk with an old man who had run out of matches to light his pipe. The sound of a violin drifted through the tunnel. To all but a few it didn't mean a lot, but to Troy it was a welcome distraction. He closed his eyes, this auditorium was not of his choosing, but having said that, the acoustics were second to none. He smiled.

Glyn was annoyed that the siren sounded when it did. He was not averse to an occasional dalliance with a pretty girl and had thought he was on to a good thing. Being forced to leave the pub was shit. He had a choice either to stay or go. The girl he had been paying attention to was succumbing to his advances. Maybe the wings on his uniform had a lot to do with that. His charm was a little above average but, indeed, a blue uniform denoting that the wearer would, at some stage, be fighting for his life above their heads, was a draw like no other.

The Elephant and Castle pub had been full when the boys had entered. It was three thirty on a Friday afternoon and everyone inside was singing Happy Birthday. As they entered, a man swearing like a trooper was in the process of being ejected by two burly men, with one each side of him, he was unceremoniously thrown outside. The ejectee, an intoxicated man, in his forties, had been accused of inappropriate behaviour toward the lady who was celebrating her 50th birthday.

"The bleedin' git squeezed me tits I don't like geezers bein' too familiar with them," she shrieked, crying with laughter.

"Well not in the Elephant and Castle," shouted another well-endowed lady who jiggled her own breasts. This was done to the approval and cheers of her friends.

The sole purpose of the boys' visit to London was to lose their virginity. Stories of willing ladies in the clubs and pubs where airmen drank abounded. To lose your virginity before losing your life became a priority and it didn't really matter to whom you lost it. The question of chastity for Michael was one of, when such an action would take place, not if it ever would. It had been on his mind ever since the death of Jimmy Harris and Archie. He knew that Jimmy had never slept with a woman, as he'd told him so, and as for Archie, he didn't know. All in all, did it really matter?

"Of course, it fucking mattered," said Troy as they sat in a train carriage on the way to London.

"To know what I know now, I think it should be mandatory that all pilots should exercise this rite of passage before putting their arse in a cockpit and flying into fuck knows what." For a moment no one spoke. Glyn shrugged and with a deep sigh made the statement.

"Well gentlemen," he said smiling. "I would concur with that last statement, but with one proviso."

"And that is?" added Michael.

"That one should announce the fact in their local newspaper."

Two hours had elapsed since the boys had entered the pub and during that time the three had engaged in conversation with three young ladies. It was obvious from the beginning that they were what may be called 'fallen women', not words commonly used for women that wanted payment in exchange for sexual favours, but if their mothers were of a religious persuasion, then that is how they would have been referred to.

After a few drinks and while watching the party goers having a knees up and singing, My Old Man Said Follow the Van, the boys were on first name terms. There was Katy who had taken a fancy to Michael. Jen, who sidled up to Troy and Sue, a pretty girl who, between drinks, got Glyn up to dance. After a while Katy, in her white and red spotted dress and red shoes; "what other colour would they be?" Michael thought, rested her hand on Michael's arm. After finding out where he came from, she'd informed him that she had never seen a cow, or a sheep and would be hard put to know what animal milk came from. In contrast, she appeared knowledgeable in the Arts, putting Michael at a distinct disadvantage. Michael didn't know a Rembrandt from a Van Gogh. He was intrigued. Katy explained that, as a child, before her father died, he'd taken her to museums and exhibitions and that, ever since, she had followed his love of Art. She seemed rather sad talking about her father, but soon smiled and asked Michael why he was in London.

When the air raid siren sounded, she looked up and shook Michael's hand.

"Thank you for your company," she said with a nervous smile.

"Will I see you again?" He found himself saying.

"I…I don't know." She answered, "I don't know."

Michael was confused. The girl in the pub, she bothered him. He followed the boys into the underground. Were the girls behind them? He was annoyed with himself, why hadn't he grabbed her hand and got her to go with him? He wanted more of her and this isn't how he had planned it. He looked both ways on the platform but there was no sign of the girls. Unsurprisingly, the birthday party people were there, having turned left in the tunnel as the boys had turned right. Michael could hear them singing. He thought that they might have stayed in the pub since licensed premises were allowed to stay open during an air raid.

"Shit," he said as he sat a seat away from the man with the pipe.

For two hours they sat, Troy and Glyn each giving an account of the conversations they had with their prospective partners. Maybe partners was the wrong word, but there was something about the girl, Katy, that Michael had talked to, that wasn't quite right. When the all-clear siren sounded the boys returned to the Elephant and Castle, but the atmosphere had changed. The birthday party crowd had stayed in the tube station and the girls didn't show up.

"They just left. Got a lift to Soho," said the bar man, giving Glyn a knowing wink and adding, "that's if the car they were in can get there. You boys missed out, pretty girls too," he said as he placed Glyn's fourth pint on the bar.

"Soho?" Enquired Michael.

"Don't ask," said Troy with a grin.

"The girls have gone to Soho?" Michael said wanting an explanation.

"The Piccadilly Commandos."

"The Piccadilly Commandos? Jesus Troy what the hell are you talking about?"

"That's what they call the girls in Soho."

"The girls we were talking to are called the Piccadilly Commandos?"

"God Michael, you really are a country bumpkin. The girls were prostitutes and probably still are."

"Street walkers," Michael interrupted.

"Yes, I gathered that, I'm not totally stupid, but how do you know they have joined the army?" Michael said with a grin.

Troy put his elbows on the table and hung his head in his hands.

"They haven't joined the fucking army, Michael, that's what they call the street walkers in Soho, the Piccadilly Commandos."

Michael noted Glyn's confusion as he looked from Troy to Glyn and back again.

"Had him going there, didn't I?" said Michael as he burst out laughing.

"You bastard!" said Troy, putting emphasis on the word bastard.

"To be honest," Glyn was shaking his head, laughing at the same time, "I thought the girls had joined some London brigade for women. I've never heard of the Piccadilly Commandos before."

"Well, you have now and that's where we will be heading after a couple more of these."

"How far is it?" asked Glyn, pouring the last of his beer down his throat.

"About three and a half miles."

It wasn't long before the pub was full again and this time it was the turn of the early evening crowd. The boys had overheard, from someone who had just walked in, that a bomb had exploded in the middle of a row of houses not far away and a family of five had been killed while sheltering in the cellar. Their bodies would be taken and placed in the crypt of the local church to join others that had died. The Very Reverend John Markham, the resident vicar, and by all accounts a decent man, would have people stand watch over them to prevent the unspeakable, the theft of personal items from their bodies. There were other stories told of the 'unforgivable', opportunists who took advantage of any situation that was presented. There were lots of those and there would be a lot more as long as the bombs kept falling.

Michael wanted to know more and there were plenty of people who would tell him. A smart looking gentleman with an ace of spades playing card stuck behind the band of his black trilby hat told him, between shots of whisky, that he knew someone who knew someone that was going about masquerading as an Air Raid Precautions Warden. He had acquired, by dubious means, a warden's helmet and other items, including report forms, and armband, in fact everything a warden was issued with to do his job.

"To what ends?" Michael enquired.

"Well, you know, he tilted his head, a warden is first on the scene when homes and shops are bombed?"

Michael didn't reply, assuming that the chap thought, quite rightly, that he knew nothing of the duties of an air raid warden.

"They make out a report on what services were needed, that sort of thing." The man continued, "his first job was to keep the public well away from the area."

Michael nodded.

"And the difference between the goodie and the baddie warden?" Michael asked, the gentleman looked at Michael and smiled.

"While the goodie warden keeps everyone away, the baddie warden lets his mates steal what's worth stealing before the authorities get there. The war has changed everything." He looked blankly at the weekend revellers, pushing, and shoving their way to and from the bar.

"It's made good people a little bit bad, and a little bit bad people, even worse. A shopkeeper I know told me that he's lost more to looters than to the German bombs," he paused and took another shot of whisky, "it's hard to watch a grown man cry … he had a clothes shop."

He went on to tell more tales about looters and cheats in positions of trust, auxiliary firemen, ambulance personnel, stretcher bearers and even doctors. For money, they would sign disability papers intended for those who didn't want to join the army. "You have the desperate and the greedy," he rolled his eyes. "You could say that one's as bad as the other and I suppose they are, but the desperate are desperate, and the greedy," he shrugged, "are what they are?"

Troy came over, placed another pint on the table and suggested they leave after this one.

"And what's with the ace of spades in your hat?" Michael asked, turning to the man he was talking to.

"That…" he said smiling, "was good fortune. I won a Rolls Royce on the turn of a card."

Michael looked the man in the eyes and hesitated, "And what were you prepared to lose?"

The man pursed his lips and stood.

"The shirt off my back … everything." He held out his hand, Michael rose from his seat and offered his.

"Mind how you go," he said, and looking up at the ceiling of the Elephant and Castle then adding "while you're up there, in the blue yonder, watch your back. Always watch your back." And with that, the gentleman with the ace of spades in his hat, gave Michael a wink, drank the last of his whisky and left.

It was a long walk to Old Compton Street, Soho. On the way there, they passed burning buildings, people standing on the street looking at the crumbled dreams of their lives, firemen holding hoses ready for the water that sometimes, like the trains, didn't come. Then there were the men and women, who, amongst the dust and smoke and with bloodshot eyes could be seen removing bricks from their bombed out homes, salvaging what they could from the rubble.

On their arrival at Compton Street the air raid sirens, as if on cue, sounded. It was a five minute walk to Oxford Circus underground. It seemed to Michael that the bowels of the earth swallowed up thousands of people in the underground stations of London, only to spew them out again on the say-so of the sirens that had sent them there in the first place. Once outside again, the boys did a walk of Compton Street and amongst the devastation they had seen, Michael found it hard to understand the logic of the people, their town was being bombed, on fire, destroyed. Yet the pubs were full, and amongst the people on the streets were the buyers and sellers of mostly black market goods, going about their business. The spivs in their brown suits and trilbies, set at an acute angle on a head of Brylcreemed hair, finished off the ensemble with a garish tie, matched by an equally garish shirt. They carried a small leather suitcase, usually brown to match their suits and inside, offered for sale, were dodgy ration coupons, nylon stockings, whisky, the customary Swiss watch, along with packets of Lucky Strike cigarettes and other hard to acquire items. These people lived by their wits and although illegal, their means of earning a living was accepted by society and society embraced their presence.

The boys walked into the Coach and Horses. Same people, different pub. All had an attitude of, I'm all right Jack, or I would be, if I had a bit more of what you've got. The Piccadilly Commandos were there, each one proclaiming they had the deepest shelter in town and nothing would dissuade them from propositioning any man that could give them the benefits of a short time spent in their company. Sins of the flesh paid for much more than food on the table. The scent of cheap perfume and cigarette smoke hung like a toxic cloud. No one noticed as men in army uniforms made their presence known with rowdy behaviour and ungentlemanly comments, mostly towards the Piccadilly Commandos, some of whom would end up in the beds of those who'd directed the comments. It dawned on Michael that some of these girls were only a few years older than his own sisters and this realisation made him question his need to be there at all. But the desire of young men outweighed any moral issue that could have been raised.

"See anything you fancy?" asked Troy, eyeing up a girl whose auburn hair was a mass of curls. Her long, lithe body in a pencil cream skirt and seamed stockings, reminded Michael of another lady in a cream skirt and seamed stockings, but that was a very long time ago. This lady was preoccupied with an intoxicated young army private, who, by the looks of him, would be on his back long before he intended. His two mates stood holding each other up while singing 'We'll Meet Again'. The problem being that everyone else in the room was singing 'Lili Marlene'.

Michael couldn't help but smile seeing them having such a good time and thinking that sex at that minute was probably the last thing on their mind.

"No, I haven't, " answered Michael, getting back to Troy's question, but then I haven't really looked." Troy grinned.

"Jesus you can't bloody move in here …" said Glyn in a raised voice, at the same time catching the eye of an attractive barmaid who had just told a squaddie to watch his language.

"Three pints of bitter please."

Time spent in the Coach and Horses would be short. So, with Troy having limited time to impress the lady with curly hair, he sidled up to her and asks.

"Do you come here often?" She looked at him with wide eyes, then closed them and shook her head.

"That's a shit question," she said, "or are you being flippant?" She curled her lip and gave him a false smile, then added. "Don't be coy, just ask me how much, that way it saves us both a lot of time, and trust me on this one, I don't want you as a family member and you wouldn't want me to be one of yours." Troy shrugged. Ten minutes later the four of them

were on the street.

"Follow me," she said, "are your mates coming as well?" Suffice to say that all objectives that night were realised. To the satisfaction of all was debatable. Troy had it away with Shirly Temple, the girl with the curly hair. Glyn bedded a lady called Mata Hari and Michael was welcomed into the new world by a lady who had an uncanny likeness to Nell Gwyn, according to Troy. The process was repeated again the following night, before returning to base, where tales of their exploits were told time and time again.

11

Billie's stay in Hawaii affected her for many months. She became restless, unsettled and angry. Her patience was short lived, as noticed by her nursing colleagues and tutors. It would be safe to say that most of them had no idea of the carnage that bombs and bullets could do. Even Sister Sandy had become aware of the change in Billie. No matter how subtle, the change was there. Nurses who had worked on victims of car crashes, industrial accidents and the like, who had 'patched up' those who'd entered hospital not necessarily in one piece, those were the nurses who had seen similar things to Billie. They were the ones that understood. The ones she could talk to and help ease her mind.

In the first few months after the bombing of Pearl Harbour, a major recruiting campaign urging nurses to join the military, got underway. Posters and pamphlets were handed out stating that nurses between the ages of twenty one and forty, with no children under the age of fourteen, would be taken on. Three of the nurses Billie had confided in about her experience in Hawaii had left. They had joined the Army Medical Corps. Billie couldn't for the life of her understand why they would go voluntarily into a situation like she'd just left. The ironic thing about the whole business was that Billie wasn't yet a qualified nurse and wouldn't be for the next seven months.

On the 9th July 1943 British and American troops invaded Sicily, the largest island in the Mediterranean and just off the coast of mainland Italy. Three days later, nurses of the 10th American field Hospital and the 11th evacuation hospital arrived on the island. Amongst the many nurses sent was a very confident young woman, who was two months short of her twenty second birthday. She was slim and walked tall and with an optimistic air. She was a woman who knew about the things men needed when confronted with the uncertainty of life.

Billie Fleming turned her head and looked to the sky. Her presence there had come about through a dogmatic will to help. Her experience, however limited, and the aftermath of her involvement in the Japanese attack on Pearl harbour over two and a half years earlier, had left her with an overwhelming need to scratch an itch that wouldn't go away. Her participation in the events of Pearl Harbour were, of course, unplanned and Billie had felt she never again wanted to see the sights she had seen. However, she'd thought long and hard about her situation, working through the rights and wrongs of it all and felt the need to do 'something.' Not to do anything, played heavily on her mind. She wanted to be where she was needed and being needed was something she couldn't easily walk away from.

Five and a half weeks after the bombing of Pearl Harbour the Lenox Hill Hospital started recruiting medical personnel for what would become an Army Evacuation Hospital. This became officially activated the following August. During its time of conception and its deployment abroad, Billie had finished her training and had, as often happened, been transferred with others to the 11th Evacuation Hospital, whereupon she'd found herself on the shores of Sicily.

Their arrival was met by German Stuka dive bombers, so for the first few days the nurses were in and out of foxholes and slit trenches as the enemy screamed above their heads. Other nurses scheduled to support the US army were delayed for a further nine days while waiting for transport. Evacuation Hospitals covered a large area. Each was staffed by up to 53 nurses and up to 750 patients could be treated at any one time. Doctors operated on patients transported in from field hospitals closer to the front, whose length of stay depended on the severity of their injuries. Postoperative patients were routinely kept for ten days, some longer, before being sent on to larger facilities that could handle the volume and care that evacuation hospitals could not.

Billie and her fellow nurses were frequently transferred to other evacuation hospitals. One of these was a new hospital being established at Cefalu, east of Palermo in Italy. Due to the region's intense heat, increasing numbers of soldiers were being infected with malaria. Mosquito nets were put in place in an attempt to control the disease, but with little success and medical personnel also succumbed. Despite the outbreak of malaria, doctors and nurses routinely worked twelve hour shifts. At one point, the hospital admitted 300 patients in one twenty four hour period. Front line battle injuries have not changed for hundreds of years, the outcome of a musket ball fired from one of Napoleon Bonaparte's soldiers into the chest of an enemy, would have the same result as any bullet fired from any gun in any war. If death is the answer, it makes a nonsense of the question. And the question? Usually, I want something you've got and if you won't give it to me, I will take it. In that same twenty four hours, 200 patients were evacuated to North Africa for further treatment. Critical patients were flown out by plane, but most went by train to the coast where they were placed on hospital ships.

The rains came early in Sicily. Three days after being transferred to Salerno, a rainstorm raised the canvas tents of the evacuation hospital to the ground. Up to 1,000 patients were moved to an abandoned tobacco warehouse nearby. Field Hospitals were constantly on the move, sometimes at short notice. The front line of soldiers moved forward, leaving death and mayhem in their wake and the hospitals followed on behind. Billie and her colleagues picked up the pieces of shattered lives as a mother would, gathering discarded clothes and toys her children had left on the floor. Billie had become hardened to the cries of men and boys begging for their mothers in their last throws of life, where there was nothing she could do but hold their hand. Many men were saved by the doctors and nurses. Most would, eventually, be transported home never to return. Some recovered at hospitals in England and elsewhere, only to again face the bullets and bombs of the enemy when fit to do so.

In thirty eight days, Sicily was taken. The field and evacuation hospitals were there for some weeks after, taking in and transferring patients. The American 7th Army, under the command of General George Patton, moved on.

On the 9th of September, the Italian mainland was breached at Salerno by the advancing allied armies, and where the armies go, so do the medical teams. Every now and again existing teams would be replaced. New people would arrive on hospital ships, calling at ports as the invasion carried on northwards. On a few occasions these ships, although displaying recognised hospital ship markings, were bombed, and strafed by German planes causing casualties, including patients being shipped out and the nurses travelling with them. Billie stayed another six months with her unit. The mobile field and evacuation hospitals were uprooted when and wherever it was necessary. By mid-February Billie was in Anzio, relieved to be away from the butchery happening in Monte Cassino. Her unit was now only 37 miles from Rome, but it might well have been a 100 miles away. As far as Billie knew, they would be in Anzio for a long time. A beach head had been formed there since the 22nd January, ready for the big push to Rome. Italy had already surrendered, but the German army had a big presence in Italy and were putting up a fierce resistance. Six weeks later Billie, along with ten other nurses, boarded a hospital ship bound for England. They were to oversee the well-being of patients who needed further medical treatment and themselves would, at long last, have a rest that was well overdue, providing they were not intercepted by German bombers.

The ship arrived at Southampton docks the first week of May and after the evacuation of troop casualties, the nurses and all relevant medical staff were taken to an American clearance hospital where they were to stay until told to get ready for the next move. Billie found it strange being in another country, although she was born in Birmingham, she was only six years of age when her parents had emigrated to America. She found herself telling her story to her colleagues, as they told theirs to her. Each story was remarkably different. Billie told of her trip to America on board a steamship and of her first meeting with a young Welshman on the train taking them to the docks. She called him Uncle Sam. There was another man her parents had met on board ship, he became her Uncle Curtis, now a highflyer in the banking world in New York.

Billie had worked with her team of nurses for many months and the bond that had developed between them was not like the friendship that she had with the nurses at the Lenox Hill Hospital. There was an accepted feeling of comradeship, a sense of looking after each other. The differing ranks amongst these nurses and their male colleagues was purely a title that one held and didn't impede the respect they had for each other in the wards. Each nurse knew her job and, to a large extent, knew something of everyone else. But now and again human feelings would get the better of them. Many times, nurses would shed tears for the men they looked after. Those people in positions of authority and in the halls of teaching, those who advocated that it was unethical for nurses to become emotionally involved with their patients were, to say the least, a little short on compassion. Human emotion being what it is, even an exterior veil of indifference can slip when alone at night with your thoughts. In fact, those thoughts could happen any time, any place and in any situation. No one is immune to personal feelings and if it is a failing to cry, then that failing is common to all.

12

Connie looked at the full glass of rum and lime perched on the edge of the table between a brass ashtray and a packet of woodbines. Just a little nudge of the table and it would end up on the floor, but she wasn't bothered, she'd had enough. She glanced up as Imogen reached out to put down her empty glass, missing the table by a couple of inches, and at the same time, knocking over Connie's rum and lime. Both glasses fell onto the sticky carpet without a sound. Billie bent down and picked up both glasses with one hand, spilling her own drink from a glass she held in her other hand.

"I think it's time to go," she said with a giggle. Five intoxicated US army nurses filed through the door of the Kings Head into the bright sunlight that shone on the little pub down an alley off Oxford Street. It wasn't often that alcohol had played any part in what leisure time they'd had since leaving Sicily. The last real session being when they found a hoard of champagne bottles hidden in an old barn just outside Salerno. The barn had been acquisitioned as an evacuation hospital for the expected wounded that would soon arrive. There were times when other field and evacuation hospitals took the brunt of incoming troops, this was the lull before the storm, The bubbles were passed around to all that dared to drink it. Knowing that repercussions would follow, failed to deter all concerned in having a recreational tipple, or two.

During their first seven days in London, Billie and her group of nurses visited the 'must see' tourist spots. They walked in Hyde Park, stood at the gates of Buckingham Palace and strolled the bombed out ruins of central London. They gazed at the Royal Albert Hall and wondered if it would survive the war. They saw the disenchanted look on people's faces and the determination of others to live to see their city rise from the ashes. They were told of Soho and its bawdy reputation, not a nice place for good girls to go. So they went and for one evening they joined the Piccadilly Commandos as honorary members, courtesy of two well established associates of the fictitious club who they had all joined up with.

"You're not really dressed for the part" said one.

"Ah, but the boys like girls in uniform," quipped Billie, not convinced that what she said was true.

"Don't they ever," replied the girl with a red boa, who looked a million dollars in her classy pencil dress with large prints of red roses.

"I want to marry a Yank," said her friend in a distinctive cockney accent.

"What did she say?" Connie asked, not understanding.

"The lady would like to marry an American G I."

"Well, you're in the right profession to get one," answered Connie, half joking.

Billie looked at the girl who wanted to marry an American. She was tall with dark thick shoulder length hair, good looking, like her friend and just as classy. She was dressed in a strappy, expensive looking, pale blue sleeveless blouse and dark blue, wide legged trousers, finished off with a pair of white flats. The thing about her was that she didn't look cheap.

When was the last time Billie looked like that, if she ever did? It had been a long time since she had admired herself in a full length mirror, but she could never look like these girls. She glanced down at her brown brogue shoes and her earthy green military jacket and skirt. She wore a khaki shirt and a tie, her cap matching the colour of her jacket. For the last two years she had felt like Cinderella's sister. Was she jealous of these girls? No, envious? Yes, not of their lifestyle, as exciting as it may have been, but of their appearance compared to hers.

They were standing outside a pub. The Coach and Horses. It was six thirty, a warm breeze blew across the street, lifting a newspaper that once held fish and chips. A group of British soldiers passed by. They stopped, one of them introduced himself as Colin,

"Can I buy you a drink?" he said, looking Lesley up and down.

"I'm sorry, I'm with my friends."

"And I'm with mine, so let's all go in and let the dice fall where it will."

"Not the kind of answer one would expect from a British soldier," said Shelly interrupting, "but hey, I'm in for the long hall. Come on girls, don't look this gift horse in the mouth. No offence young man, I mean, referring to you as a horse."

"Non taken miss. Are you American?"

"Kentucky born and bred, and don't think by buying us a drink you can get into our pants."

"I wouldn't dream of it."

Shelly stopped suddenly, turned, and looked Colin square in the face. "You wouldn't?!" she exclaimed, raising her eyebrows. She smiled, a slowww… smile.

"No, Ma'am, certainly not," the soldier stammered. Shelly turned and walked into the pub.

"How disappointing…! Landlord, the boys are buying the girls a drink."

The early evening turned into a late evening and the drinks flowed. The two girls of the Piccadilly Commandos were in deep conversation with Billie and Imogen. With a sense of humour, they discussed each other's work.

"You must have seen a lot of men's willies in your profession" said the one with the red boa. Imogen gave a little giggle.

"Not as many as you in yours," she answered.

"But unlike you two," Billie was already laughing, she knew what was coming, "we don't look at men's willies in monetary terms." All four burst out laughing. With tears running down the faces of the London girls. The one wearing the trousers and wanting to marry a G.I. uttered.

"I have never thought of it like that". Her mate added through her tears, "You mean every time we see a willy, the till drawer opens?"

"And a bell rings," said Imogen, doubled up in laughter.

In no time, the conversation turned to the war.

A lad, who looked not old enough to put a rifle to his shoulder and with an air of his own importance, spoke loudly, just like others who are an embarrassment to themselves, drunk or sober.

"It's good that your boys have come over to help us. A bit late," he said with a grin, "but we will beat the bosch in the end."

"I hear you girls have just arrived from Italy, how were things over there? By the way, I'm Tom." Connie looked at him curiously.

"Tom", she said matter-of-factly, "have you been to the front? I mean have you even left these shores yet?" The hint of bravado he had seconds ago vanished. Those in the group that had heard Tom speak, and that was most of them, were silent.

Tom nervously answered "no, no, I haven't, but I've heard the stories."

"Look Tom, with all due respect, the stories you've heard, as true as they may be, have little relevance to the shit you may encounter in the next twelve months, so put aside this cocky attitude it seems you have. I will give you some advice. Keep your mouth shut, your head down and learn. I've seen boys like you who'll never see their mothers again. I hope to God you will. Now drink your beer and enjoy the moment."

As it turned out, Colin and his mates all chipped in to buy the girls a drink. Shelly was quick to point out that it wouldn't be right to expect one guy to pay for all the girls, including their new friends who'd joined the party and were now in deep conversation with two of Colin's friends, prospective clients no doubt. Shelly wasn't the type of girl to be flattered or impressed by any man, but like all girls, there were moments when, being starved of the company of said men, she would succumb to an easy approach and a genuine interest. Being wanton for the company of men may sound an exaggeration, as they had been surrounded by them for a long time, but a war setting was not conducive to a long term romance. Whereas short, lustful encounters were commonplace under these circumstances.

Billie looked at Shelly, she was twenty six years of age, the daughter of a coal miner from Jenkins, Kentucky and the eldest of eight children. She had told Billie her story, of being molested and abused aged fifteen, of her journey to become a nurse and now, finally, to be in the safe company of friends that respected her. Her saviours had been her uncle and his wife, who had taken her in and guided her, setting her on a road that was beyond her dreams. It was ironic, to begin a new life in a war and that it was war that had set her free from her past.

"And you Billie, what has life got in store for you?" The question was posed by a young officer who was not of the group that had walked in off the street and must have overheard her name being mentioned. He spoke softly, unlike some, the 'tally-ho' type who wanted to be heard as well as seen. Billie smiled, taking the drink he offered.

"I don't know," she answered, "I've never really thought about it."

"And you?" She guessed him to be in his late twenties, smartly dressed, as officers usually are.

"Let's get the war over with first." He didn't smile.

"You've been there, haven't you?" Billie didn't smile either. She had a feeling about this man. She guessed that he had seen some of what she had seen, only from a different perspective. As, like others on the front line, he had walked forward, not really knowing what was left in their wake.

"From the beginning," he pursed his lips, tilted his head and lifted his shoulders. "We were dispatched to France in late autumn four years ago and, four months later, found ourselves on the beaches of Dunkirk. It seems like a long time ago now. I've seen and done a lot since then, but in my head it was yesterday." He stopped talking and looked around.

"Would you mind if we go over to that table?" he nodded in the direction of a little table across the busy, noisy room.

"I don't feel in the mood to celebrate, not tonight, unless of course it's your birthday?" It was his smile that intrigued Billie, it was warm and genuine and showed in the misty blue eyes that lingered on hers.

"It's not my birthday," Billie laughed, diverting her eyes, "when it comes around, you will be invited." Again, that smile. She followed him, he pulled out a chair and she sat and looked up at him. He was older than she had first thought, maybe thirty, maybe older. He was confident, positive, seemingly well-mannered and carried his thick set frame like a lumberjack. Billie prompted the conversation.

"You mentioned Dunkirk."

"Ah yes, Dunkirk, the whole episode was a bloody nightmare. An old man and his two sons hauled me and twenty others out of the water and into his fishing boat.

As he talked, he lit a cigarette and looked at the pint glass of beer in front of him, toying with it, turning it around and around with his fingers. His cigarette burning in a porcelain ashtray with the words Players Senior Service printed in blue around its edge.

"There were lines of men on the shore, dozens of them every hundred yards or so, all walking into the sea. Above us, Stuka dive bombers strafed the beaches in straight lines, their bullets lifting the sand every eight feet from one end of the beach to the other. This happened time and time again. Their attacks were not confined to the beaches, they flew low across the shallow sea and you could hear the zip sound as their bullets hit the water. Every now and again a body would leave the line and float away, like the one who was two yards in front of me. The screams of men filled your mind." He stopped talking and lifted his gaze from his beer, raised his head, took a drag of his cigarette, and then stubbed it out. Billie looked into the haunting eyes of a frightened soul and, in her mind, relived scenes of her own. He was somewhere else now, maybe he was back on that fishing boat heading for home.

"You know," he hesitated, "of all the things I've seen and all the people I've met, there was never a man like that fisherman and if I never see tomorrow, he showed me what courage is." He paused, "I'd like to tell you more about it someday." For a moment there was silence between them. In the background, above the din, squeals of laughter could be heard, and someone started singing 'Rule, Britannia'.

"I'd like to hear it." Billie found herself saying, not realising that she had all but accepted an invitation to see him again, and she didn't even know his name.

The build-up of American troops in London, preceding and during the nurses stay in the city, was due to the impending invasion of the European mainland. It was well known that an invasion was on the horizon, the question was, when? It wouldn't be long. In the meantime, the furlough the nurses were taking was welcomed.

When they wanted entertainment, the girls went to the West End. The American Red Cross Club was the first stop for many US troops. It was situated at the Piccadilly end in the Lyons Corner House, Rainbow Corner, 23 Shaftesbury Avenue. The club provided recreational activities, meals, accommodation, a laundry and a barbers. It had two large dining rooms and, in the basement, a snack bar which stayed open long after British establishments had closed their doors. The snack bar was a home from home for the

US troops. It served doughnuts, hamburgers, coffee and rivers of coke, American gum and chocolate bars. It was a little piece of Uncle Sam in the centre of London. The boys shot pool and played the pinball machines, while listening to the latest music coming from a Wurlitzer jukebox. The dance hall, at all times, were accustomed to the swaying bodies of young people in uniform, dancing to the sound of the big bands and entertainers from across the sea, singing into microphones they were born to hold.

The British didn't seem to have this same zest for living, but then they'd been at war for four years and had known nothing but heartache. Now, a new dawn was in the air, a feeling of optimism and the young wanted more than bombs, bullets and bedlam. The Dead End Kids Institute, a youth club in the northwest of London provided a place to go where local teens could be who they wanted to be, a place where they could have fun. This 'hive' for the young was well attended and dancing was the main attraction; its allure brought on by the mass popularity of swing music that was sweeping the country. Young girls pretended to be Ginger Rogers and the boys had plenty of American actors to choose from. They'd seen their films and quoted their lines. The club was a utopia the young had dreamed of. The older generation may have complained of the Americanisation of their country's youth, but for the growing number who wanted it, it was too late. The yanks were here. America showed that there was a new way of life that was glamorous and with, seemingly, no restrictions. It was a way waiting to be taken and, come hell or high water, some would take it. In the dark days of the war, what else was there?

During the second and third week of their stay in England, Billie and her fellow nurses saw hundreds of allied planes fly overhead preparing the groundwork for the invasion of Europe. Everyone was on edge, knowing that the moment of waiting would soon be over. After spending five days in their initial quarters, the girls had moved a few miles to establish a tent hospital for the mass influx of casualties and were now billeted in Nissen Huts adjacent to the hospital.

On the second Sunday afternoon, Billie got on a bus to Hyde Park to meet a man at Speakers' Corner. She knew his name. He'd told her in the Coach and Horses four days earlier. Kenneth James Stanton. For four days he had been on her mind and she didn't like herself for it. What the hell am I doing here? she uttered to herself, as she stepped off the bus. I really don't need this, not now. She had seen where the results of new or old relationships had ended, she had seen the 'Dear John' letters. It happened often, too often and she didn't want a bar of it.

"Hello Ken… have you been waiting long?" Don't smile, please don't smile.

"About ten minutes," he smiled. They walked, talked, sat on park benches and walked some more. This was the first time in a long, long time that Billie had been alone with a man. She'd been 'asked out' many times and had, as many times, reluctantly denied herself, some for good reason and others for no reason at all.

"I won't be able to see you again after today,' he said as he reached for her hand, "we're confined to barracks until we move out."

"When will that be?"

"Rumour is, any time after the fourth."

Billie stopped walking.

"What date is it today? she asked.

"The twenty fifth."

"That's in ten days' time?"

"Yes, I know. Listen," he glanced at his watch, 'I have eight and a half hours left. Where would you like to go? We could get a cab... I don't know London very well, and you probably even less, and remember it's Sunday, everywhere will be closed."

"Take me to a hotel," Billie blurted. She had no rhyme nor reason to say it but say it she did.

They had already walked down Park Lane and Piccadilly Road, turned right onto St. James' Street, then found themselves outside the Stafford Hotel on St James' Place. They looked at each other, then at the three arched entrance to the hotel. It had a large stone carved frieze above the canopy and two steps each side with ornate wrought iron railings running parallel to the building.

An American flag hung limply in the midday sun. It hung on a staff, angled at a degree relevant to its showing and fixed to a metal plate bolted to the red brick wall of this pre-Victorian building. The Stafford, discreetly tucked away at the end of a quiet enclave seemed busy with the comings and goings of American and Canadian military officers. Undecided as to venture inside, the sound of an air raid siren suddenly echoed over the rooftops of nearby buildings. Immediately, there was a scurry to the hotel entrance and the only person to come out was the hotel concierge, encouraging everyone to enter the building, including Billie and Ken. Officers of all ranks and military forces were guided through the foyer, down a flight of steps and into the vaulted brick cellars, where seats had been arranged amongst the racks of wine bottles that served the hotel. Mutterings of disgust could be heard as Germany had stopped bombing London twelve months earlier. As they sat, Billie reaching for Ken's hand, nonchalantly whispering,

"It's a nice cellar, isn't it?"

"Not exactly what I had in mind." He squeezed her hand.

"Me neither," she smiled.

"Excuse me," a gentleman sitting next to Billie turned, "are you staying in the hotel?"

"No, we were ushered in from outside," she paused, adding, "this beats the underground shelters though, doesn't it?"

"Doesn't it just and you'll find a better class of people down here." They both laughed. As they talked, Billie noticed the rankings on his uniform, a commander no less. He was from Queens in New York and had been in the army for many years. As he talked, Billie looked at the men seated opposite. One in particular seemed to be looking at her with more than a passing interest. Another, had an array of insignias denoting his rank. Billie paid little attention to him and avoided his stare.

The concierge then appeared and announced that the air raid siren was a false alarm. Everyone stood to leave and as they did, the man who Billie felt uneasy about, followed her. At the top of the steps, everyone spilled out into the foyer and went their separate ways. Billie and Ken turned right into the lounge bar.

"Excuse me miss," she heard a voice behind her and at the same time felt a slight tap on her shoulder. Billie squeezed Ken's hand, stopped, and turned.

"I hope you don't mind," he spoke tentatively and slowly, "but I think I have seen you before." He frowned. Billie stood, not knowing what to expect.

"You're a nurse are you not?" There was a hint of a smile on Billie's face.

"Yes, I am, but I don't think we've met."

"No, no…, you're right, we haven't met, but I have seen you, and unless I'm mistaken," he was smiling now, "you were in Hawaii, at Pearl Harbour, four years ago, at the Tripler Hospital, do you remember? It is you, isn't it?" Billie was dumbfounded, she beamed a smile that spread across her face.

"Yes, yes of course I remember, how could I forget?"

"I knew it," a broad grin spread across his face. The man looked at Ken.

"If I'm intruding and taking liberties, I apologise, but it would be an honour to buy you both a drink." With that, he raised his hand and caught the barman's eye.

"Three martinis, Clive, if you don't mind? We'll sit at the window."

Ken looked blankly at the man calling the shots and wondered what was going on. Although he had gathered that this officer, which he plainly was, had seen Billie before, he was now looking forward to an explanation for his interest in her.

"Firstly", he said as he sat down, "I would like to introduce myself, my name is Henry McPherson, Colonel Henry McPherson. I'm here…" he tilted his head and smiled, "well, why are we all here? But that has nothing to do with my wanting to talk to this young lady," he looked at Ken "and you are?" He asked, the smile not leaving his face as he spoke.

"I'm sorry," interrupted Billie," this is Ken and my name is Billie."

"Pleased to meet you both, now as I was saying, or was about to say… I had been in Hawaii for six weeks before the Japanese attacked Pearl Harbour and was attending a meeting on the day when the bombs started to fall. The upshot of it all was that I was taken to the Tripler Hospital…" he stopped talking as a waiter placed three drinks on the table.

"I had dislocated my shoulder; falling over a curb trying to get away, nothing serious. There were a lot of people outside the entrance to the hospital and I sat in a chair and watched them file through into the main building. Then it all went crazy, with stretchers arriving one after the other. As I looked on, I saw a girl in civilian clothes rush to a lad whose arm was severely injured, then the man she had arrived with suddenly went to a bush and came back with a short stick. She had already ripped the young lad's shirt to make a tourniquet and applied it, using the stick the man had given her. After that an orderly came out of the hospital, put a nurse's hat on the girl's head and gave her a white apron." All the time Colonel McPherson spoke he was looking at Ken, as Billie sat motionless reliving the moment.

"Then two men carried the stretcher inside, followed by the girl. She stopped, turned and looked at the man that had been with her and I distinctly remember her saying, I'll see you when I see you, dad. The Colonel turned his gaze to Billie.

"When you went inside, I looked at your father standing amongst the mayhem that was going on. He stood alone and I think that was the moment he lost his daughter to the world; he could do nothing to help you. You may wonder why I remember so well what happened that day? You see, I also have a daughter and she is also a nurse. She is much your age and at this moment is still in Italy. The similarity between your father and myself is not hard to understand," then pausing he added "and if there is anything I can do for you, then I will."

"No thank you, colonel, there is nothing I need, but I am grateful for your concern," Billie placed her hand over the colonel's. "And have no fear of losing your daughter, sir. She's like me. We've just stepped outside for a moment."

Colonel McPherson said nothing, he just placed his free hand over Billie's, before looking at them both and, with a knowing smile, whispered.

"Are you looking for a room?" Billie and Ken passed a fleeting glance between them but said not a word. Rising to his feet the colonel told them he would be back in a moment. On his return he dropped a key on the table, on its tab was the number twenty three.

"With the compliments of myself and the general manager, Mr Louis Burdet." Leaning forward he again whispered. "He's a spy."

Billie and Ken both rose and offered their hand. Throughout their meeting Ken had not spoken a word. There was no need, except for now and that was to say goodbye, and I will sir, when told to look after the lady he was with. When he shook hands with Billie, Colonel McPherson thanked her for her reassuring words regarding his daughter. In return, she thanked him for reminding her that she too had a father, from whom, whilst having stepped out for a moment, she'd sometimes been too long away from. Before he turned to leave, the colonel suggested that, on their departure, Billie and Ken take a staff car to their next destination; he assured them that everything would be in order and to see the hotel manager when checking out. He wished them well for the future and Godspeed to wherever they were going in life. They watched him walk to the reception desk. Then, as he strode out, he glanced in their direction and raised his hand. Billie and Ken looked at each other, then at the table Billie smiled, reached out and, with some apprehension, picked up the keys. With Ken following behind her, she walked up the stairs to room twenty three.

13

Early November saw Michael in Gibraltar, having re-joined 111 Squadron. Troy and Glyn were still with him. A few had left to join other squadrons, some had been withdrawn for various reasons, and while some had failed in their endeavours to stay alive, others had joined to keep up the numbers.

Michael opened an airmail letter from his sister, sometimes he could go weeks without receiving a word, then three or more letters would come at once. He had found a bench, a quiet spot, overlooking the Alboran sea and behind him was the rock that dominates the peninsula it stood on. To the west, was the harbour and the Strait of Gibraltar, leading out to the Atlantic Ocean. In the evenings, sixteen search lights cast their beams into the night sky, as the rock's artillery lay in wait. Their purpose in Gibraltar was to provide air cover for the invasion of North Africa and to that end 111 squadron was vital to its success.

Dearest Michael   *21st September 1942*

I hope you are well. I received your last letter on the 18th of August and you sounded a little more cheerful than you have been in some of your previous letters. Everyone here is well, apart from Mum who is in bed with influenza, but she is on the mend. You seem to have been travelling around a lot. I expect you never thought you'd see other countries the way you'll see them being in the RAF. You'll have so many stories to tell when you come home. We get picked up by bus for work each morning, calling at Abermule as other women get on along the way. Accles and Pollock now employ over one thousand people.

I told you in my last letter that Sally, myself and some other girls from the village would be starting work at Accles and Pollock, didn't I? The factory is so big. The vast majority of employees are women; some even come up from South Wales to work there. At the moment, I'm on a line doing welding. One of the women, Mary Jones, has taught me and others how to weld. Her father had taught her before she had ever set foot in the factory and they pay her more to teach others. The money is good, far better than anything we could earn elsewhere else. And besides, it means we can do our bit for the war effort. We're building Sten gun barrels

*and parts for aeroplanes you could well be flying!
I do hope the war will end soon as we're all getting
rather tired of praying for it to be finished with.
Jenny got married last Saturday and asked to be
remembered. I thought she might have waited till
you got home to see how things would work out. I
know she rather fancied you, but it wasn't to be.
I often wonder if the good times are gone and if
we'll ever see the likes of them again, or is it all in
the memories that we cling to? I do so hope we can
all be together again soon.*

Your loving sister,

Esther.

*P.S. Mum, Dad, Sally, and Dan send their love.
Looking forward to your next letter. Look after
yourself.*

Michael folded the wafer thin paper and placed it
back into the wafer thin envelope that had already been
opened by officials. He was aware of the need for letters
to be censored and he had a pretty good idea of the full
contents of his sister's letter. It was rumoured when he
was last home that a large factory would be built in
Newtown, something to do with the war effort. No one
knew what was to be manufactured there, top secret he
was told. There was another business in Newtown doing

work for the war ministry. The Penstrowed Sawmills, situated on the fringe, east of the town. Jones and Leaches, manufactured thousands of tent pegs and ammunition boxes for the army, along with wheelbarrows and other timber merchandise.

In 1942 a fourteen year old boy, one of a family with twelve children, who lived in an isolated cottage 2 miles from Llandyssil, had started working at Penstrowed Sawmill. He'd found board and lodgings in the attic space of a house in Stone Street, Newtown. Michael's mother had told him, in one of her letters, that she knew the family. She'd sometimes see the children in the village shop, picking up loaves of bread and placing God knows how many into a pillowcase to take home. One of them, the fourteen year old, had told her that it'd take him twelve months to save up to buy a bicycle, so he could cycle the seven miles to his job at the mill in Newtown, thereby saving himself the money it cost him in board and lodgings. His working companions, a mix of Italian prisoners of war and local men, laboured long hours to furnish the ministry with their required numbers of pegs and boxes.

Michael looked up and out to sea, catching sight of a yacht, whose sail hung, not moving, on its mast, awaiting a wind that would blow it on a course that it had surely travelled before. Michael smiled and wondered if Esther was right in thinking that the good times were gone. He knew things would never be the same. He had changed and the world was changing too. But around the corner, he felt sure more good times were to be had and, God willing, he'd be there to enjoy them. For now, he must remain strong and take whatever wind of change blew his way. He also knew that good men were still to die before this was all over. But he thought as a bittersweet smile spread slowly across his face, unlike them, he would survive. Oh yes, he would survive and maybe, just maybe, there was someone out there, that in the future would be his friend and companion, someone to share his life at the moment, that was something he didn't want.

In that same month 111 flew to Algeria, where they stayed for four weeks before moving on to Souk-el-Khemis in Tunisia. Five months later, in June of 1943 they were summoned to Safi Air Base in Malta, then onto Comiso in Sicily a few weeks later. It was from here that they covered the Italian landings before moving to Montecorvino, near Salerno on the mainland of Italy in September. On the eighth of that month, Italy surrendered to the allied forces. From September into October the squadron was in Battipaglia. From October to January in Capodichino where a fighter base was set up just outside Naples. And so, it went on. It was all a bit like follow my leader as they hedge-hopped from airfield to airfield, up the Italian west coast behind the American and British ground troops working their way north.

111 Squadron landed at Piombino Air Base, 155 miles north of Rome in June 1944. It had been twenty months since they'd left Gibraltar and along the way, a few Spitfires had gone missing, accompanied by the pilots

that flew them. Some were found and some were not. New men joined and some moved on. Those that were left became the backbone of the Squadron. There were times when nothing seemed to be happening, where the planes sat in hangers getting a good look over by the men that kept them in the air. And the pilots? They wrote, read, played football, ate pasta, sang, danced and cavorted with the Italian ladies, whenever they could. It mattered little that these ladies could cook like their mothers and when need be, that they'd cast aside their Catholic faith for a moment's indiscretion-indiscretions that could be repented by saying three Hail Mary's, seemingly a fair trade off. And in any case, those moments of indulgences could bring financial rewards beneficial to the women's family. This wasn't always the case, of course, but who dares wins, says Troy.

From Piombino they flew to Calvi in Corsica and in August moved, on again to an airfield in Ramatuelle, 4 miles from St Tropez in France.

Dear Mother and Father   *8th August 1944*

Just to let you know that I'm well, as I hope you all are. We are now at a little advanced airfield close to St Tropez in southeast France. The city was liberated on the 18th of August, and at this moment of writing, I am sitting outside a café with the ocean in front of me. Across the street American soldiers of the 45th Division are in good humour, celebrating the taking of the city. It's been a long haul to get this far. Still some way to go, but there's a feeling of optimism that the war is going in our favour. Troy and Glyn are still with me. We've been doing patrols over Vichy France, an area that had sided with Germany. And at this moment. We're awaiting our next move.

We've had some uplifting moments though, especially during our run through Italy following the ground forces. We flew low over American troops and dipped our wings and they acknowledged us by raising their hands. We did the same over their field hospitals, showing off by doing victory rolls. There was a feeling of nostalgia when we did this, as the nurses would come out and wave. I'd like to think we brought a little hope to their lives. Last night there was a big party in town, at a café. Troy played the piano, a sheet of music was placed in front of him and the local tenors accompanied him singing Drink, Drink, Drink, apparently a song from an opera, The Student Prince.

The American air force were also in town and I spent a while talking to one of the pilots. They were covering the ground forces and, like us, were flying Spitfires. We raised a glass of red wine as the singing and dancing went on and as he left, the American handed me his Ray Ban aviator sunglasses, something I will always keep. Must go now, as the boys have just joined me. Look after yourselves and give my love to all.

Michael.

On the 26th August, 111 Squadron flew north on a 110 mile trip to Sisteron, still in France, from where they made attacks on railways and roads. September to October saw them in Lyon, there they rested for a couple of weeks before returning to Italy, landing in Peretola, Florence. They moved on in November and saw in the New Year in Rimini on the west coast. They stayed there until February, then moved, yet again, this time just down the road to Ravenna, a move of only 32 miles. Their workload as fighter pilots was becoming less and less, as reports were coming through that Germany could never hold back the advance of the allied forces. From now on, 111 Squadron were unlikely to meet any serious opposition and were enjoying the moment with the end of the war in sight. For the latter end of February, all of March, April and into May, the squadron stayed in Ravenna. On the 8th May, one day after the surrender of Germany, 111 Squadron left and flew to Klagenfurt in Austria. Thirteen days later, Michael witnessed Yugoslavian troops, an ally of Germany, march out of Klagenfurt… everyone was going home. And for the boy who'd started work as a mechanic in a little garage in mid Wales, the war was over.

Seven days after the 6th of June D-Day landings, American nurses waded ashore on the beaches of France and immediately began setting up field and evacuation hospitals. They were kept busy dealing with the many casualties resulting from the invasion, and an influx of victims of the parachute regiments, dropped behind enemy lines. These regiments were trying to unite the two beaches that the American troops had landed on. The beeches, code named Omaha and Utah are situated on the coast of Normandy in France. The beaches, by road, were 29 miles apart. Billie, like the rest of the nurses, was dressed in an American GI field uniform, as supplies of their own uniforms had not arrived in time for their departure. Being men's uniforms, the girls were having to do a lot of alterations to make them fit. The boots were another matter, as even the smaller sizes in men's footwear created a problem for some. But necessity being the mother of invention, they managed to make them fit by putting on three pairs of socks, anything to make them more comfortable to wear.

If the nurse's lives were miserable before the landings, it was now made more so by the rain and subsequent mud created by the comings and goings of troops and vehicles. In the busy times, they worked fourteen hour days, rest was impossible and every day became a Monday, or whatever day they chose to call it. The pain and screams of men didn't stop on Sundays, any day was not a good day to die, would a Sunday be any different?

Finally, the front began to move east and living conditions improved. The hospitals began to grow, meaning they needed more medical staff, nurses, doctors, surgeons and orderlies. These were drafted in, as and when needed. It was at this point that Billie and four of her fellow nurses were transferred again. This time to rejoin the 12th Evacuation Hospital, whose wards were now taking in German wounded prisoners, free French soldiers, injured French civilians and children. This only added to the heartache of those charged to look after them. Thankfully medical supplies were more forthcoming than they were in Italy. And so they moved on. Allied forces from the South and the North pushed east and the nurses followed.

The front moved at a pace. High numbers of casualties occurred in pockets of resistance but these were handled by other evacuation hospitals and Billie's unit were not needed. For almost a month, Billie and the rest of the 12th followed the US troops through France. There were periods of inactivity, with no incoming casualties that the nurses found frustrating. The German front line was retreating. Often, hospital equipment could not keep up with the advance, so Billie, like others, slept out in the open without tents and spent days looking for their medical apparatus. Deliveries were sporadic and delays inevitable. In mid-September at the Siegfried line, the Allies met the Germans and casualties mounted. The 12th followed the US third army and established operations at Bonneval, 75 miles southwest of Paris. Here it admitted over 1,200 casualties in under a month. The 12th then received orders to deploy to Rheims, 44 miles from the German border. Their medical unit was set up in an abandoned American Memorial Hospital, which the retreating Germans had left in a sorry state. They worked hard setting things up, only to be ordered to evacuate, leaving it all to another incoming evacuation hospital. Moving became the norm, but to everyone's relief they were still advancing in the right direction, or so they were told.

In a field near the Argonne Forest, a long strip of mountainous and wild woodland in north-eastern France, 'The 12th' set up their evacuation hospital and stayed for a month. Field kitchens were deployed to all hospitals, serving two hot meals a day, whenever possible. As well as food brought in, cooks sourced it wherever they could, including from the Argonne Forest, where wild boar, red deer, rabbits and hares were shot, butchered, roasted and served. Pork and venison were a particular favourite. As a one off, and perhaps making light of their situation, Billie, under the supervision of a surgeon, had learned how to skin and dissect a rabbit in under one minute using a scalpel. This, she pointed out jokingly, added to the other culinary skills she had acquired during her stay in Europe. This variation of meat was welcomed by everyone, medical staff and patients alike and for a moment it helped unite the fragile minds of all. During this stay, the 12th moved thousands of troops to the rear.

Then on the 29th September an order was given that they move 87 miles southeast to the City of Nancy. At this new site was a French military hospital that had been used by the Germans, a modern facility, but more beds were needed and delivered. On the 1st of October the hospital became operational and by nightfall, over 300 casualties had been treated. The 12th were now closer to the front line and were receiving casualties straight from the fighting.

General Dwight Eisenhower the supreme commander of all American forces called in on the 12th, as did a number of two star Generals. Their visits lifted the morale of the entire hospital, since such high ranking officer's visits didn't happen all that often. Seven days later General Eisenhower called again, this time in the company of General George S. Patton who had been transferred to command the US 3rd army. They walked the wards, talking to patients with combat injuries and assuring them that the war would be won.

Nurses and medical staff were apprehensive of General Patton's visit as his reputation preceded him; he had slapped a soldier in an evacuation hospital in Sicily, accusing him of being a coward and threatening to send him back to the front line, or to have him shot. This, to many, was an unforgivable act since the soldier was suffering from shell shock and battle fatigue.

However, on this occasion General Patton's behaviour was exemplary. Although flamboyant, he was also well-mannered. He had walked past Billie and she'd noticed a silver Colt 45 handgun on his hip with his initials GSP carved on its white ivory handle. Wearing this gun was his trademark, or a visible identification of who he was. Everyone knew General George Patton by his handgun alone.

Weeks later, word had reached the 12th that General Patton had been injured in a vehicle accident. He died twelve days after. On the 21st of December, thirty six days since his visit to the hospital. It was rumoured that he would be buried alongside his fellow soldiers, those of the 3rd army in the American Cemetery in Hamm, Luxembourg. Although Billie didn't think much of him, she was still saddened that such a powerful man, who she had actually seen, now lay, at the age of sixty years, in a foreign land, forever to be in the company of those he had led.

Winter was now upon them, so the 12th stayed in Nancy, spending Christmas and the New Year of 1945 there. Starting on the 16th of December 140 miles south, the front line of the American 3rd army had been breached in the Ardennes and casualties were increasing. The German army had made a successful counterattack and, on a front that was miles long, they were now advancing.

Three weeks later, the 12th packed up and moved to Luxembourg, a distance of 52 miles from the Ardennes. There they took over three large buildings taking a number of days to adapt them for hospital use. By the 15th they had started taking in patients. Some days later, the battle of the Ardennes was over. The 12th Evacuation Hospital spent two months in Luxembourg City and many personnel took the opportunity to visit Paris. Quotas had been introduced at this point, for some long serving men to be sent back to the US. Billie was pleasantly surprised to find that a contingent of medical personnel from the Lenox Hill Hospital Manhattan, a number of who had been in the army long before the Lenox Hill contingent were mobilised, were given leave to return to America.

By mid-March, Luxembourg had become surplus to requirements, as the German army had retreated more than 37 miles further east. It was time to move out. The town of Trier, in Germany became their next stop a distance of 43 miles from their present position. The building chosen for the hospital was in need of repair and once this was done, The 12th moved in. The problem was that this position had already become too far behind the front line of fighting to be effective. It was now late March and apart from the occasional intake of locally inflicted injuries, there was little to do but enjoy the early spring sunshine. Baseball teams were picked and games were played in a vacant lot, only to be interrupted by intermittent sniper fire, which rather put paid to the enjoyment of the players. By late March, orders came through to undertake the journey to Frankfurt, where the 12th took over a sports stadium. In the first week of April, an advance party left Trier and were followed by the rest of the unit when transport became available. On the 5th April, the hospital was again accepting front line patients.

But as the days went on, fewer and fewer patients were arriving. There were more patients with diseases and injuries from accidents than surgical cases. Respiratory and contact diseases were the most common. In the coming weeks, the 12th were called upon to check on the health of Allied prisoners of war, who were now coming in by the drove. Some of these men had been incarcerated since 1942. As soon as they were medically cleared to travel, they were sent to France on special flights and from there, to destinations unknown. But all were going home.

Billie, who still had the company of Shelly, Connie, Lesley, and Imogen, admitted to them all that, without their friendship, there were times when insanity had been but two steps away. They all agreed. The bond and the memories they now held, would stay with them for the rest of their lives.

On the 7th of May, Germany surrendered and the guns fell silent. Those on both sides lowered their heads in respect to the fallen, then lifted them and rejoiced in the knowledge that it was over. Billie and her fellow nurses stayed on for a further two and a half months after the war's end, returning to the UK in mid-August.

The 12th Evacuation Hospital had moved eleven times in two years and in those two years Billie and her fellow nurses had sung, danced, drank, cried and, in between, put together the broken bodies of men in their care.

15

Michael arrived home three months after the war had ended. In many ways it was an anti-climax to the initial foray of returning servicemen. The celebrations of that return diminished as the weeks went by. He had notified his parents that he would be home sometime in the last week of August, not mentioning when, as up until the day before, he didn't know himself.

It was late afternoon on a Wednesday when he found his mother in the front garden of his home, cutting some sweet peas from the hazel sticks they had climbed. On seeing him, she burst out crying. It was a muffled cry. She had dropped the scissors she held but clung to the flowers like she would have done had she won first prize at Montgomery Horticultural Show. He clung to her, fearing she might fall. She repeated his name several times before holding him at arm's length.

Michael removed his hat and she held his face in both hands. For the few moments she looked at him. He could smell the fragrance of the sweet peas she still held. It was a moment they had both looked forward to. His mother, ever since the first time the wheels of his aircraft had left the runway, had feared for his life. Throughout the war the anxiety she had felt had been well founded. With stories of RAF airmen being killed. Oh, how she had wished that's what they were, stories. But the reality was, they were all true. Now as she held her first born, a fleeting thought of déjà vu entered her mind of when she had held another man who had returned from a war. Still holding the flowers, she turned and ran screaming into the house shouting for Bill. Michael stood not moving, his mind unclear. Shrieks of joy could be heard as Sally and Esther came running with outstretched arms. They held him, then standing in the doorway, was his father. Bill smiled as he walked forward, with hand outstretched, a hand Michael hadn't shaken in a long time.

Michael's homecoming was joyous but tinged with the knowledge that there were local men who didn't make it home. Apart from the familiar words of sadness expressed, Michael said little, but thought a lot. The relationship with his father had changed, not physically or emotionally, but it was as if they had climbed two separate ladders. His father had reached the top of his twenty seven years earlier and now… now Michael had caught up, they were standing on different ladders but on the same rung. There was no talk of heroic deeds, and the sorrow of fallen companions, they kept to themselves. It was hard to come to terms with what had happened over the past few years. So, Michael's conversations were of the places he'd been and the people he had met. His friends, Troy and Glyn, who had been with him since the beginning would always be with him.

Alone at night in his bed, Michael stared into the darkness. Nothing stirred. The sound of the silence was unnerving. He remembered the stories of how his father walked the hills at night after he came back from his war in Egypt. Would history repeat itself? No, Michael did not walk the hills at night, but with pencil and paper he wrote down the names of people he'd met and where he had met them. Doing this seemed to steady and calm his mind. Images came clear to him as he recalled the story of his life. His early childhood, in hindsight, was one of excitement and learning.

His mother's brother, Uncle David the blacksmith, still swung a hammer, striking hot metal on his own father's anvil. Michael smiled as he remembered the times he would pump the bellows in the workshop, blowing air under the hot coals of the furnace. It was something that David had said the day after Michael had returned home, following his initial greeting. He'd looked him in the eyes and asked the question.

"And now what are you going to do with the rest of your life, Michael?" He grinned as he said it, but it was a statement that caught Michael's attention. Michael shrugged.

"I don't know," he replied, "I really don't know!"

For many days Michael thought about his future, just what the hell was he going to do. For the first time in his life, he was lost. The war was over, his service no longer required. He sometimes looked proudly at his uniform, now on a coat hanger displayed like a discarded piece of clothing on the door of his wardrobe. He often ran his finger over the silver wings sewn to the jacket. Flying had become part of him, it had been his life, this is what he did, indeed this is who he was and without it?

The reality of his dilemma came a week later when his official papers of discharge came through the post. Michael was twenty five years and eight months of age. He knew, when for the last time the wheels of his Spitfire touched the concrete on an English runway, that his life as an RAF pilot had come to an end and that he would have to move on. Like a lot of experienced pilots, he had been offered positions, like the initial training of cadets, administration jobs and posts that excluded any flying whatsoever. No, his future would be elsewhere. He had come too far to stay on the ground.

For three months, Michael did the rounds of looking for a job, anything that he could get some satisfaction from, but there was nothing. As it was summer, he did find farm work helping with the hay harvest, for the limited time that harvesting lasted. He followed a thrashing box from farm to farm, feeding it with sheaves of corn, barley and oats. He did find some satisfaction in doing that work, as he saw full hessian bags of grain being taken to the grain store. Even work at the big factory in Newtown was a nonstarter, as Accles and Pollock had closed down due to their products not being needed since the end of the war. Sally had, again, told of the welding she had done on the

Spitfires and Hurricanes, ones Michael may have flown and, jokingly, suggested that it was her welding that had kept him alive. But, as luck would have it, a new factory was being set up. Phillips Cycles were coming to take over Accles and Pollock's factory and would have work for those that had been employed by the former company. Whether he could get a job there or not, he didn't know.

The Christmas of 1946 came and, just as quickly, passed. Children of the village had done their rounds of carol singing, collecting a few pennies for their endeavours. It reminded Michael of the cold winter nights he'd done the same when he was a child, walking with friends through the snow, carrying a jam jar with a lighted candle in the bottom to see their way. The pub, as expected at this time of year, sold more beer than they had done for a long while But, it seemed to Michael, that, apart from the few local men that didn't come home, as sad as that was and the rationing of food and suchlike, the war had not really touched the lives of local people. He had been told that on some nights during the war, villagers would walk to Montgomery Town Hill from where they could see the orange glow in the sky over Liverpool as it was being bombed.

Unsurprisingly, a large gathering of people attended the village church on Christmas day to observe the end of hostilities. Prayers were said for the fallen, but unlike past Christmases, this one had a feeling of acceptance in that it was time to move on, time to live for the future. Michael was taken by the genuine sadness the parishioners showed in their grief for the families that had lost loved ones but felt that he'd become hardened to death and the causes of it. Many times, he'd knelt at the altar of sadness and thanked God for his deliverance, but enough was enough and he would now live his life as best he could.

On Monday the 25th February 1946 the first 1,000 ladies and gents' black bicycles rolled off the production line at Phillips Cycle factory. Michael, after a week's training, had managed to get a job in the paint spraying department. He needed to earn money and as it was a permanent position with the prospect of overtime, he took the job. Michael had already passed his driving test during his stay in the RAF and with the money he'd saved, bought a Morris Eight motor car from Abermule garage. Now he was free, independent and ready to be let loose on an unsuspecting world. Was this what he wanted? Deep down he missed the adrenaline rush of yesterday, the panic, the uncertainty and the camaraderie of his fellow pilots, those who were all so different to each other, yet in the sky, they were all the same. He wondered how long his insecurities of not 'living on the edge' would last.

Michael's social life had become one of indifference. He felt he didn't belong in the village dances and pubs anymore, it was all a charade. He had made friends at work, but they spoke a different language to him. It was hard, damned hard to be one of them again. He engaged in conversation only to find that he now had nothing, or very little in common with most. As for the women, it seemed that in the past all they'd wanted was to be seen on the arm of a pilot in uniform, to be shown off like a trophy they had acquired. At the time, that was fine by Michael as he could take his pick with most of them. But now… in civilian clothes, he was lost in the crowd and that was fine too. Was it the uniform that defined who he was? Indeed, had he become the uniform itself? It was this question that bothered him, had he changed that much as to doubt himself?

Every so often, usually at night and in the solitude of his bedroom, Michael lit his Tilley Lamp and put on his RAF uniform, along with the Ray-Ban aviator sunglasses given to him by the American pilot in France. Immediately he would have a feeling of being where he belonged. He would look at himself in the full length mirror on his wardrobe, stand to attention, click his heels and for a moment pause, slowly raising his right hand to salute his own image. In that posture he'd close his eyes and be transported back to who he used to be, who he always wanted to be, then a voice in his head would say.

"Will the real Michael Jones please step forward?" At that moment he was content, but the clouds in the sky would always haunt him.

Michael kept in touch with Troy and Glyn through letters. Both had stated in returning letters that they missed the company of each other, almost to the point of despair, wrote Glyn. Troy was now the head of music in a grammar school in Kent and Glyn, still in the RAF, had taken up a position training cadets, travelling from base to base, all rather boring he stated. Their marital status was still the same, however Troy was now courting a fellow teacher. Glyn was still playing the field, his expertise in that department he attributed to the Piccadilly Commandos. Michael smiled at the memory.

In the spring of 1947 Sally got married. Her husband, John, the butcher from Welshpool; the lad who'd taken Sally, Esther, and their friends to Newtown to see the film The 39 Steps. They had been seeing each other on a regular basis since that night and had now exchanged vows in the same church where her mother and father had married twenty seven years before. Michael was glad to see his sister so happy and wished them well for the future. Although sad at the thought of her leaving home, he knew that one day both he, his remaining sister and brother would also make that move. It was inevitable that this would happen. When the opportunity and the reason enough for leaving came, he would have little alternative but to go.

That opportunity and the reason came three months later.

As the time went by Michael became more and more restless, he spent more time at home, aimlessly walk the roads, to break the monotony. He'd drive to the coast on weekends. But even so, after a time, he found it all very boring. His mother had tried to talk to him, to find a way through the determined nature that had always set him apart.

"Go and see your RAF friends," she suggested. So, he went. He had made arrangements and bought a return ticket to Paddington Station meeting the boys there at eleven thirty on the following Friday. Their meeting was all welcoming. It wasn't a matter of just shaking hands, it was much more than that. These were men of substance, a breed of men that encompassed all that was missing in Michael's life.

"So where shall we go?" Troy asked with a smile.

"I suggest we get a taxi and head to The Elephant and Castle," answered Glyn.

"Where else?" Michael said, lifting his hands.

The boys had arranged to stay for two nights. Where? They didn't know. Not that it was important, their delight was to be together again. The three of them were in civilian clothes, each carrying a small suitcase for their stay. The taxi driver dropped them off at the Elephant and Castle. Just to stand outside it was a tonic in itself. Michael looked around. Properties that had been damaged during the blitz had been torn down. All the roads were clear and now busy with cars, bicycles and anything with wheels, darting hither and thither paying little or no attention to other road users. "A little like Phillips Cycle factory at knocking off time," Michael thought. They decided to book in and went to their rooms. Some minutes later they were standing at the bar with a beer in front of them. It seemed strange to be in each other's company again and, apart from their initial greeting, Michael found that, in a very short time, it was, as it had always been.

The boys had moved from the bar to sit at a table in a little room where they could speak undisturbed, away from the conversations of others. There they talked of the good times, the bad times, the fear and relief, the tears and laughter. It all came spilling out. Michael was not alone when he spoke of his feeling of isolation, the boys felt it too. Troy would lose himself playing his piano and said that the room could be full of people, but sometimes he felt alone when his fingers struck the keys. Glyn, he wanted to be around people, not necessarily for their company or conversation, he had the ability, he said, to switch off, their talking becoming a background hum to his thoughts. This wasn't always the case, he explained, but he could do it whenever he needed to. Glyn talked of his lady friend, a history teacher in the school where he taught.

"Will you marry her?" Asked Troy, raising a smile as he glanced at Michael.

"Probably, she's a nice girl, we get on well. We're compatible and all that."

"I suppose it's a little pointless to ask you any questions regarding the opposite sex?" Glyn, sporting a large grin, was looking at Troy as he posed the question.

"Well, you know me," he said, leaning back in his chair, "it's the uniform that pulls them, it always did. But I must admit, I don't know if I want that life anymore. I don't know if I want my job either. Nothing is like it used to be. The kids I'm training to fly now are different", he hesitated, "maybe not, I don't know anymore. But it was a different time then. Remember, we were thrown in at the deep end, it was sink or swim, that's why so many died.

It was over seven years ago, Jesus Christ, we were only kids ourselves, not a bit of wonder that we're all screwed up. Some lads, may I add, are worse than others. I've seen them." He looked up, "you have no idea how much I've looked forward to seeing the two of you." He smiled.

"Michael, you remember that 109 you took out, the one that was on my tail? I can't remember where it was, over southeast England I think, I couldn't shake him off. You saved my life that day. And you Troy, always the sensible one, the wing man that was always there, like a fucking limpet. Christ, it was damned hard to shake you off sometimes." Troy raised his eyebrows.

"Well, you needed someone to shadow you, but you did lose me some of the time."

And so, the conversation went on. Stories retold, and some that had never been mentioned. The weekend, for Michael, was a revelation, as it was for his friends, each taking away from their meeting a sense of wellbeing, one that they had given to each other. They said their goodbyes at the railway station, vowing to meet again in a couple of years. But, in any case, they would write.

Within the next couple of weeks, Michael had regained some self-esteem. He became more outgoing, more like his old self. He still wanted to leave home and do something that he was good at. That opportunity came in a letter from Australia two weeks after his London trip. It read.

2nd Dec 1947   Delta Downs, South Australia

Dear Michael,

I hope you are well. I don't know if you remember me, but I flew with you for a spell with 111 Squadron out of Salerno in 1943. I'll always remember getting drunk with you and the boys before going on a sortie, how the hell we all came back I'll never know. You helped get me out of my Spit before it caught fire. I don't remember having thanked you. As you may recall, a day later me and my buddies flew on, not to see you again. We were only with you a few days, but I know a bloody good flyer when I see one and you were one of the best. I don't know if you made it through the war or not, but if you did and are reading this, I would like to remind you of our chat over the few beers we had at the base. It went something like this.

"And what are you going to do when the war is over Michael."

"I don't know Silvester, hadn't really thought about it, but I'd still like to carry on flying."

Now I don't know if you're still pulling the old joystick back, but word over here is that, in the very near future, more pilots will be needed for crop dusting on the wheat belt stations. You could come out on assisted passage. It would only cost you £10, and it'd be great to see you again. But, like I said, if you're not reading this and your mother is, I send my condolences. If you're still with us, living on the right side of the turf, drop me a line. In the meantime, cobber, look after yourself.

Silvester.

To say this letter was a surprise would be an understatement. Of course, Michael remembered the incident. Three Australian pilots who had been with them a short time were being transferred to another squadron and, to Michael's recollection, they had flown with 111 Squadron six, if not seven times. The last time being when Silvester's Spitfire was hit. Michael followed him down. When he had landed, Michael was right behind him and reached his plane, sliding Silvester's canopy open just as the Spitfire went on fire. He and another pilot got Silvester out and clear of the aircraft as it went up in flames. Silvester had a large gash on his forehead and was bleeding badly but they got him out. He was a lucky man. And for the life of him, Michael couldn't remember giving Silvester his address or why, but he must have done.

Michael, after having a talk with his parents about this opportunity to go to Australia, decided, with their blessing, that he would take the chance and go. He had no reasons to stay and the positives of the venture outweighed the negatives. So, with no reservations the decision was made. Michael wrote back, saying that he was still very much alive, that he remembered Silvester and the incident mentioned. He spoke of other events during Silvester's short stay with 111 Squadron before moving on to talk about his eagerness to travel to Australia to do a spot of flying. He missed the open skies and to be paid to fly, would be a bonus. An opportunity not to be missed.

Michael posted his letter, affixed with a blue airmail label, alongside the relevant number of King George stamps needed. As his letter disappeared into the dark open mouth of the letter box, he made a point of wanting to remember this day.

Things moved fast, assisted passage to Australia had been going on for the last three years and had now become the norm. Thousands of people took advantage of the £10 cost to secure a ticket. Michael had been interviewed at the Australian immigration office in Birmingham, after receiving a letter from Silvester stating that he was more than welcome to stay with him until he got himself sorted and that a job flying with Silvester was not a problem. Michael had taken a medical report of his health with him, received from his doctor in Newtown, not that he ever went to the doctors, but it was a mandatory document for all migrants. Michael stated his preference of State, the port he wished to disembark and the nature of work he acquired. The interviewer looked at his medical report, read his military record, then smiled and stamped the word APPROVED on the relevant papers in front of him.

These papers would ultimately put him on a ship, one that would take him halfway around the world. Michael already had a passport and now, all that was left was to wait for the immigration authorities to get back in touch with dates for embarkation and a boarding pass.

On the 21st of Feb,1948 at Tilbury docks in London, Michael boarded the RMS Ormonde, a ship of the P&O line, an immigration ship that also carried mail. It had been a troop ship during the war, as it had been in the Great War. All that was in her past and now she was to take hundreds of people to a new life, transporting them to a country that had taken in thousands of people before them. Some would be disappointed and would regret their decision, but this was all in the future. All Michael's farewells had been said. But he was leaving with anticipation and excitement, rather than a heavy heart. Coloured paper streamers caught the wind as they were thrown over the ship's railings to the crowd below. The ship was moving now, slowly but deliberately away from the wharf and Michael found himself remembering the moment he'd walked through the gates of Shawbury RAF base and reminiscing on the first time he had taken to the skies.

Megan busied herself cleaning the house after Michael had left, every now and again, she would stop. The realisation that her son would not sleep in his bed that night was not new. She had this feeling many times while he was away and knew that this melancholy mood would pass, as it had done before. Her youngest son was now living at the farm where he worked and although he called in every weekend, things would not be the same.

"I must get rid of these old newspapers," she said, "I don't know why I keep them." On the top of a pile of newspapers she'd retrieved from under the stairs were some Picture Post magazines. She placed the pile on the table and looked at the topmost magazine dated the 16th May 1942.

"This is five years old!" she exclaimed.

"Don't throw that away," Esther was hovering over her mother's shoulder, "It's a photograph of Cecil Mason from Llanidloes. I haven't seen him in a long time, nice lad."

"He looks so young." Megan touched the picture of a youthful soldier with a full pack and rifle on his back, climbing a rope. "It was taken while he was doing an assault course at Southend and the magazine had a report on it."

"He was twenty one when that was taken. Apparently, he was that good on the course, better than the instructors, so they made him one, an instructor." Megan put the magazine to one side and placed the rest into a sack. Then sifting through the newspapers, she paused at the headlines of the local paper. Sunday 23rd January, three years earlier, at twenty minutes to three on a cold stormy afternoon, a Halifax Bomber had crashed into a field six miles from Newtown. All nine of the Canadian aircrew were killed. What it was doing there, no one seemed to know. Some said it flew low over the Mochdre hills before coming down. Megan thought of the families of these boys.

"How sad," she said as she placed it with the rest of the papers in the sack.

16

After spending two months at an evacuation hospital in Kent, Billie received notice of her own evacuation back to the US. She travelled on a flight accompanied by two of her nursing friends, both of whom had been with her for, what now seemed, an eternity. They had seen and done a lot in their time together and now they could make plans for the future. As soon as they had set foot on British soil, Billie, having never heard from Ken, had wondered about finding him; she had a contact he'd given her, a friend of his. She thought it strange that he had never given her his home address but had asked her to contact his friend when the war was over. Billie had thought about going to see his friend in person but decided not to, as it could look as though she was being a bit pushy, so she wrote instead. Within a few days, she received a reply.

Dear Billie,

I regret to inform you that Ken died on the first day of the D-Day Landings. He was with the

*3rd British Infantry Division and was killed on
Swensord Beach, Normandy. We had been friends
since primary school, so I knew him well enough to
know that he was an honest and genuine person.
He will be sadly missed. He told me about an
American nurse that he'd met and seemed quite
keen to renew his acquaintance when the war
was over. I am so sorry to be the bearer of bad
news. Wishing you a happy life and a safe trip
back home.*

*Regards,
Walter.*

Ken's death wasn't a complete surprise to Billie, she had written to him, care of his friend a number of times with no reply and had wondered if she was just someone that had passed through his life, never again to meet. Well, they would never meet again now. She was sad to learn that he had died. At least he had thought of prolonging their relationship, however realistic that would have been. She didn't dwell on his death but often thought of their frenzied few hours making love in a hotel room, paid for by a man who had, in the past, probably been in a similar situation himself. "Ah, the reckless behaviour of the young," she said to herself, adding, "I think for the next few years, I'm going to have some more of that fun, I damn well deserve it."

For the first few months after the war, the merrymaking and 'do as you please' attitude of the masses became the norm. There were consequences, but for the young, especially all those in uniform, it was time to take stock of their lives. Many British women had married their GI lovers and, having said goodbye to their families, moved to America. On an impulse, Imogen had married a US doctor and, four days later, they were on their way to America. They had known each other for just eight weeks. Lesley decided not to return to the US and went to Ireland as she had an aunt who lived in Dublin. For Billie, Shelly and Connie it was party time. They threw caution to the wind and danced all night to the sound of the big bands. They drank the cocktails, wines and beer being offered by hormone ravaged men. Every so often they would succumb to the attention of the silver tongued talk of the men in their company. The outcome being a night of passion, some memorable, some not so. There were a few regrets, but not enough to dissuade them from flitting from one hunter to another. They were fully aware of their flirtatious and outrageous behaviour but, like everyone else at this time, they were having a ball. After all, they were just, window shopping, as Shelly said. The three of them knew that it wouldn't last and that it would come to an end when they stepped aboard a plane heading home.

Home for Billie came two months later on the third of January 1946. Accompanied by Shelly and Connie, they boarded an American transport plane flying from

RAF Croughton in Northamptonshire to the 'Mitchell Air Force Base', Long Island, New York. Billie's feelings at the time were two fold. On the one hand she was going home, joy of joys, on the other she would be saying goodbye to everything she had known for the last three years. This flight would be the last event in a chain of events that was outside what she had perceived to be 'normal.' She looked around. Everyone seemed deep in thought. Shelly turned and smiled.

"Penny for them?"

"My thoughts?" Billie answered, returning her smile. "Just wondering

where do I go from here?"

"Me too, I'll go and see my parents, but I won't be staying. I want a better life for myself than to go back to Jenkins. I don't have fond memories of that place." For a moment she was silent. "Jesus Christ Billie, I'm twenty eight years of age, what the hell am I going to do?" You lot are, were," she corrected herself, "like family to me." With tears filling her eyes, Shelly reached for Billie's hand and with a slight smile gently squeezed it.

"Apart from all the bad times we went through, we did have some good times, didn't we?"

"Yes, we did, Shelly and there will be more good times in the future. Maybe you could come to New York and we could work together again."

"Do you really think that could happen? I mean me come to New York?"

"Why ever not, you're my friend and sometimes that's all you need." Billie was surprised at her own proposition. She had said it without thinking it through, but on quick reflection, what was there to think about? This was someone who didn't want to go home, someone who needed something to look forward to and if she could give Shelly that something, then that's what she would do.

And so, they flew on. Shelly now had something positive to think about and Billie was pleased with herself for making that happen. Connie would be getting off at Mitchell Air Base to catch a plane to Chicago, where she'd be reunited with her family. And Connie, being Connie, like the rest of them, would, no doubt, carry on doing what they were all good at doing and that was nursing.

On a cold Monday mid-afternoon, they landed at Mitchell Air Base, everyone eager to again stand on home soil. The girls held each other and, with tear filled eyes, said their last goodbyes. Connie caught her plane to Chicago and there were Greyhound buses waiting to take passengers, all of whom were medical personnel, to various parts of New York state and beyond. It would be a long haul for Shelly, but she was in a better state of mind now, knowing that Billie was there at the end of the phone. What little possessions they had, they carried. Billie couldn't wait to see the skyline of New York and it wasn't long before she did.

She got dropped off in the city and was choked up and teary as she stood on Main Street. A cold wind brought colour to her cheeks. She needed a coffee, she needed to sit down, so she walked into a cafe and did both. Billie was halfway through her coffee when she felt a soft tap on her shoulder. On turning she gazed into the smiling eyes of the gentleman that had served her.

"It's Billie, isn't it?" he said. She was confused. "Billie, Billie Fleming, Joe's daughter? I knew it," he seemed excited.

"Yes … yes, but who are you, do I know y … "

"It's Dean, you remember… Deans cakes? A friend of your Uncle Sam. The last time I saw you was at Willena's funeral. My God, of all the cafes in all the world you had to walk into mine. Sorry Billie, Humphrey Bogart, Casablanca and all that." As soon as Billie recognised him, she burst into tears.

"I … I …" Dean, seeing the state she was in, took her by the elbow and, carrying her case, led her into a room at the back of the cafe.

"Jan, it's Billie, Joe and Pageant's daughter, would you get her another cup of coffee please, she looks half frozen. That's Jan, you don't know her but she knows your mother and father, they call in from time to time."

"I'm sorry Dean, I don't know what came over me, a little overawed at being back home I suppose." Billie dried her eyes with a handkerchief given to her by Dean.

"I've just arrived from London and wanted to see the city before going home." She looked up. "There, I feel better now," she smiled. "Is this your place, Dean?" she said, changing the subject.

"Yes, it is. It's taken a long time, but I knew one day I'd have a place of my own". He looked at her. "You've changed since the last time I saw you," he sighed, "where did that little girl go?" Billie looked up.

"That little girl disappeared a long time ago. She grew up." Still smiling, she handed Dean's handkerchief back.

"Believe me, sometimes I wish I could go back to being her, but a lot has happened since then." Billie stood.

"And a lot of water has passed under the bridge," replied Dean. For a moment Billie paused and looked around, with servicemen still coming home from the war, Dean she thought, didn't really have a clue. Then, she added with a smile.

"That bridge got washed away when I saw the bombs fall on Pearl Harbour." With that, Billie picked up her suitcase.

"You'll be going home from here?"

"Yes, I'll get a taxi."

"You will do no such thing, I'll drive you, Jan will manage things here." They left the café, making way for an elderly couple going in.

"My car is parked just around the corner; I'll have you home in ten minutes." Billie asked to be dropped off one block from her home, as she thought she'd like to walk the rest of the way. Dean obliged and pulled away from the sidewalk, waving as he went.

"Call and see me again," he shouted.

"I will," she answered, raising her hand.

"That was Billie?" he said without knowing he had said it. "I must be getting old, or that kid is older than her years. Wherever she'd been, in these last few years, she'd altered. I think her mother and father will have a bit of a shock… Billie Fleming, I'll be damned."

Billie lingered for a few moments, taking in her surroundings. The trees with their leaves falling, most of them lying on the road and sidewalk, the vehicles on the street, people walking, going about their business, not knowing, or caring that she was home. She felt like yelling.

"Hey, it's me, Billie. I live here. I've been away and now I'm back."

People would smile, say hello and walk on. In the time it took for her to walk to her house, every conceivable emotion passed through her mind. The predominant one was that she would be overjoyed to see her parents again. On reaching her front door she knocked, then burst out laughing, realising that she had just knocked on her own front door. On opening it, her mother, not realising who it was, smiled.

"Hello, can I hel …"

"Hello Mom," with her voice breaking, Billie rushed in and threw her arms around her mother, while sobbing and laughing.

"I don't believe it, I've just knocked on my own front door," she cried.

Pageant led her daughter into the house, insisting that she ring her father and within half an hour Joe walked through the door. He stood and just looked at her, hardly recognising her. They hugged for many minutes. Joe repeated over and over how happy he was to see her. The Fleming household, once more together, talked well into the night. Alan, Billie's twelve year old brother, who she could have passed now in the street and not known, asked her questions that she found difficult to answer. They were questions he wouldn't understand the answers to, not at his age, so she glossed over them. The war had its place and this was not the place to discuss it, if it ever would be. She didn't want her home to be witness to any talk of suffering, her nightmares and recollections of such events would be enough. During the evening Joe rang Sam and when he answered, he'd passed the phone over to Billie.

"Hello Uncle Sam, it's Billie, I'm home."

"Billie!" There was a pause, then she heard him call, "Grace its

Billie, she's home."

That night she slept in her own bed. She was now too tired to cry and too tired to laugh, she slept in a dream that faded into the darkness of the night. Billie awoke late, unsure of what the day would bring. She lay there and looked at the ceiling, then snuggled up and closed her eyes, not to sleep, but to savour the moment. She thought of many things. When she'd go back to work. The friends she'd had here in Manhattan and the new friends she'd made since she'd left What would become of Shelly, Connie, Lesley and Imogen? Billie thought she would give Shelly a week before getting in touch. It was at that moment that the realisation came that, maybe, when Shelly came to New York, they could get a place together. The idea of moving out of home didn't shock her as much as the idea itself. She had already mentioned to her parents that a friend of hers might move to New York. Billie swung her legs over the edge of the bed, walked to the window and, hesitantly drew back the curtains. "Like opening the curtains of a new life," she thought. She looked out and smiled at the morning.

17

"Billie will have some stories to tell." Sam replaced the telephone and looked at Grace.

"Why don't you invite them all over on Saturday night?" she said. "We have nothing on and I'm sure they would like to come around, you know how much Billie likes this place."

"Yes, she spent a lot of time here when she was younger."

"And the reason for that?" Grace raised her head above the paper she was reading.

"Willena, I suppose," Sam shrugged. "Billie missed her terribly after she died."

"We all did, we all did and maybe you more than anyone."

Sam looked wistfully at Grace. She was right, for a long time after Willena's death the kitchen had seemed an alien place to be. That was her domain, always had been. Even today, there was a picture, amongst others, of Billie and Willena hanging on one of the kitchen walls. Sam sat briefly in his chair, then stood and went into the kitchen. He was thinking about the intervening years since Willena's death. How long was it now, eight years, was it really that long ago? To familiarise himself with the passage of time, he went through the ages of his children since Willena had gone. Henry was twelve, Sarah ten, Mary eight and Jimmy seven. They would all be home from school shortly. My God where has the time gone?

The week passed for Billie like a whirlwind, flitting about like a fairy with a wand. Her army pay, as little as it was, had mounted up and there was the additional money her parents had banked for her while she was away. This meant that she had more than enough to do some serious shopping. Pageant was the one to know how a dress should hang on a woman of pleasing proportions and, according to Pageant, Billie had pleasing proportions. She took great satisfaction in passing on her gift of the catwalk fashions to her only daughter. Billie, who stood two inches taller than her mother and two inches shorter than her, fathers five feet ten inches, Billie was a prime example of femininity. Billie and Pageant did the rounds of the New York fashion houses, Philip Hulitar, Cristian Dior, Traina-Norell, and Norell.

Because of her father's position at the New York Times newspaper, Billie's parents moved within the circles of the well to do. Dinner engagements, parties and functions were the norm. Now Pageant had an attractive daughter to show off and she wanted to make the most of it. It wasn't that Pageant was a snob and she would always remember her humble beginnings, but, she did enjoy the finer things in life. Billie, on the other hand, didn't do posh. She did nice. She didn't want to disappoint her mother and would do anything for her, but she found it difficult swanning around in ball gowns, strappy cocktail dresses and glitzy padded shoulder jackets that her mother insisted she try on. There was a moment when she recalled the Piccadilly Commandos in Soho. She smiled to herself remembering their classy look, or was it a slutty look, either way, at the time she, would have swapped outfits. Thinking about them now, her mother would have been mortified. In the end Billie and her mother came to a compromise. Billie would buy a few items of posh, then go to Claire Mc Cardell's and walk out with bags of nice, ready to wear, clothing.

It was an emotional greeting. When Sam opened his front door, Billie threw her arms around him. He was family. Sam responded in kind. It had been twenty years since he'd first met this vivacious young woman. She was a little girl then and had become someone special, a link to his past and now as he held her, a lump came to his throat as he mentioned her name. Billie stood back but still held Sam's hand until Grace intercepted to give her a hug.

"Welcome home Billie, it's so nice to see you again, please come in." Billie with the rest of her family followed Sam into the living room where other acquaintances of Billie were gathered. Her Uncle Curtis and Aunt Isabelle, Eddie, one of Sam's old friends who Billie hadn't seen for years but still remembered with fondness, Grace's mother and father and a number of others that had, however remote, been part of Billie's childhood. The afternoon went as expected. Irrespective of the ages there gathered, Billie was the centre of attention. She found the children amusing and, to her surprise, a little tiring. She hadn't been around young people for a long time and there was a moment when she wanted to be alone. She excused herself, saying she was going to the kitchen to have a few words with Willena. No one was surprised at Billie's comment, as they knew how close the two of them had been. Billie closed the door behind her and gazed at the large table in the centre of the room. She felt sad but smiled as she walked over to it. She remembered the times Willena had chased her around the table, both squealing with delight. Billie went to look at a picture of them both, hanging on the wall. She touched it and found she wasn't sad anymore. There was a tap on the door, it opened slowly.

"You alright Billie?" Sam's smiling face appeared.

"Yes, Uncle Sam, I'm fine. I just wanted a few moments with Willena."

"Would you like to, have it?" Sam asked as he stood by her side.

"The picture?" Billie answered without looking at Sam.

"Yes, the picture. Would you like to, have it?"

"Yes, I would love to have it. I have a few little things Willena had given me, but this photograph would mean a lot to me."

"Then it's yours." Sam reached up and lifted it off the nail it hung on.

"Thank you, Uncle Sam, those were happy times, weren't they?"

"Yes, they were. Ones I'll never forget."

Billie hadn't noticed the Christmas and New Year of 1946 go by. She was too busy with other thoughts to pay much attention to what was going on around her. She just enjoyed the company of her family and the few acquaintances she had. There was a snowstorm in late January and with that having passed, Billie was looking forward to Shelly's arrival sometime in March.

Billie started back at the Lenox Hill Hospital, a few days later, and again went to visit her Uncle Sam.

"Your father tells me you have a friend coming over from Kentucky to join you?"

"Yes, but I've got a problem with that," without stopping, Billie looked down and anticipating a comment from Sam. She carried on, "when Shelly comes it will put me in an awkward position in having somewhere for her to stay. So, I have decided to get a place for the both of us." Billie looked up "I know it may sound selfish on my part, I mean to move out so soon after arriving home, but I can't stay, as much as I'd like to. I think that, after being away for so long and having my own independence, it may be time to move on."

For a moment Sam didn't answer, he could see in Billie's eyes that she wanted approval and that approval could come only from him.

"Where would you go?" Sam asked, sounding concerned.

"Not far," Billie smiled, "within walking distance from home."

"And do your parents know of your decision?"

"No not yet, but I have hinted… just a little two bedroom place, maybe you could help me find somewhere?" Sam picked up a little apprehension in Billie's voice and wanted to assure her that he understood.

"I will do everything I can Billie, but I would prefer it if your parents were to ask me to help you, if that's all right?"

"Thanks Uncle Sam, I wouldn't have it any other way."

"You two been reminiscing?" said Grace as she walked into the kitchen. "I thought I would make us some coffee."

"Billie has a problem," Sam smiled. "With her friend coming over, she has decided to find a place for them both to live and has asked if I could help her out."

"That wouldn't be a problem would it, Sam?"

"No none at all, I'll find you a place, Billie." He smiled.

Another week passed during which Billie had the heart to heart talk with her parents about leaving and finding a home of her own. Pageant was upset but accepted that sooner or later this was going to happen. She had just wanted it to happen later, rather than sooner. Joe rang Sam to ask if, with his contacts, he could find an apartment for Billie and within a week, Billie held the keys to a comfortable second floor, two bedroom apartment with the first two months' rent paid by Sam, his reason being that this was what he believed Willena would have wanted him to do.

Shelly arrived in the last week of March. Joe and Pageant looked at each other when they saw their daughter and Shelly hug each other as they stood outside the Greyhound bus. Billie had told her parents of Shelly's past and of their close friendship, hoping that they'd better understand the reason she'd asked her to come to New York.

"Billie, it's not for me or your father to approve or disapprove of your friends. You're old enough to choose and we think you did the right thing. Without true friends, you can live a lonely life and you are not the kind to live a lonely one."

For the first two days Shelly stayed at Billie's home. It was a getting to know you time. Both were a little nervous, Shelly wanting to appear acceptable in the presence of Billie's parents. Billie's home life was a far cry from her own. Of course, money was a factor, along with education, etiquette and how to live in a loving environment. These were things Shelly had known precious little of. Thank God, she'd left that life behind her a long time ago. To have to go back to that would be sad beyond words.

For the following twelve months, Billie and Shelly lived a life of contentment. Shelly had lost some of the rough edges of her past but not completely and Billie was thankful for it. She didn't want to lose that part of Shelly that had made her what she was, the dearest of friends. The Lenox Hill Hospital had become a different place to what it had been when Billie had first started working there. The biggest change was the gradual respect that nurses were given, generally and politically. There was now an overall acceptance that these women were in a profession that demanded the respect they deserved. No doubt the service they provided during the war had a big impact on this initial change of attitude, but it was happening and Billie, Shelly and the thousands of other nurses who went away to serve their country, were glad to see it.

The Thanksgiving holiday of 1947 was a low key affair, as both girls worked double shifts on the Thursday and Friday of the last weekend in November and did likewise on Christmas and Boxing Day. It wasn't unusual for nurses to cover for each other over the festivities, as time given would be returned in kind. The lead up to Christmas, with its family parties, invited gatherings, visits to the theatre and general goodwill to others, was heart-warming. This activity was interrupted with working at the Lenox Hospital, but this did not lessen the joy of the season for Billie. Coloured chains of paper and tinsel were hung on the walls of the wards. People exchanged small gifts, with a lot of hugs and kisses between family and friends and all donations of toys for the children's ward were welcomed.

The voice of Bing Crosby singing 'White Christmas' and 'Let It Snow, Let it Snow', drifted through the wards and added to the festive spirit. People with minor injuries were patched up and sent home and those who had to stay, made the most of it.

On New Year's Eve, Billie, and Shelly, like most young people of New York were out in the bars, dance halls and night clubs. Movie theatres were full. It's a Wonderful Life, a film starring James Stewart and Donna Reed was showing at the Globe Theatre. The girls fast danced to the jazz bands and to blues songs by Ella Fitzgerald. The Ink Spots did a few numbers and Perry Como sang some of his slow songs. The girls heard them all and, between songs, drank the cocktails offered to them. Shelly had a French 75 in her hand and Billie had just finished two Hawaiian moonshines when they moved on to something that the barman had conjured up. They danced to the sound of Buddy DeVito and the Tommy Dorsey Band. And when it got late, Shelly would always quote:

"Get yourself a big steelworker type of man, at least they'll look after you." Billie looked at Shelly as she slow-waltzed with her arms wrapped around the neck of a man she'd just described. As they exited into the street, Billie repeated a line from a song she'd heard earlier.

"Why does it get so late so soon?" They summoned a taxi and arrived home in the early hours.

"One hell of a night," said Shelly, collapsing into her bed. "Thank you, Billie, you're one in a million." Billie sat on the edge of her bed and looked at her friend.

"Thank you too, Shelly." Shelly didn't hear. She was fast asleep.

Then the blizzard came. On the 26th January at twenty past three in the morning, it started to snow. In less than 24 hours, twenty five and a half inches had fallen.

Traffic came to a standstill, people were stranded and as the day wore on, long lines of automobiles were buried at the curb. Four hundred people rode a chilly, Long Island train that took ten hours to make a twenty minute run. People sought refuge where they could, in the subways where services were stopped, in public buildings and bus shelters. Seventy seven people perished in the blizzard. A few days later it was all but gone.

It was midday on the first Sunday in February and it was snowing again. The flakes fell silently, disturbing nothing, not even the air through which they fell. Billie closed the taxi door; the driver had dropped her off outside Sam's home. Then, after promising to pick her up in two and a half hours, he slowly drove away. Billie had taken the weekend off work to visit Uncle Sam and Grace. She hadn't seen them since Christmas and since Shelly had gone to Long Island with Oscar, a man she had met on New Years Eve, she was on her own at the apartment. Billie didn't mind being on her own, in fact, she rather liked the calm and the quietness that it brought.

"I hear Shelly has a man," said Sam as he offered Billie a ham sandwich from a plate Grace had placed on the table.

"Yes, she met him at a party."

"And what do you think? I mean, is he a good sort? Do you think it will last?" Billie smiled.

"Yes, that would be nice. They've been seeing each other for over a month now. He seems like a nice man."

Billie hesitated, "he's a few years older than Shelly, not that that's an issue. I think he'll be good for her."

"What does he do?" Grace asked.

"He's a captain, or something in the New York fire service, stationed in Manhattan somewhere."

"And you, Billie," Sam raised his head, "are you seeing anyone?"

"No … Uncle Sam, I do not have a gentleman friend, if that's what you're asking." Billie's answer denoted a certain defiance, immediately regretting the tone in which she spoke to her uncle. "And at the moment, I'm not looking for one. I don't know," she groaned, "but most girls of my age are married, or going steady. It seems to be compulsory that if a girl isn't married at a certain age then she's left on the shelf. Well, it's a damn big shelf, Uncle Sam and there are a lot like me who don't want to get off it … well not just yet." Grace giggled.

"Well good on you," said Grace. "Don't you be pressured into something you don't want to do."

"There are things I want to do and places to see and if I have to do them alone, then so be it." Sam looked at Grace, obviously he had touched on a subject that was out of bounds and he apologised to Billie for bringing it up.

"It's not you Uncle Sam and I do appreciate your interest in my life. Maybe one day. If I do meet someone I intend to marry, you'll be the first to know." Billie smiled, then changed the subject.

"Nice ham Aunt Grace, do I detect the taste of honey?"

"You do Billie, would you like another sandwich?"

During their conversations, Sam mentioned Michael, his Aunt Megan's son.

"Isn't he my age?" asked Billie with a surprised look. "And wasn't he a pilot in the RAF? I remembered that being mentioned."

"Yes, he took part in the Battle of Britain, then went over to France and goodness knows where else."

Billie gave a soft smile.

"I remember them flying over us in Italy. Is he still flying?"

"Well, he made it home to Wales and is currently working in a bicycle factory there. Did you go to Wales when you were in the UK, Billie?"

"No, I never made it, but I'd like to one day. That would be nice."

It was still snowing as Billie's taxi came to a stop. She brushed the snow off her coat, opened the taxi door and stepped inside. Back at home she turned on the radio and looked at the clock hanging above the door that led to the kitchen. Shelly would be home in another five hours, she thought, till then she intended to enjoy the peace and quiet. She hung up her coat, replacing it with a thick jumper, a Christmas present from her mother. She made herself a hot water bottle, retrieved a blanket and then, fully stretched out on the settee, and closed her eyes.

For five hours, in between cups of coffee, something to eat and a little sleep, Billie thought of her future. The past had been done and although there had been moments of fear and frustration, it had been altogether an exciting time. The uncertainty of everything had been exhilarating. It was the trains, boats and planes that had exposed her to people, places and things that she'd had no knowledge of. Experiences she would never have witnessed had the war not happened. It was the little things that sometimes came to mind. A gold chain with the image of St. Christopher congealed in blood, around the neck of a nineteen year old. An arch of pink roses over the front door of someone's home, a home that had been blown apart and only the door, its frame and the arch of roses were left standing. A discarded shoe. A walking cane, still in the hand of its owner, lying in an undignified manner in the mud of a country road. "Little things," she thought… maybe they weren't that little.

Sleeping in her own bed and knowing her surroundings brought Billie back to the reality of the life she now lived. At the moment she was content, but for how long? She was a person who knew herself and would not conform to what was expected, or desired of a young lady. If she'd have wanted a man, it wouldn't have taken a lot to find one and if love were to enter the equation, then she would deal with it, as and when it happened. As for the future, she was already getting itchy feet. She could get a nursing job anywhere, there were sick people all over the world. Maybe she would go back to Europe, maybe Canada or the islands in the South Pacific, anything was possible. She smiled to herself, thinking of the palm trees and white sandy beaches in Hawaii, a different place now. Then she closed her eyes and drifted off.

In May, Shelly announced her engagement to Oscar. He had accepted a position in the Chicago Fire service and had asked Shelly if she would go with him. It was a short engagement and within six weeks, they were married. Billie was the only bridesmaid; a small reception was held at the Manhattan fire station and, for the umpteenth time, Shelly apologised to Billie for leaving her.

18

Michael arrived in Port Adelaide, some six weeks after setting sail. The voyage, for the most part, he found rather boring. Many times, while standing on deck, he imagined what it would have been like for the sailors during the war. For him, the sea held little interest, except that it looked somewhat different when flying over it at thirty thousand feet. From the sky, it seemed there was no sense of movement, nothing could be seen but the ship itself and the wake it left behind as it propelled itself through the waves. He tried to visualise what it would have been like to be bombed by attacking German aircraft, torpedoed by submarines and to be on board a sinking ship. He looked at the bow of his ship as it rose and fell in the troughs of water. "No," he thought, he would much prefer the freedom of the sky than to sail the sea. Probably, a sailor would think otherwise, with the names of his ships forever etched in his heart. Once a sailor, always a sailor. He had heard that a number of times and wondered if that applied to pilots. Once a pilot, always a pilot. On reflection, he didn't think that pilots were as attached to their planes as sailors were to their ships; there were too many planes, in too many places.

As the ship sailed through the Straits of Gibraltar, Michael looked at the peninsula, with the rock, being a dominant feature and smiled. He'd been there before and remembered sitting on a chair at the RAF base, looking out to sea. The boats and ships he'd seen pass the rock took him to a different time. He had thought that he would ever see the place again, yet here it was. He tried to remember the time he had spent on the rock. Who was there that he could remember apart from Troy and Glyn and, of course, the rest of the squadron? No one really came to mind, except maybe the little terrier, a dog abandoned and then adopted by the RAF base as their mascot. Sooty, so named because of his colour, had wandered around the place with an air of his own importance, making friends with everyone who had the time to make a fuss of him. Sooty often sat and watched the pilots take off, then come to sit in the same spot to see them come home again. It was as though he counted them out and counted them in, not moving until the last one had landed.

The ship's first stop had been Port Said in Egypt. Passengers had disembarked and wandered for a while through the markets, buying fresh fruit and trinkets, anything that would be a memento. With the ship refuelled and resupplied with provisions and whatever was needed, it was time to move on. Then, with all on board, the bow of the ship had inched its way forward into the Suez Canal. While sailing through this narrow waterway,

Michael had thought of his father. Thirty years earlier he and Michael's Uncle Jim, along with a certain Jack Davies from the village, had patrolled parts of this 120 mile canal that linked the Mediterranean Sea to the Red Sea. Michael found it sobering to watch the desert sands drift over the dunes. They rose and dipped like the seas that had brought him to gaze at a sight his father had seen many years before. The warm wind kissed each grain, then sent it with others to and beyond the horizon, creating a moving landscape that would not rest. Only when the tiresome breeze paused, did the desert cease to move.

The weather, sailing through the Red Sea, had been balmy and warm. Daytime temperatures in the mid-twenties, dropping to eleven or so degrees at night. On the ship's port side and beyond the horizon for most of the way, was Saudi Arabia. On the starboard side, the countries of Egypt, Sudan and Eritrea. To most passengers these countries were of little importance, they didn't feature in their day to day lives, not that they should. What did feature was their daily routine. Getting up in the mornings, going for breakfast and taking a look at the ship's notice board to see what activities were scheduled for the day. Michael was no different. His travelling companions were a mixed bag of building workers, factory hands and office administrators who specialised in various professions, but there was not one ex-pilot to talk to, anywhere.

By the time they arrived at Port Aden after passing through the Red Sea, Michael had become friendly with a man who had fought his way through the war as a driver, taking supplies to the front line wherever they were needed. He was originally from Australia, in his forties, single and, in his own words, he was going home. In the evenings, Michael visited the bars with his newfound friend, who had introduced himself as Colin. They talked, mostly, of their background, their homes, what they had done and where they had been. It was enlightening to talk to someone who'd led a different life to his; it reminded Michael of the boys, his fellow pilots, whose lives also differed from his.

It seemed everyone had their own agenda. Like Michael, they were all starting over. Even the girls on the dance floor looked like they didn't have a care in the world. Young men at the bar looked anxiously in their direction, their minds far from the pint of beer in front of them. Each was thinking of their next move in getting acquainted with a girl they'd taken a fancy to. It was the mating game all over again. Nothing ventured and all that, Michael excused himself and walked over to three girls who were dancing together. A slim, leggy girl in a blue dress and matching stilettos, pleasing to the eye and with long auburn hair, hesitated, but didn't back away as Michael slid his arm around a waist that was hardly there. They danced to a slow Nat King Cole number. Then danced to another and another. There was no fumbling of feet; she followed Michael's lead like they had danced before and the more they danced the more she relaxed. When the timing seemed right, Michael took her back to the table where her friends were sitting. He thanked her and she smiled.

"My God you can dance as well as fly." Michael straightened his tie.

"Flying and dancing are one of the same." Michael grinned, "One drifts across the dance floor, as one drifts across the sky."

"And?" said Colin, almost laughing.

"And what?"

"Details, tell me about her? It's called sharing information."

"I don't share that kind of information, not to anyone." Michael was grinning from ear to ear.

"Has she got a name? I can assure you, I'm no competition."

"It's Kerry, her name is Kerry."

Port Aden had been a short stop. with just enough time for the ship to be resupplied with provisions. Then it was out into the Gulf of Aden; ahead lay the Arabian Sea and the long haul of the Indian Ocean. Michael's encounters with Kerry were based on companionship. She was fun to be with. Although he enjoyed Colin's company, Kerry had the edge on him simply for the fact that she was of the opposite gender. Michael had decided that he would not pursue a romance with Kerry and this surprised him. At that moment, he didn't want anything too complicated in his life. But, it would be nice to have a female friend for the rest of the journey.

Kerry was a schoolteacher. She was twenty three years of age, very intelligent and had an answer to everything. She would be getting off at Fremantle in Western Australia to expand her career yet showed no anxiety about her move to Australia. She'd said that classrooms were the same the world over. The only difference were the children. She seemed to apply logic and lateral thinking to most things, which annoyed some people. But Michael found her amusing and damn good company.

Saying good night could have been a problem. On the first night after walking Kerry to her cabin, Michael bent, kissed her on the cheek and uttered, "Nos da". She pulled back with smiling eyes and asked what he'd said.

"It's good night, in Welsh," he answered with a smile. For a moment she was silent. Michael could see the wheels of her mind turning. Then she held his arm and standing on her toes, she reached up and whispered.

"Buenas noches, Michael."

"I've never had that said to me before."

" Ditto," she replied as he opened her cabin door.

After that, saying good night to each other was as easy as saying it in a foreign language. This seemed to ease any tension. However, it did have one drawback in that they both had to learn the words in different languages, just in case, they had landed on the same one.

The ship had already crossed the Tropic of Capricorn during their run through the Red Sea and with the equator some distance ahead, Michael, at a loose end one afternoon, had gone on deck. It was three days after meeting Kerry.

She was on his mind as he sat in the sun on a deckchair vacated by an American passenger who, after exchanging a few words, had handed him a novel to read. The Iceman Cometh, by Eugene O'Neill, an author Michael had never heard of. It told the story of some alcoholic men living in a doss house in New York in 1912. Halfway through the second chapter, Michael happened to look up and noticed an elderly lady lying on a deckchair some feet away. She had a wide brimmed straw hat covering her face and wore a white pleated skirt, the hem of which she had risen above her knees. Her pale blue top had a low neckline and the fingers on her hands were linked into each other and resting on her stomach.

There were not that many elderly people on board the ship and he got to wondering the reason for her being there. Probably travelling with family, he surmised. He was about to carry on reading, when he noticed a slight shake in her hands, then the woman's legs started to do the same. Immediately he jumped up, something wasn't right. He dropped his book and rushed over. He noticed she was sweating and her skin was pale and clammy. She sat upright, her breathing was fast. She said that she felt dizzy and nauseous. Michael laid her gently back and grabbed the towel lying by her chair. He called for water and someone handed him a bottle. Michael suspected that it was heat stroke and told her to stay calm as he poured water onto the towel and began wiping her face. He then poured a little water on to her legs to dampen them down. The last of the water he sprinkled on the collar of the blue top she wore. Someone then brought over a sunshade, for which the lady was most grateful. A number of people had now gathered, some giving advice, others having a look before wandering off. Another bottle of water was handed to Michael. He held it to the lady's lips and encouraged her to drink. Within a few minutes the ship's doctor was by her side. He kneeled and did a quick examination, then leaning back told the lady that she indeed, had heat exhaustion. The lady looked a lot better as the doctor and a nurse assisted her to the ship's hospital where she spent a number of hours under observation. Nothing more was said as the curious onlookers went their separate ways. Michael went back to his deckchair, picked up his book, sat down and carried on reading from where he had left off. A half hour later, Kerry passed by.

"Would you like some company?" she asked. He looked up, folded the corner of the page he was reading and placed the book on the ships deck.

"The best offer I've had all day" he smiled, "apart from an offer of a drink from Colin, which I declined."

Michael rose and dragged over a deckchair, placing it next to his. Kerry was dressed in a one piece, canary yellow bathing suit with a wrap around orange, light cotton skirt. She sat with a sigh, placing a summer beach bag by her side.

"I hear you've been busy saving damsels in distress?" Michael looked at her and grinned.

"An exaggeration in numbers, I'm afraid."

"An exaggeration?" Kerry said smiling.

"Yes, there was only one damsel and to say I saved her would imply I had performed an heroic deed. All a misconception, I'm afraid to say." He laughed.

"In any case," he frowned, "how did you know what happened?"

"My friends passed by and saw you preoccupied with an elderly lady."

"I didn't see them."

"Like I said, you were preoccupied." Michael laughed.

"Are we dancing tonight?" she asked, "Or do you fancy a film?"

Kerry was laid out now, with a rolled up towel supporting her head. She had unwrapped her skirt, with her bare legs now exposed to the sun. Michael made a comment about her legs being in the sun and to cover them up.

"Don't you like my legs?"

"I refuse to answer that, in case I incriminate myself."

"So, you do like them," she giggled.

"That's not fair. I'm just concerned that in this heat, you'll burn and calamine lotion on red legs is not a pretty sight."

"Take no notice of me," she said with a little laugh. "But then again, you could rub some lotion on my legs if I burn them. I have a bottle in my bag."

"Kerry! You are an incorrigible young lady and if you carry on with that line of talk, I'm afraid temptation will get the better of me. Anyway, this isn't the time."

"Nor the place," she chuckled.

"Maybe we can do both," said Michael after a moment's pause. "Do you know what film is on?"

"The Big Sleep. I don't know anything about it, other than it came out last year and that a friend of mine went to see it. We could go for a drink after the film. By the way, we have eight days left on the ship."

"More than enough time for me to impress you."

The film, starring Humphrey Bogart and Lauren Bacall, was one of fast paced intrigue, and was worthy of its reviews. Michael and Kerry left the theatre holding hands, as they had during most of the film. It seemed a natural thing to do.

Kerry's past romances, she had told Michael, amounted to some fleeting relationships. Apart from one that lasted for a period of nearly two years. That had ended when her lover, a telephone engineer, fell from a telegraph pole and broke his back. Six months later, Kerry found herself on a ship on her way to Australia with no intention, whatsoever, of getting romantically involved with any man. It was ironic that two people most decidedly, not looking for something, should find themselves in a situation where a relationship could have developed. They danced and talked till dawn, neither knowing how their story would end. That night it ended with Buona Notte and Bonne Nuit. Having an Italian crew on board was helpful and Kerry's French was impressive.

Crossing the Equator had been somewhat of a novelty. The ship's entertainment crew put on a show that involved some of the passengers. At midday, on the Monday, part of the upper deck was festooned with imitation objects of the seabed, seaweed, sunken treasure chests and all things connected to King Neptune. Some of the crew were dressed as king's guards and ushered six passengers across the deck. The passengers were all dressed as prisoners. One of them was Kerry who was nominated to take part by her friends. All were led in a line, tied two yards apart with rope. King Neptune was another passenger. He wore a crown of coral and robes of green seaweed, with a long white beard and held a long, forked trident. He was seated on a throne of old ship timbers with two mermaids, half lying, each side of him. A short distance away was an empty chair, again decorated with seaweed.

The ship's band played music as the first prisoner was freed from the rope that bound his wrist and was placed upon the chair. King Neptune gave his order. The prisoner was sentenced to death by chocolate, his crime? Spreading a false rumour that the ship's Captain was really an alien. Three volunteers stepped forward and were given paint brushes. A bucket of liquid chocolate was placed beside the prisoner and he was painted from head to foot. As the band played sombre music, the crowd of onlookers cheered and chanted in unison, death by chocolate, death by chocolate. After being freed he was taken to stand under a shower as the next prisoner, a lady, was being prepared for her demise. This lady's troubles had started when she attempted to bribe a crew member into giving her the keys to the ship's library. Her sentence was death by custard. This procedure was repeated six more times.

The sentences for various alleged, crimes only separated by the choice of toppings and puddings that could be poured or painted onto each prisoner. Kerry's alleged crime had been that she broke into the ship's bar after closing and drank all the gin, a charge she vehemently denied.

Unfortunately, Kerry was also found guilty and punished accordingly. Death by rice pudding. King Neptune oversaw the sentences, it was all carried out to the cheering and baying of the assembled crowd. The bloodless deed was done. This 'crossing the line' ceremony ended to thunderous applause from the ship's passengers.

During the next few days Michael spent a lot of time in Kerry's company; he was growing fond of her. He tried to deny his feelings by concentrating his thoughts on her impending departure in just two days' time. Kerry's thoughts were similar. Once she had departed the ship, she knew that she would never see Michael again. Intimate thoughts of him were constantly on her mind and if he were to pursue the same line of thinking, she would be doomed. It would be a shipboard romance, one that ended when suitcases were collected and passports stamped. Parting is such sweet sorrow, that I shall say good night' till it be morrow. Kerry quoted Juliet and conceded that this is how it would be. Their last night together was one that memories are made of. Kerry's friends had kindly vacated their cabin for the evening and so the couple sang, danced and made love with no regrets, tears, or recriminations.

RMS Ormand weighed anchor and sailed into a new sea. With the Port of Fremantle fading in the distance and with over 1,000 miles still to go, the Great Australian Bight lay ahead. With another five days' voyage in front of them, sailing on, what they were told, could be an angry sea. Everyone hoped for calm waters. As the horizon loomed on a forgotten part of the world, the ship ploughed on. With Kerry gone, Michael began wishing the days away. There were no forwarding addresses given, no way to keep in touch, nothing to distract them both from the adventure that they had sought when first stepping on board at Tilbury Docks.

It seemed that everyone disembarking from Port Adelaide, especially single people, had pallied up with others who were doing the same. This was as much for the company as anything else. Some had people to meet them, while others were on their own. Once on dry land they all went their separate ways, some to various parts of the state but most to the city of Adelaide. On the day of leaving the ship, Michael had said goodbye to Colin and other acquaintances he'd made during the voyage. He wished them well for the future, as they did him. Some hours later, as he walked down the ship's gangway to set foot on the Australian Continent, he, again, thought of his father. It seemed that at poignant moments of his journey, he would relate his vision and feelings to his father, whose life on such a voyage as a young man had been equally life changing. The similarities ended with the final destination. From here on in, Michael's respect for his father and those that had stood beside him, would always be a part of him.

On their arrival, the weather in Port Adelaide was a warm sixty five degrees, with the summer heat having passed and winter approaching. As he stood in line for immigration, Michael found himself thinking about the months ahead, just what do crop dusters do in the winter? He had gathered as much information as he could from various sources, but crop dusting in Australia was still in its infancy and he would have to jump on the bandwagon while it was still moving, so to speak. In any case, he'd be meeting someone who was in the middle of it all, and Silvester knew all that there was to know.

After the Immigration process had been dealt with, Michael was ushered along with the others who had disembarked into a large hall where he stood in alphabetical order beneath a large board with the letter J printed on it. This depicted the first letter of his surname. In front of him, at some distance, a welcoming crowd of people had gathered, some holding cards with the names of passengers they were there to meet. Michael strained his eyes. Opposite him was a man with a sign that read 'Michael Jones Pilot'. Michael recognised Silvester immediately. Their meeting was heart-warming and they hugged each other like the old, fleeting, friends they were. Michael stood back and looked at Silvester. He was tall, his face well-tanned with a scar on his forehead that brought back memories.

Silvester was not on his own. He had brought his father and brother along for the ride. He introduced Michael as the man that had saved his life in Europe. Gilbert, his father, a lean man of average height, whose weather-beaten appearance gave rise to a body that had spent many years in the sun, stood in a blue vest and khaki shorts. On his head was an equally weather-beaten Australian, wide brimmed Akubra hat with a sweat stain that ran along the part where his forehead made contact with the felt. He smiled as he shook Michael's hand.

"We are indebted to you, Michael. It is a pleasure to meet you," his handshake was firm and prolonged. Silvester's brother, Tim, who was dressed much the same, offered his hand.

"G' day, Michael, welcome to Oz. Did you have a good trip?"

"It was fine, just fine." Answered Michael, a little overwhelmed with the welcome he was receiving.

After leaving the port, with Michael's cases in the boot of the Ford V8, the men headed out on a 120 mile drive to Delta Downs, Silvester's hometown.

19

The snowstorm in New York on the 26th January 1947 was the worst in modern times. Sam shut his business down for three days, allowing his workforce to see to their own immediate needs, as well as doing chores for the elderly that lived in the vicinity of the workshop.

Henry, Sam's eldest, was always at his father's side; he spent his weekends at the workshop even when his father wasn't there. Academia was not his calling, but his ability to turn his hand to practical learning was noticeable. He was a lad well-liked by his peers and his ambition was to take over his father's business. There was little doubt that's what he would do.

Sam and Grace's social activities amounted to going to the theatre at least once a month and, as the children grew older. Had more time at weekends to visit various restaurants in the city. They had kept in touch with Louis and Charlotte Fontaine, the French Americans they had met in Paris while on honeymoon fourteen years earlier. On the last Saturday of August, Charlotte had invited Sam and Grace to Louis' sixty ninth birthday party.

She had booked two tables at a ground level restaurant beneath the Chelsea Hotel, 222 West 23rd Street and afterwards at the bar next door. The restaurant, which both couples had visited on a number of occasions, had an atmosphere unlike any other. Its rather avant-garde decor reflected the hotel's occupants. The Hotel Chelsea was a place of intrigue and Sam had learnt a lot about the community that lived there. It was home to story tellers and artists in all their variations. The not so intellectual intellectuals, who discussed their theories on subjects that meant little to the unprepared. The writers of poetry, who couldn't quite get their message across and whose pencilled words were often discarded in hotel baskets, or cast into gutters somewhere along the way, but still, undaunted, the writer wrote on. The Hotel Chelsea thrived on its utopian lifestyle. Its inhabitants and visitors, be they singers, sculptors, writers of dreams, drug dealers or the men that walked the steel beams far above the heads of the ants that scurried in the streets below, these were the characters producing the heartbeat of the Chelsea. Effeminate men, with the mannerisms and flamboyant clothes more suited to a Broadway musical, walked without fear through the corridors of the hotel. Will they ever find what they seek?

The hotel was a place where lonely souls, people of means and people of little means, came and mingled with past winners and present losers. Some of whom took their own stories to darkened rooms where, to the annoyance of all, they would end their lives. Methods used varied from rope, pills, a bullet and sometimes ingenious ways beyond rational thinking. After all, this was the Hotel Chelsea.

In its sixty three year history, the hotel, named after a retirement village in London, had seen the likes of painters, Jackson Pollock and John Slone, walk its landings and stairs, along with other artists whose minds were full of abstract or impressionist visions, but whose creations were not worthy of wall space in any gallery. All could find a corner at the Hotel Chelsea to hang their masterpieces. Writers, the calibre of Mark Twain, Thomas Wolfe and Sherwood Anderson, drank, dined, danced and made love to heiresses, actresses and ladies of the night and, often, ladies of the day, whose morals were compromised by the very presence of such men in their midst.

Other people, like Sam and Grace, visited the Hotel Chelsea to absorb the street entertainment outside. None of it advertised. The performances that took place on the sidewalk, in the bars, even in the hotel's lobby were spontaneous. Performances were, as often as not, controversial, where maybe a scene from Shakespeare would be played out to their own interpretation. Residents held discussions on the latest musicals being performed on Broadway. Sometimes theatre agents of such productions called by, often securing the talents of people who they thought could make it in that world of auditoriums and thunderous applause. The hopeful often performed recitals of their own musical or literary works. Some made it, most would not. Few saw their names lit up in the neon signs of Broadway, but the dreams lingered. As long as there was a dream, there was a sense of belonging and the Chelsea became a byword for a hotel of dreams … or nightmares.

In early November 1947 at the Playhouse Theatre Sam and Grace, again in the company of Louis and Charlotte, were fortunate to revisit a performance seen once before at the Joanne Les Pins review bar in Paris. The vocalist, a waif-like little lady with short dark hair, wearing a plain black dress and black patent shoes, stood like a lost soul before two thousand eyes. All were ready to give their verdict on a performance that would either raise her profile or crucify her. Edith Piaf had come a long way and not just in miles. Louis had followed her career since first seeing her on stage as a young girl, but never thought he would see her perform again. Her rendition of La Vie en Rose brought tears to Louis' eyes. He said later that the song, its French words spoke of seeing life through rose coloured glasses, reminded him of the poverty of his childhood in the back streets of Paris and the gratitude he owed his parents for leaving that pitiful place. Nine weeks later, Charlotte awoke to find that Louis had died in his sleep beside her.

Every so often Sam heard from his mother and Aunt Megan, both gave accounts of the births, deaths and marriages that had taken place in his little village in Wales. He smiled to himself when Megan told him of Michael; anything to do with Michael or Billie was important to Sam. Maybe they reminded him of himself, that part of him, his adventurous side, he lived it now through them. His own children didn't feature in these thoughts, probably because they were too close and far too young to make adult decisions, even if they were old enough, he would be too judgemental. He was very proud of them, of course, and maybe his subconscious didn't want them to be like him, but he didn't dwell on that.

Australia, where Michael was destined to go, was a country distant in mind as well as the seas that separated it. Much like America, it attracted immigrants from all over Europe. Its sparse and isolated cities needed people to populate them and to bring them screaming into the twentieth century.

"South Australia", Sam placed his finger on a world map he had hanging up on his office wall.

"Crop dusting in the wheat belt of the southern region of the State. Is that where Michael is?" He suddenly said, surprised and not fully understanding that Michael was not a kid anymore. As it was, Sam couldn't forget the image of him pointing to an aeroplane in the sky and saying" I want to be up there, I want to fly". Sam sat down. It was only yesterday that Billie had rang to tell him that she was thinking of moving on too. She explained that since Shelly had left, she felt under no obligation to stay in New York. She had no commitments and as much as she loved her parents, their life was not hers. Ever since she had left home to train as a nurse six years earlier, she hadn't found one place she'd like to go back to. Or maybe she had but didn't realise it.

"Jesus Uncle Sam, I feel like a bloody wandering albatross". Billie cried as she spoke. "You are the only one I can talk to, why is that Uncle Sam, why is that?"

"I don't know Billie," Sam answered. "It could be you have already lived a lifetime most people haven't. It can be hard talking to those who haven't walked where you have. In a different way I've been there too, remembering times and people who've stood with me. Times when I needed reassurance in the things I was about to do. In your case it was different, your path differed to mine in that you were told what to do and where to go. Now, Billie, you're free to follow your own dream wherever it takes you. You don't need advice from me. Don't look back, Billie. And remember, I will always be here, whenever you feel the need to talk."

Billie hung up, leaving Sam a little sad but with a warm feeling that she could achieve anything that she had a mind to.

20

Pageant helped Billie pack her suitcase.

"I'm going on holiday Mother not to the other side of the moon." Billie said as she handed her mother four pairs of socks.

"It might as well be the other side of the moon," quipped Pageant, "why on earth do you want to go to Australia, a land of kangaroos, snakes, spiders and creatures that want to eat you?"

"It isn't that bad Mother; crocodiles and dingoes don't exactly walk down the streets."

"What about the sharks?"

"They don't walk down the street either and it's a working holiday I'm going on, not an exploration of the outback. Father's excited about me going. He says he wishes he could come with me."

"Your father! I'm afraid he likes his home comforts too much to go camping in the bush and to watch a Billie-can coming to the boil. My God, he wouldn't last two minutes. I've read about the flies; they will eat your cornflakes before you put your spoon into the bowl." Billie laughed.

"Very good, Mother but I think you exaggerate a little."

Ever since Billie had discovered that Michael had emigrated to Australia, she had pondered on the possibility that she would go. It was a country that had never entered her thinking, least of all to visit, but the more she thought about it, the more intrigued she became. She had found out that the Australian immigration policy was encouraging US citizens, as well as Europeans, to migrate and that the assisted passage applied to all. Billie's dilemma was that she didn't want to emigrate but would like to spend some time there, working, if possible, to pay her way. If she were to go under assisted passage and found it wasn't to her liking, she would have to stay for two years, or reimburse the Australian government for the cost of her passage if she were to leave in under that time.

What part of Australia to visit, was another question. It was a big country. Brisbane in the State of Queensland looked as good as any. She had read that about 230 miles to its north, lay over1400 miles of coral reef.

It stretched along most of the Queensland coast and there were miles of white sandy beaches to walk on. Billie thought it sounded like heaven. This was the place she would like to visit. It was going to cost the earth to get there, but once she had made up her mind, there would be no turning back. Billie wasn't as brave as Michael in wanting to emigrate, but she would go for six months and see what happens. Work was her priority and the information she had gathered from the Australian immigration office in

New York was reassuring. The administrators of a new women's hospital, opened some years earlier in Brisbane, were always looking for trained nursing staff to fulfil positions and accommodation was included as part of the appointment. Billie learned that after the war, thousands of US citizens, including ex-servicemen, had settled in Australia. She was surprised how smoothly the application process went and it occurred to her that the world was now a very different place than it was a few years earlier. As long as she had her health and enough money to get herself home from wherever she and her suitcase resided, she could traverse the globe. Sailing was the only realistic option, as flying was for the wealthy and celebrities. She was neither. Just how she got to Australia mattered little to the authorities. So, she flew to Los Angeles, boarded a ship with passengers of various nationalities and professions and sailed the east west passage. It was a long haul but she would get there in the end.

Some weeks later Billie placed her luggage on an unfamiliar bed. In total she had three suitcases. The rest of her possessions, stuff she didn't need, she had left at home in New York. She was met at the port of Brisbane, after immigration formalities had been observed and recorded, by a representative of the Brisbane Women's Hospital, William Turnbull. William was a short, thick set man with wavy blond hair, impeccable manners and a white set of teeth that made his face light up. After formal introductions were over, William put Billie and her cases into a taxi and then accompanied her on the twenty five minute drive to the hospital. Billie's observations of the city suburbs from the taxi's open window were typical of Australian homes, or so William told her. The white picket fences, almost as white as Mr Turnbull's teeth and the verandas, with ornate Victorian cast iron lacework panels and corner brackets were, he informed Billie also typical of Australian homes.

These verandas that ran the full length of the single story dwellings were repeated street after street and were fronted with well-manicured lawns and tropical plants. Eucalyptus trees with pale smooth bark looked ghost-like as they stood motionless in the shadows of each other. They grew on each side of the road, making streets and avenues of eucalyptus trees.

On arriving at the hospital, Billie noticed an Australian flag on a white pole. It was motionless in the midday sun, not even a light breeze was strong enough to lift its corners. Billie's cases were placed outside the administration office. Then after bidding Mr Turnbull farewell, another man stepped out of the building. He smiled at Billie and gestured for her to follow him.

"Your cases will be alright there," he said, as she matched his steps into an office on the ground floor.

"Please take a seat Miss Fleming, this won't take long."

As Billie took a seat, she noticed a folded card on his desk that read Mr Clive Anderson. After introducing himself, he proceeded with an official welcoming speech that had obviously been rehearsed and, in all likelihood, said many times before but this didn't diminish the genuine message it conveyed.

"I've read your work history, Miss Fleming and, may I say, nurses like you don't come along that often." He looked up and smiled.

"You've seen a lot of trauma in your working career and would be an excellent example to our student nurses. Have you thought about teaching?"

Mr Anderson was a slim man of average height, in his mid-forties, Billie guessed. He was clean shaven with slick black hair but there was nothing distinctive about him to recognise, even if he were in a police line-up. He wore a pale blue, short sleeved shirt and cream shorts. He smiled at Billie as he looked over the sheet of paper he held. Billie raised her head on hearing what amounted to a short evaluation of her working career.

"No, I haven't," she said, "it's never entered my head."

"Well, during your stay here maybe you might think about it?"

Another twenty minutes were spent going over hospital regulations and Billie's general duties. Mr Anderson then stood and handed her a pamphlet on another set of rules and regulations, this time on living at the nurses' complex. Then, stepping outside, Billie accompanied Mr Anderson on a five minute walk to a building three floors high, with each floor containing six, two bedroom self-contained units, a small kitchen, lounge, shower, and WC. It was a new building and as yet not all rooms had been taken. Billie's living quarters were on the ground floor. She turned the key to her pale green front door and walked in. After a quick look around, she decided it was better than she had expected and was now looking forward to her stay in the land of koala bears and kangaroos.

Billie had already read the itinerary for the first week of her stay. She used it as a period to settle in and to explore her surroundings, to meet fellow work colleagues and to discuss the working systems of the hospital. Not that it was a lot different to hospital procedures back home. From the medical magazines she had read, facilities of this nature and the way they were run had, over the past few years, become more universally standardised than ever before. The results of studies of nursing practices were passed on, irrespective of what country the initial research had been done. Thereby, the treatment of patients gradually became standardised throughout the countries that had recognised and accepted the research findings.

Billie awoke to the sound of kookaburras and glanced at her watch - six thirty.

"Bloody hell, it's the middle of the night," she thought. She looked up. A ceiling fan swirled cool air around the room. Acting on her first impulse, Billie got up, had a shower and washed her hair. Surprisingly, she had slept well, her last thoughts being, of what she would do the following day. The temperature the day before had been seventy degrees, rather warm, but Billie liked it warm and if today were to be the same, that would be just fine. She had already placed her clothes in the wardrobe and had chosen a blue cotton dress to wear along with a wide brimmed straw hat.

The kookaburras were still calling as she closed the door of her new home and walked the few yards of a stone slabbed path to the road where she turned right. While walking, it dawned on Billie that she hadn't had breakfast and that last night's meal of a meat pie, two rounds of toast and a slice of carrot cake, had served its purpose in satisfying her appetite. The meal was kindly given by Tessa, a woman from next door who had seen Mr Anderson leave and had called round to introduce herself before going on a late afternoon shift. Tessa Crawley was thirty two years of age and a paediatrician. She had been at the hospital for over two years and had emigrated from England with her parents after the Great War. The first thing that Tessa had asked Billie that evening was if she had eaten, while at the same time, handing her a plate with the goodies on.

"Must dash," she said, "I'll see you tomorrow."

It took Billie forty minutes to walk into the city. The cool morning breeze she had noticed was just strong enough to lift the flag outside the hospital that she had passed the day before. The city was, as she had expected. She had seen street scenes of the place in magazines advertising Queensland as the state to emigrate to. The only thing different was the splash of colour that the various shops, restaurants, numerous coffee outlets and ice cream parlours used on their advertising boards and canopies that shaded the pavement. Billie walked up and down Queen Street where she popped in and out of shops, just for a nosy. She did more streets, having a look at other shops until it was time to go home. But first she needed a coffee. She found it strange to be handling money of a British denomination; she had used it once before in London. But this time there were different pictures stamped on the coins and notes. She unfurled a five pound note from her purse. On the front was a picture of Sir John Franklin, whoever he was, and on the back, in pale blue, was a picture of the heads of two merino sheep, a cow and a bull. Billie reasoned that as these were two of Australia's main exports, why not put their images on a note of currency.

She did some people watching from a seat outside a coffee shop. Concluding, once she had finished her drink, that people the world over were pretty much the same as they went about their daily business. From the mother of a toddler, who ran away at the first opportunity, if the thought arose within the child to do so, but isn't that what children do? To the gambler checking his T A B ticket for any winnings that may come his way and the smartly dressed businessman carrying a briefcase, wondering if he had screwed up on the deal, he had just shaken hands on. Billie could have stayed there for hours, surmising how people lived their lives, but she had some living of her own to do. So, she left her seat and walked home.

It was two thirty when Billie got to her unit. She had called at a convenience store not far from the hospital on the way, just to get a few things, bread, butter and milk, but it didn't end there. She was laden down with two bags of groceries and other items she would need. When she got home, she saw Tessa sitting in a chair on her ground floor veranda reading a book. Tessa looked up, smiled and placed her book on a little table in front of her.

"I've been into the city," said Billie smiling back.

"And how did you find it?"

"I followed the signs," answered Billie with a chuckle. Tessa laughed.

"No, I meant how did you like it?"

"I liked it fine. When did you get home?" Tessa stood and told Billie she had been home for a few hours, that her front door was open and to come through and join her for a cup of tea.

"I'll just pop my shopping into the house first, and I'll be with you."

Billie pushed Tessa's door open and walked in. At a glance Tessa's lounge looked 'lived in'. There was no sign of another occupier living there, that wasn't to say that Tessa lived on her own though. On opening the fly screen door Billie stepped out to join her new neighbour on the veranda.

"I'm sorry I had to rush off yesterday, Billie. I didn't want to be late on the ward."

"That's fine. Thanks for the pie and carrot cake."

Over the next two hours, between cups of tea and afternoon biscuits, the topic of conversation shifted from their nursing career to family life, to their current situation regarding men. Tessa mentioned an ex-boyfriend in Mt.

Isa. Then they talked about what they expected from life in the future. Tessa was in awe of Billie's stories of the last five years, the places she had been and the things she had seen and done. Tessa had not been asleep for the last five years either. There had been a steady flow of convalescing soldiers pass through the hospital, but that was a few years ago now. For a long time, they came, first for assessment before being sent to various convalescent centres across the city. The last influx was a shipload of Australian prisoners of war from Japan, being dropped off at the ports from whichever state they came from.

"These men had been to hell and back," said Tessa, "but I hadn't seen them at their worst. You saw them, Billie. You saw them with their broken bodies and screwed up minds. My God Billie", she said, "don't you have nightmares? Don't you want to stop and settle down?"

"I've tried to," Billie answered, a little unsure as to how to explain her thinking. "Firstly, I don't have nightmares and yes from time to time, thoughts cross my mind mostly about the terrible things I've seen, but I wasn't alone. I had my bad dreams then, Tessa but it may surprise you, that those thoughts don't come in the shape of nightmares. As for settling down. For the last two years I've lived with a fellow nurse in Manhattan. She'd been with me through the fighting in Europe. Then she ups and gets married and moves to Chicago. I could have stayed where I was, but I got itchy feet and being here is only an extension of how I've lived since the end of the war. You may be wondering why I'm here? Like I have said, I got itchy feet.

Maybe with all the moving about I've done, the places and people I've encountered along the way have made me unsettled… Where it will all end I don't know, but for now this nomadic lifestyle suits me. As for settling down, that will happen when it happens."

As Billie spoke, Tessa was aware of something she felt missing in Billie's life, or was it in her own life that something was amiss? Tessa had told Billie that she had never left Brisbane, never been to any of the big towns up north. The reality was that she had done nothing 'worth mentioning' in her entire life. Yes, she was a nurse, and she believed a good one. Alongside her colleagues, she had saved the lives of many children and to the children's parents, she was a hero. But she felt that it was the Billie's of this world that would set the bar at a height not all could reach. As for America and the Americans that Billie had told her about, only one thing came to mind, an American soldier that had forced himself on her six years earlier. Tessa was to recall this 'incident' in more detail later that evening.

"The laundry." Billie suddenly said, "Mr Anderson mentioned something about a communal laundry. I do need to wash some clothes."

Tessa drank the last of what was left of her tea and stood.

"Follow me, I'll show you where it is, as you know this is a brand new building and our laundry has been fitted with Bendix washing machines."

Billie followed Tessa down a short passage into a courtyard that housed the laundry. Washing machines had become popular over the last couple of years, only for the fact that they were more affordable so people could buy them. Billie's mother had one installed at the beginning of the year and thought it was the 'bee's knees. It saved a lot of work for Billie, as she would take her own clothes to her mother to wash. After seeing the laundry, Tessa was about to explain the situation regarding the tenancy in the complex, when Billie told her she had already read the rules, even the bit about men being strictly prohibited. They giggled about that. Billie then went to her unit and checked its contents more closely. It was adequately furnished, had cooking utensils, cutlery, bedding, everything that was needed for her to stay for as long as she so wished.

It was six o'clock when Billie knocked on Tessa's door.

"Come in." Billie turned the handle and walked in.

"When are you back on duty?" Billie asked, throwing Tessa a chocolate bar as she was lazily sprawled out on her settee.

"Thanks," she said, looking surprised. "I have tomorrow off, then I go in for the weekend. I'm covering for a friend who's going up to Rockhampton for her sister's wedding."

"Rockhampton?"

"It's a small town 350 miles north." Tessa moved her feet for Billie to sit.

"That chap you were seeing, the one you mentioned earlier, the one that went to Mt. Isa, what happened to him?" Tessa smiled, got herself more comfortable and started to tell her story.

"Well, after he got demobbed and left the army, there was a lot of work to be had in the copper and silver mines up north. Jesus, Billie, it's over 1,000 miles to the God forsaken place. We'd been going out since before he went to war and we picked up again after he came back. It wasn't the same anymore, but we made a go of it. Then he decided to earn some decent money and I don't blame him for that. Anyway, he went to Mt. Isa and I never heard from him again. That was three years ago. I did hear some time after that he'd got some Sheila in the family way and, thinking back, I'm not sure if I loved him enough to have married him."

"But you would have?"

"Probably."

"Has there been anyone since?"

"No not really. I had a bad experience while my man was away. Maybe that's partly why it wasn't the same when he came back."

"In December of 1942, the yanks were in town and had been for a long time. There were thousands of them, spread all the way up the coast. Our government had requested them to bolster our troop numbers in readiness to repel any invasion from Japan. Since, at the time, a lot of our men were in Europe, New Guinea and other parts of the Pacific region, we needed their help." Billie sat in silence. "Tension had been building up for months. The American GI's military pay was a damn sight more than our boys got. They had stores in their camp that sold things that our boys couldn't afford. Alcohol, cigarettes, ice cream, chocolates, even nylon stockings, and other luxuries. Our boys weren't even allowed to go into those shops, even if they could afford to. The local girls didn't really stand a chance. They would take what the yanks offered them and that was plenty."

"There was a time, when a good looking American guy could have his cake and eat it, or to put it another way, he could have the cake and the whole bloody shop window it was placed in. Believe me, Billie, a lot of young girls and their mothers succumbed to a box of chocolates and a pair of silk stockings. Oh yes, those GIs could show the girls a good time, all right. All this caused resentment against the Americans, and it wasn't long before fighting broke out. Our hotels were only allowed to serve alcohol twice a day, for an hour at a time and that time was of the hotels choosing. Can you imagine the shit that caused, with gangs of Australian servicemen, rushing from one hotel to another, drinking as much as possible before the hour was up? This was happening all the way up the coast, as far as Townsville where things got so bad that the Aussies set up a machine gun in the middle of the bloody high street. Then in late November, all hell broke loose. There was rioting throughout Brisbane. It wasn't just the servicemen, a lot of civilians took part. They'd had enough too. At the end of it all, the official number of dead was one Australian soldier, but hundreds of servicemen on both sides were taken to hospital. I know, I was there when they came through the doors. Like I said, the official report was one dead, the truth..." Tessa shrugged, "was somewhat different. No one knows the real number, but it was a damn sight more than one. Soon after, the number of American GIs in Brisbane was reduced and the ones still here were confined to barracks for longer periods. That all happened six years ago, but the repercussions of it lasted a long time. Hundreds of local girls married American servicemen and moved to the US. There was a saying about the American GIs at the time, they were overpaid, over sexed and over here."

All the time Tessa was speaking Billie never said a word and it was only when she looked up that Billie spoke.

"And you Tessa, how did all this affect you?"

"I was twenty six at the time. A week before the riots, I was out with the girls celebrating my birthday. We'd just left the Dunmore Arms on Queen Street when we were approached by three American Military Police who wanted to see our papers. Although very arrogant, everything seemed fine. Some of the girls in the crowd were playing up to them, so the MPs tagged along. One of them came on to me, I told him I wasn't interested, but he wouldn't listen."

Tessa was becoming agitated as she spoke. Her voice was hurried and growing louder. "Then they went away, but that wasn't the end of it. We were on the street between hotels when a fight broke out. A line of American MPs with batons in hand came from nowhere and were met by dozens of Aussie servicemen. We split up, not wanting to get caught up in it all. It was utter panic, with women screaming, losing their shoes as they ran away. Tanya and

I ran down a siding and coming toward us were, yes, the same three MPs. I knew we were in trouble. The bastard that had come on to me, grabbed my shoulder, ripping my dress. I fell down with him on top of me. He started grabbing my breasts and lifting up my dress. I remember yanking his head back by his hair and he slapped my face. We both got up and all the time he was pulling at my dress. The top of it was ripped open. He reached out to grab my brassiere and that's when I kicked him. His legs were open and I lashed out as hard as I could. I was wearing my sensible sturdy nurses' lace up shoes and he hit the ground faster than a dead bullock at a slaughterhouse".

Tessa smiled. "By this time Tanya was screaming her head off. The other two guys had her on the ground, tearing at her clothes. Before I knew what was happening three Aussies came running down the alley and set about the men assaulting Tanya. The guy that attacked me was still rolling around on the ground holding his crotch and cursing me. One of the Aussies came over, gave him no mercy, he beat the shit out of him. Then he bent down and whispered something in his ear, then left him with such a blooded face that his mother wouldn't recognise him. The thing is Billie, I took great pleasure in seeing those guys crawling on the ground. They deserved everything they got."

"And now," Billie enquired, how do you feel about what happened?"

"Well, for a long time I didn't go out in dressy shoes," she laughed, "and I don't go to places with no people about, but apart from that I'm fine. Don't get me wrong, what happened frightened the life out of me and it would've been a lot worse if those Aussies hadn't turned up. But you can't dwell on what might have happened. The worst didn't happen and that's that." Tessa tilted her head and looked at Billie. "You know," she spoke wistfully, my father used to say that hindsight was a wonderful thing, but then he would turn it on its head, and say that if there were more foresight, the word hindsight would be a word less often used." Billie smiled.

"Your father is a wise man, Tessa."

"Was, a wise man. He died from a stroke four years ago. I miss him terribly but it's getting better. My sister and her three children now make my mother's life worth living and for that I am happy. Now, that's enough of my rambling. I suggest we have a little something to eat and tomorrow I'll take you to the hospital and introduce you to the girls." Billie was told that Mary McCloud, like most matrons, was strict but fair, in that she always took the side of a nurse, until such time that nurse proved her own incompetence. Even then, she never embarrassed anyone in the company of others.

That night Billie found it difficult to sleep. She was bothered by the warmth of moving air disturbed by the ceiling fan. The mosquitoes with their high pitched sound when flying close to her ear before landing and maybe taking a sample of her blood. She also thought of Tessa's talk on the Brisbane, she'd known six years earlier. Tessa's experience of sexual assault was something new to Billie.

She had never encountered anything remotely like it. Of course, there had been times when men, had looked at her with eyes that suggested lust was on their mind, or with a wanton gaze that had lingered a little longer than was necessary. That look, Billie had come to recognise was, in part, what some men were about. A dirty old man, being someone not necessarily dirty and not necessarily old, just someone you didn't 'fancy'. As Billie's mother had often told her, a gentleman was a gentleman until he proved himself otherwise. "Yes," she thought, "the older she became the more interesting men were." You didn't have to like them all, but to be aware of them being different was at least a step to understand them. Of course, some would disagree, but that's the way she saw things and she was happy to think the way she did. "AMEN to all that," she whispered to herself before closing her eyes.

21

Michael gazed at the flat land of the Yorke Peninsula. They had been travelling for over an hour. The bulldust that billowed out behind them from the dirt road, rose and drifted out across the endless acres of corn fields that grew on each side of the track. Gum trees and Australian bush appeared every so often, along with brackish pools of water where white cockatoos and grey galah's sometimes rose in small flocks to fly amongst the roadside trees.

There was an answer to every question Michael asked. Was he likely to see kangaroos and emus? The answer to that came a couple of miles clear of the last town they passed. They were in open countryside when five kangaroos appeared amongst some paper bark trees three hundred yards from the road. He spotted a similar number of emus 5 miles further on, when they passed another water hole. After this, there was a stretch of 20 miles of natural bush on both sides of the road where eucalyptus trees grew thirty feet in the air, but at ground level the bush was sparse. Not dense like a rain forest, but mostly grassless with low scrub, easy to negotiate and strangely inviting.

The boys stopped for a break and Michael took advantage and went into the bush for a little walk about. At this point, there were no fences to keep anything in or out and there was a sense of calmness that isolation can bring. He could see why people could get easily lost. Wherever he looked, in any direction, the bush was all the same. A woody smell, tinged with a flowery and eucalyptus scent hung in the air. The smell reminded him of the times, as a child, when he had the sniffles or a blocked nose and his mother had sprinkled eucalyptus oil on a hanky for him to inhale.

The subject of bushfires came up when they had settled back into the rhythm of the road.

"Everything that lives in the bush is threatened when a fire goes through," explained Tim. "Especially the koalas, they've little chance of getting out of the way. Roo's fair a little better," he said as they passed one standing on the side of the road, curiously looking at them as they drove on. "You have to be on your toes all the time. They're unpredictable critters, especially at night. They'll jump out in front of you and you can't do a damned thing about it. Hit a big boomer and he can smash your car up. That's why we have roo bars bolted to the front. Strewth, I heard a story about a roo that went through the windscreen of a Chevy and the bloody thing wrecked the car from the inside and that's fair dinkum." Michael smiled, he thought Tim's Australian terminology was enlightening, but he did get the gist of what he was saying.

After passing the bush section of their journey, they came across a clear landscape and another waterhole. This time Michael noticed what appeared to be a number of rabbits drinking.

"Are those rabbits?" he asked. "You have a lot of them over here?"

"Yes, the damn things are all over the state, north to south, east to west. Over the years we must've killed thousands. They're in plague proportions throughout the country. The Government's looking into getting rid of them by developing some kind of contagious virus. They've tried before but nothing really came of it."

Gilbert went on to tell Michael about the damage the rabbits did to grazing land, affecting sheep and cattle numbers and costing millions of pounds.

"How many are there?"

"The Federal Government reckons about five hundred million, maybe more."

"Tell him about the rabbit proof fence in WA," blurted Tim.

"Do you want to know how we keep the bastards out of our back yard, Michael?."

"You built a fence?"

"You're damn right, we built a fence."

"But surely, all the rabbits have to do is to hop to the end and go around it?" Michael wondered why all three men laughed.

"Good thinking, Michael, but they'd have a bloody long walk," said Gilbert. "The fence is over 2,400 miles long. It was built over forty years ago and they've been maintaining it ever since. I once knew a man from the North

West who worked on it. He was a line runner. Worked in one of the gangs that kept their section in good order. The gangs lived a lonely life, patrolling and maintaining their stretch of 100 miles on horseback. They used camels to pull drays loaded with supplies. He was a first world war veteran and worked alongside loners and guys who'd spilled out from countries he knew nothing about. He used to say that the bush was good to him and that he couldn't live in the society he'd fought a war to preserve. Poor bugger, I don't know what happened to him, but there were lots like him at the time. They'd been to Gallipoli and other places in Europe, not all of them came back."

"Do you think the isolation of the bush was something he was looking for? He would have had no contact, or conflict with anyone except the rabbits, maybe he needed that kind of peace." Michael said.

"You could be right, Michael. You could be right."

"Getting back to this rabbit proof fence, it must have taken one hell of a time to put up." Michael queried, not being able to comprehend the distance mentioned.

"Now, I'm going to be precise about this," answered Gilbert. "It took four years in all. Fence No1 stretched from somewhere on the south coast of Western Australia to the Eighty Mile Beach, just below Broome in the far north. That's a distance of… Christ knows how long. Fence No2 ran somewhat parallel, maybe 200 miles apart from Fence No1 and re-joined it after some 700 miles. Fence No3, only a little one, left fence No2 at right angles and headed for the Indian Ocean, 160 miles away."

For the rest of the journey not a lot was said, except when a wedge tailed eagle, pointed out by Silvester, flew out of a large gum tree. Tim explained that you didn't see them that often on the peninsula. 2 miles further they turned left, pulling up in a cloud of dust. Gilbert got out and checked his mailbox, a post in the ground with a miniature dog kennel fixed to the top of it with a roof that flipped open giving access to the mail placed inside. What mail Gilbert had, he placed on the dashboard, then drove off in another cloud of dust. Another mile and Delta Downs came into view.

The first thing Michael noticed was the Southern Cross windmill that stood by some gum trees all pretty much the same height. The windmill's galvanised metal blades and tail fin shifted on a spindle, moving in whatever direction the wind blew. For a few moments he watched it lazily turn, drawing to the surface the most vital of a farm's needs … water. The second thing Michael noticed were two jacaranda trees with their vibrant violet flowers. He had been told that the family home was roughly seven hundred and forty acres of good wheat growing land that had been in the family since 1880. Some of that land was not under seed, but year on year, they had tried to increase their yield.

Michael was met by Silvester's mother who stood holding a jug of iced water. His two sisters handed out glasses to the menfolk. Hettie, Gilbert's wife, was overjoyed to meet Michael. Her gratitude for Michael's part in the saving of her son's life was such that Michael felt obliged to mention that, had the situation been reversed, Silvester would have done the same.

"Maybe so, Michael and I'd like to think he would have, but the fact is, if not for you and your friend, Silvester wouldn't be here."

Nothing more was said about the subject and Michael entered the home of Hettie and Gilbert Thomson. Before the light faded, everyone was seated on the balcony, eating a meal that Hettie and the girls had laid out. It was a 'help yourself' kind of meal, with cold meat, potatoes, cheese, biscuits, grapes, raw carrots and a variety of other edibles and, of course, cold beers to drink. But the day was not finished. As the sun set, Michael walked on the lawn and gazed at the big sky; it seemed to go on forever. He'd seen skies similar to this before but only from the cockpit of an aeroplane. In the west, the heavens were glowing. Michael had never seen a sight quite like it. On this canvas in the sky, from left to right was a scene with a dozen shades of orange and a myriad of reds that ran into purples and blues. The clouds looked as if they were on fire, with a hue that blended into the night. The brush strokes of this scene defined the meaning of Art and Michael looked at it in wonder. Silvester stood with Michael, then asked him to follow him as he walked past two outbuildings, then a barn. They turned to their right and at fifteen paces against the fading fiery sky was the silhouette of Michael's boyhood dreams. A Tiger Moth sat on an apron of dusty earth, its propellers motionless, seemingly asleep.

"Good God," Michael uttered. He stood rigid. "If I never see another sight, this and the sunset will stay till the end of my days." Walking toward it, he raised his hand and reached up to touch the smooth curve of the wooden propeller blade.

"We'll be up in her tomorrow, Michael," Silvester said, as he ran his hand along the plane's lower wing. "Then we'll have to modify it to a single seater by replacing the front cockpit with a hopper."

Michael awoke to the sound of a gipsy engine above the box room where he had slept. The room was small, but everything he needed was there. His suitcase was empty, a wardrobe now contained his clothes and his socks and personal items were in the drawers. He had placed his pilot's logbook on his bedside table. He looked at it now and wondered when he would write his first entry. He quickly dressed, putting on the working clothes that Rebecca, Silvester's youngest sister, had placed on a chair in his room. She had been through a pile of the men's old clothes, saving Michael the trouble of buying any.

Hettie was at the kitchen table with a teapot in hand when Michael entered.

"Good morning, Michael. I hope you slept well. Would you like a cup of tea?"

"Yes, Mrs Thomson, I slept well and yes please, I would love a cup of tea."

"Silvester's popped over to see our neighbours, he'll be back in an hour; he's gone for some parts for the hopper. Dad and Tom are doing some maintenance on the corn drill. Rebecca is milking the cow and Patience is feeding the chickens and checking on the pig. She had a litter last week, that's the pig, not Patience," corrected Hettie. "She lay on two and killed them. Again, that's the pig, not Patience." She laughed, "and if you want eggs for brekkie, she'll be bringing some back with her."

"That will be Patience, not the pig?" Michael added. Again, Hettie laughed.

"Sit yourself down and I'll put the frying pan on. Two eggs and a piece of steak with some fried bread, be ok?"

"Steak for breakfast?"

"It's what my boys have."

"Then it's steak and eggs for breakfast. Who am I to question the habits of a lifetime?" Michael didn't use the Australian term brekkie, as he thought it would not have sounded quite right coming from him.

Within the hour Silvester was back. Michael was in the yard when the Tiger Moth flew overhead. The prop stopped turning and the dust settled a few yards from the barn where it had stood the previous night.

Before an act of vandalism was perpetrated on the Tiger Moth in taking out of the forward cockpit seat to accommodate the new hopper, Silvester suggested that he and Michael take the plane up, for what Silvester's father called, a reunion flight. Michael, although a little apprehensive, was keen and Silvester even keener. It'd been three years since Michael had been at the controls of a Tiger Moth, but he didn't refuse when Silvester insisted that he sit in the front cockpit. Silvester could feel Michael's anxiety, so offered to take her up. The plane still had dual controls. Once in the air, Michael could take over and land when they were done. Everyone helped to swing the plane around and the boys got in.

As Michael lifted his leg over the side of the cockpit, he found it strange getting in without a parachute strapped about him and mentioned this to Silvester.

"Michael, you're in Australia and I can guarantee there'll be no fucker up there shooting at you."

They both laughed as the gipsy engine burst into life and, for the first time, Michael rose above the Australian sun burnt sod to see a landscape that, in the coming months, would become as familiar to him as it needed to be.

It didn't take long to convert the Tiger Moth into the crop spraying machine envisaged. In fact, the Thomson's had another such plane on a neighbour's station 50 miles away. This one, bought second hand, was advertised as a 'like new' ex-RAAF plane. It had cost £485 with a small deposit. Michael didn't really know if that was an expensive buy or not, as he had no idea how much aeroplanes cost in the first place.

"We should have it paid for within two years," said Silvester and that's where you come in." Silvester had already explained the sequence of events regarding the spreading of pesticides and fertiliser throughout the peninsula. It had now got to the point where the costs and benefits of such products on the grain harvest was considerable. Crop spraying had been done on a small scale for a few years, but it was only in the last year or so that it had really taken off. At Delta Downs corn had been sown and five tons of super phosphate had been delivered. The only thing missing was the second Tiger Moth and that would be flown in the following morning.

Five hundred acres of wheat were to be sprayed on Delta Downs and eleven other stations on the Yorke Peninsula had also contracted Silvester to spray their properties too.

Eighteen months earlier, the Thomson's were one of the first on the peninsula to invest in their own plane and it was only due to Silvester being a pilot that they had decided on investing in another Tiger Moth. Michael and Silvester were sitting on the veranda, relaxing with a beer. It was early evening as they watched the sun sink behind a group of mallee trees. A warm breeze blew the red and pink bougainvillaea flowers, the vines of which held fast to the wooden veranda post. Michael suddenly asked Silvester what had made him write to mention about him coming over to do some flying?

"I really can›t remember. I think, at the time, I was reading about an ex-pilot in New South Wales. One who'd done the same sort of shit that we had during the war. And I got to thinking how come I'm still here. How come I was alive after nearly dying in that Spitfire? How come you were alive to save me? So, I wrote, firstly to see if you were still with us and, hopefully, to meet you in different circumstances. As it turned out, you are still with us and I got to meet you again."

"And the ex-pilot in New South Wales?"

"He got killed in a Tiger Moth. Flew into a tree crop spraying."

Michael didn't say a word.

Silvester looked up, there was no expression on his face, just the sobering look of someone who, like Michael, had drawn a long straw and not the short one.

"And you, Michael, what's the reason you came over, the real reason, not the one you told people?" The question was not expected, much less the way it was said.

For a moment Michael was stuck …then raising his head he said.

"Four words come to mind, Silvester. Opportunity, excitement, fear and boredom! And you can place them in whatever order you like, but I believe we pilots are a breed apart and I don't mean to flatter ourselves either." He paused. "Why did any of us want to fly in the first place? Here, and now, if we really wanted to, we have a chance to get out of it and do something else, but we don't and we won't," he shrugged. "Why? Look no further than those four words, Silvester. That's where my answer is."

Delta Downs
Yorke Peninsula
South Australia

Dear Mother, Father and Dan,

I hope you are all well. It seems strange for me not to mention Sally and Esther. You must miss the girls not being there. Give them my love when you see them.

I am well, as we all are at Delta Downs. I explained in my last letter who everyone is, so I will not repeat myself. Silvester and I have been spraying every day except Sundays. We lost two days last week because of the wind and rain. We have work for the next three weeks and maybe another three weeks after that. A lot of enquiries have come in from further afield, so we are not too worried about work running out. It took me a couple of days to get back into flying again, and it was surprising how often I looked over my shoulder to see if anyone was behind me. Old habits I suppose.

Have I had any hairy moments, I hear you ask.? Well, there are a few things you have to watch out for. The first being that we are in the air for about three minutes above the area we are spraying and at the end of your run, you have to watch the tops of trees in order to clear them. Then we turn and drop down again to do another run in the opposite direction. Last Tuesday, after one of his runs, Silvester came back to refill his hopper with some eucalyptus leaves wrapped around his wheels. He laughed and said Rebecca had put them there when he landed. Rebecca denied it, saying he was there to spread fertiliser on the ground, not his blood.

Reading the contours of the land requires lots of attention, but it's hard when you're travelling at eighty miles an hour and eight feet above the ground. Every so often, I go for a little 'walkabout'. The boys on the ground don't really mind, it gives them time to have a fag, while I have a look around. Another thing I have to keep my eye on is my fuel gauge. We're doing about sixty to eighty take offs and landings per day. Landing in a paddock miles from home because you didn't keep an eye on the gauge would make you look incompetent. This happens very rarely of course, as the ground crew have a pretty good idea of when the tank needs refuelling. Someone suggested we have a big party at the end of the spraying season. A lot of friends and neighbours could be driving and flying in. Looking forward to it.

Must go now. All my love,

Michael

Michael posted his letter, taking it to the small town of Kadina, a fifty mile round trip. While in town, Hettie and Rebecca did their fortnightly shopping as well as getting things that were needed for the farm. Michael settled his dues by paying a small rent. Hettie didn't want anything, but Michael insisted that as he was being paid a handsome wage, so she must at least take something. Michael's relationship with the girls was cautious. He didn't want to get romantically involved; that wouldn't be a problem with Patience as she had been courting a neighbour's son for the past three years and they had set a date to be married in six months. Everyone called her husband-to-be, Tiger, although that had nothing to do with the name of the aeroplane the boys flew. Apparently, it was one of the first words he spoke as a child, so that's what everyone called him.

Rebecca, on the other hand, was a different matter. She was a bit of a tomboy and liked to mix it with the boys. She was twenty two, four years younger than her sister and used some colourful language when the need arose. The need seemed to arise quite a lot when using a spanner or wrench doing maintenance work on whatever machinery needed it. That aside she was also more refined, with a certain air that her sister didn't have. They were both equally attractive, but Rebecca was a touch fussier about her appearance and could play the part of the dutiful daughter a little better than Patience. She also had the charm of a lady who had been to an Australian finishing school, capable of walking the halls of shearing sheds and grace the tables of a bush pub. Michael was curious as to her ambition in life.

One late Friday evening when everyone had bid their good nights and gone to bed, Michael and Rebecca were in deep conversation. She wanted to know all about him, his travels during the war, not the war itself, just the travelling bit. She asked about his girlfriends, past lovers and the type of lady he wished to marry one day. Michael smiled. Rebecca, with her ability to ask questions of this nature in her calm, matter of fact way, needed answers. Surprisingly, Michael answered her. Was it the way she had asked and what was her need to know? He told her the story of his travels, his past fears and his present ones, his dreams, sometimes, for a lover, but he respectfully declined to mention the women he'd been intimate with. Not that it would have made any difference, but he was not prepared to betray a trust. He told of the friends he had found, the ones he had lost and the ones he would probably never see again.

In reply, Rebecca told him about herself. About her mother and father who had given her, from a young age, the ability to think for herself and to have a strong sense of being her own person. She was taught to think she could achieve anything she wanted to but to do it all with humility. Humility, her father had said, would make her what she would turn out to be. He had told her this before she had known what the word meant and he told her to look it up in the dictionary. She had never forgotten it. She told Michael that, as a young girl, her dream had been to marry a rich pastoralist with thousands of acres of land.

"Has your dream changed, Rebecca"? Michael asked. She thought for a moment.

"No, but I'm more realistic about the eventual outcome of my life now."

"Meaning?" Michael tilted his head.

"Meaning, I don't move in the circles of wealthy pastoralists or their sons. In fact, there are no circles of that description on the Yorke Peninsula." She paused. "Not that I'm aware of. Sure, there are those that would marry me. A few have hinted and there were a lot of fine young men amongst them but, apart from everything else, life kept getting in the way. Time is something we think we have plenty of. Look at yourself, would you have thought, four years ago, that you'd be sitting on the veranda of a farmhouse, talking to a girl who lived on the other side of the world? And four years from now, you may regret that you didn't attempt to seduce her. It might have been a memorable experience for both of us. I'm not suggesting for a moment that you try; all I'm saying is that we make choices. How they turn out is sometimes not what we would have wanted, but our choices are our own doing and we have to take responsibility for them". Rebecca stopped talking, she smiled and leaned forward.

"Can I ask you something, Michael? Can I write to you in four years' time? I think you'll have moved on by then but I have your address and even if you're not back in Wales, I'm sure my letter will eventually find you. It will be interesting, don't you think, to know where we'll both be? My letter to you and your letter to me will take us both back to this moment in time. Is that a deal, Michael?"

Again, she smiled and then held out her hand. Michael took it.

"It's a deal," he said and I'm sure whatever happens in the future, I'd like to think we'll both find a friend who'll want to stay. And… when I receive your letter, I promise, you'll hear from me. Who knows," he smiled, "I may come back and marry you."

"Wouldn't that be something?" she answered.

22

For the next two and a half months there were not enough days in the week. From sun-up, to sun-down, the boys flew hundreds of miles in their six day week. It rained a few times, once with some thunder and lightning thrown in, so the boys had a day off. They were also contracted to spray barley and potato crops in various parts of the state from the Adelaide Plains to the Eyre Peninsula and the Murray Mallee.

Rules and regulations had to be adhered to. State Government inspectors often called to check certificates and to see that all products used on the land were in accordance with set specifications. Although crop spraying by air was in its infancy, it was becoming a popular way to enhance the growth of cereal crops, by reducing competition with broadleaf weeds that took moisture from the soil. Spraying also helped to control insects and fungi that could devastate crops. Michael had heard of aerial spraying companies springing up in all states and could see that it would not be long until station owners, like Gilbert, with one or two planes would be bought out. For the rest of the season, they followed the crops as they grew, interacting with station owners all over the state.

In the first week of November, Patience got married. Due to the remoteness of its location, the vicar had travelled to Delta Downs to officiate in the proceedings. Michael stood to one side as he watched with interest as invited guests from miles around gather, with drinks in hand, to congratulate the smiling couple. As chief bridesmaid, Rebecca, with one of her sister's best friends, looked like all bridesmaids do, desirable to say the least. Michael was introduced to many people and forgot their names soon after. He and Silvester had given up their rooms to accommodate people who had travelled many miles to attend the wedding and would be staying the night. Michael and Silvester were to sleep in the shed. After they had cleared the area of red back spiders and the like, the boys set up their bunk beds. The snakes, if there were any, had already left of their own accord; they tend to stay away from places where there's too much human activity.

Rebecca, for the most part, had spent her time in the company of Michael, otherwise mingling with guests and generally having a good time. Michael had noticed a number of hopeful young men approach her, no doubt with thoughts of romance in mind and suggestions of a rendezvous, to which she would either accept or reject. As it was, she went to her bed in the early hours with an aching head and did not rise until mid-day. By that time the guests had left and everything was back to normal.

At Christmas, Silvester and Michael had planned a trip for a couple of days to the city, wanting to be back home for Christmas Eve. On Friday night, Michael awoke at one thirty, he got up and went to his bedroom window. He looked out, the only thing to move were the shadows being cast by the moon. He stepped into a pair of shorts, threw on a shirt and walked barefoot through the house. Rebecca was sitting at the veranda table that the family had vacated three hours earlier. She looked up and smiled. The light from the moon shone on the veranda and the table where she sat.

"Can't sleep, Michael?" she said.

"No," he replied, "it's a warm night."

"It's normal at this time of year."

Michael stood on the steps of the veranda and looked at the horizon, then raised his eyes to take in the big sky above his head. Warm winds seemingly blew the stars about, as they danced and played hide and seek with what wispy clouds dared spoil their brilliance. He sat opposite her, not really knowing what to say. It was easy in the company of her family, they would fool around and enjoy each other's company, but there was another side to Rebecca that she was reluctant to share. Her private life was never discussed beyond the fact that she had male friends. Nothing further than that. So, it amazed Michael when she asked his opinion on whether a girl should marry for money or for love. His immediate response was.

"Marry for money, love will come later." He grinned.

"Do you really mean that, Michael?"

"Well, it would be nice if it worked out that way. I suppose if you wanted to take that risk, then by all means. It begs the question though, has this gentleman fallen in love with the girl, or has he other motives?"

"Other motives?"

"Yes, other motives. I assume this is a hypothetical question you're asking, and if so, then for what reason did the gentleman ask for the lady's hand in the first place?" Rebecca looked confused.

"You must remember, marrying for money can work both ways. Either the lady in question will marry to acquire a comfortable living, or if the lady is financially independent, she would be willing to share her bed as well as her fortune with a man who has stolen her heart. Either way, this situation can be fraught with danger."

For a moment Rebecca sat without uttering a word. Then, straightening her back, she smiled. "So, if this situation were to come my way, what would you suggest?"

"Rebecca my dear, I am in no position to advise you on anything regarding affairs of the heart. I've kept well away from this situation happening to me. My life up until now has been a roller coaster ride. One day I'll want to get off, but until then, I'll follow the sun and do what I will."

Rebecca rose and stood behind Michael. She wanted to touch him, place her hands on his shoulders and, with her thumbs, caress the back of his neck. She closed her eyes and for a brief moment she hesitated…

"I'm going to bed," she said softly, tapping his shoulders.

"Good night, Rebecca, sweet dreams," Michael replied, not turning.

"Good night, Michael."

He watched her walk away, following her shadow through the open door and into the house. Her lythe, frame was very tempting and he guessed that, if invited, she would willingly come to his bed.

Silvester and Michael drove to Adelaide, following the same road as they had travelled when leaving the port on Michael's arrival at Delta Downs. They left early with an orange glow and a rising sun in the east. It would take over three hours to get to the city and in the meantime, Michael leaned back and took in the scenery. They had packed a bag for Friday and Saturday night, planning to be home on Sunday. It would be interesting to see how Australians celebrate Christmas. Much like back home, Michael was told, the difference being, that you can eat your turkey, roast potatoes and brussels sprouts out on the patio in the sun if so desired.

The Richmond Hotel on Rundle Street was rebuilt for the fourth time in 1926 and from 1844 was called the Plough and Harrow, or so it said on a plaque inside the lobby. Michael wondered what it would have been like living in Adelaide at that time, over one hundred and four years earlier.

Silvester had dismissed his query, saying, "How the fuck should I know", as he picked up their room key and they headed for room number nine.

Sometime later they walked down Rundle Street, the main street in the city, entering the first pub they came to. Casually standing at the bar, they were soon served, then walked away with two schooners of Coopers Pale Ale and sat at a table close by. After another beer, they made their exit into the street, now busy with shoppers. There was no mistaking what time of year it was; every store had its shop windows decorated, tinsel hung from every angle, cotton wool depicting various snow scenes and Christmas trees with presents wrapped in colourful paper tied with cotton bows spread around their base.

John Martins, one of the biggest stores in Adelaide, had its front window made up with cardboard reindeers pulling a sled with a man dressed as Father Christmas, who waved to excited children as they stood peering in. The weekend before Christmas, Adelaide, like all cities, was buzzing with people spending their money. Michael and Silvester were no different. Top of Michael's agenda were presents for the Thomson family. He had thought of getting something for the house but, on reflection, had changed his mind, deciding instead to get presents that were a little more special. But what? For the girls he bought a silver necklace with a heart which he had inscribed with their first name, the year, the word 'Love' and his initials on the back. For their mother, a brooch with a round opal at its centre and, on the back, the words 'Thanks for everything', with again the year and his initials. For Gilbert and Tim, he bought a good sturdy pair of work boots. Silvester was another matter; he had mentioned a number of times that he wished he had a pair of aviator sunglasses, like the American pilot had given to Michael in Italy. On their way back to the Richmond Hotel they had passed a shop that sold glasses, giving Michael the idea. So, the next pub they came to Michael suggested they pop in for a drink. Inside, cigarette smoke drifted through beams of sunlight that were cast through the open windows. An elderly gentleman with a beard and sporting an Aussie bush hat, one that had seen better days, stood in a corner strumming a guitar and singing bush ballads to those who had the inclination to listen.

"Two of the same?" Silvester asked.

"That's fine by me" answered Michael, straining his ears to the sound of the bush ballad singer and caught the words. 'The dying stockman'.

Then halfway through his beer, Michael excused himself.

"Do you mind if I pop out for a few minutes? I've seen something in a shop window I want to buy and don't ask me what it is."

"Sure, take your time. I'll sit and listen to the bushman."

Outside, Michael walked back to the shop they had passed before.

He stopped, something in the shop window next door caught his eye. It was a travel shop. Qantas Airlines were advertising flights to all major Australian cities. There was a list of prices and another of destinations to places like New Zealand, the UK, America, Singapore and other countries. But what he was interested in was a picture of an airliner on a postcard. It was a Lochhead DC-4. He recognised it from a picture he had seen in a book at Silvester's house and, anyway, that's what it said it was on the card. There was also a photograph of a pilot, co-pilot and their cabin crew. "Very smart," he thought. Then he entered the shop that sold spectacles. Shortly after, he went back to the pub with what he had purchased in the pocket of his coat. On entering, he noticed Silvester talking to someone.

"Michael, I'd like you to meet a fellow flyer. Donald, this is Michael Jones."

"Pleased to meet y, cobber, a Welsh Pommy pilot, never met one before, so you're flying with Silvest? He tells me you had something to do with him still being here… preventing him from getting his second pair of wings." Michael looked at Silvester and smiled.

"He exaggerates a bit," said Michael, shaking Donald's hand.

It turned out that Donald flies a Tiger Moth, crop spraying out of Mount Gambier, a place over 230 miles to the south. When Michael joined them, the two men were discussing the weather, the supply of phosphates, other pest controlling agents, and new laws that would be coming in the near future, mainly to do with safety issues. They moved from the bar and sat at a table vacated by an elderly couple who struggled with their bags of Christmas shopping. Donald, also an ex-RAAF pilot, had spent most of his time flying around the Southwest Pacific when Japan entered the war and had come home in 1946. Another farmer's son, he had learnt to fly above the corn fields of his father's station and it was due to his father's encouragement that he went to war.

Silvester and Donald had made each other's acquaintance at the ANZAC Day parade the previous year. Silvester, his father and brother, Tim had left home in the dark and it was still dark when they parked their car in a side street not far from Pennington Gardens where the dawn service was to take place. Michael listened with interest as Silvester told the story. Dawn was breaking as they stood with hundreds of other people and, with lowered heads, listened in silence as words were said in commemoration to the fallen of both wars. Silvester had noticed the RAAF wings pinned to the lapel of Donald's jacket and introduced himself. After the service and the Last Post had sounded, the three of them made their way to North Terrace to see the parade go past. Thousands of people lined the streets to watch all sections of the Australian Armed Forces file past. It was a poignant moment, as Silvester explained to Michael, but there was no need for explanations. Michael had experienced similar feelings while standing on the streets of Newtown during Remembrance Day. Silvester went on to describe how the veterans had marched four abreast.

"I go cold when I think of them," he said.

"Those poor bastards in Gallipoli didn't stand a chance, but that day with shoulders back, heads held high and with the heels of their footfall as straight as an arrow, they marched into the warm breeze like they always did. To see the emu feathers in their slouched hats and rifles slung over their shoulders, it was a sight to remember. As you know, Michael the Australian Light Horse was a mounted regiment whose last charge was against the Turkish forces in Beersheba, Egypt in 1917. They were on parade alongside other veterans who had fought in the Great War, but that was long ago, in another time and that's where we will leave them."

With that, Silvester and his two companions emptied what was left in their glasses, then with a refill, raised their beer and drank a toast to their own fallen comrades.

It was seven thirty when Michael and Silvester placed their bags of shopping on the hotel beds. Both were suffering the effects of having had a little too much to drink. Michael pushed aside his shopping and lay down.

"He seems like a decent enough chap?" said Michael.

"Who, Donald?"

"Yes, when was the last time you saw him?"

"I haven't seen him since that first time last year. Father had some business in the city at the time and Tim came for the ride. Father told me then that he thought we may have two to three years in the crop spraying business before the big boys moved in. But there will always be flying jobs, planes don't fly on their own."

The following day the streets were again full of people. At midday, John Martin's Christmas Pageant went through the streets and Michael and Silvester stood on King William Street to watch, along with thousands of others. Excited children were shouting and waving as Father Christmas and his helpers went by. Michael had not seen anything on this scale before and was impressed. At night the pubs were busy with people having a good time. Michael found it strange that someone here could die for their country at the age of eighteen, yet not legally have a beer until they were twenty one. The girls were flirting, egging on youthful, daring impatient young men who would do anything to acquire their company. Michael looked on with thoughts of the past, remembering his moments of success and failures in that department. As for Silvester, he seemed to be getting on well with a lady who had big breasts and a big mouth who was obviously drunk and not really a challenge. Michael was surprised that Silvester would contemplate seducing someone like that, let alone spend money on drinks that she did not refuse. One of her two companions was in another league, she was classy, with a touch of arrogance, not a lot, just enough to make her interesting. The other was a short blonde lady who looked rather embarrassed at the antics of her friend.

"I would've thought your standards of female companions could be a little higher?" Michael whispered with a grin. Silvester raised his hand and cupped his ear. Michael repeated his comment.

"It isn't her I'm after, it's her friend I fancy."

At daybreak the following day they headed home. Silvester had spent the night in the company of the young lady whose big breasted friend, by all accounts, was a nice girl but gets rather 'over excited' due to the effects of alcohol. Silvester had said his farewells to her on the steps of the hotel with the intention of seeing her again. Silvester slept as Michael drove home. Michael's night had ended with a kiss on the cheek and nothing more. The short blonde lady was good company but rather self-opinionated and not someone that Michael would want to see again. So, for the next few hours, and not for the first time, Michael contemplated his future. Just what did he want to do? What was it that kept him in a state of wanting to move on all the time? He knew he could stay at Delta Downs for as long as he liked, maybe marry Rebecca and live happily ever after, but that wasn't going to happen, was it?

He looked at Silvester, apart from farm work, flying was all he knew. He was flying solo at sixteen and had joined the RAAF at eighteen. His war history was much like everyone else's. Flying was their love, doing cartwheels in the sky and such like. Pressing the cannon button was just a part of it all. Get it right and you fly another day, get it wrong and 'it's two o'clock from the house'. Silvester's long term love life was, at this time, non-existent. He had split up with a neighbour's daughter some twelve months earlier, so last night could be the start of a new romance for him.

Christmas Day in 1948 was a Saturday where the sun shone on Delta Downes. At ten thirty the kitchen had more bodies in it than you could poke a prawn at.

Rebecca was at the sink shelling said crustaceans and splitting crayfish down the middle, while Michael peeled potatoes beside her. Silvester had come in after preparing the barbie for later, saying that the iron plate needed a good scrubbing from its last use. At the kitchen table, Hettie was busy with a pumpkin, something Michael had not taken to, so there wouldn't be any going on his plate. A large piece of salted ham was placed alongside Hettie. Patience looked at it and set about getting it ready for the oven. Gilbert had killed a pig a few weeks earlier and its dissected parts were salted and placed on a stone slab in a little cellar under the house. Michael could still hear its screams as it was hung upside down in the barn before having its throat cut. It was the same at home, so it was not something new to him and, as unpleasant as it was, butchers could not sell live pigs to their customers and expect them to do the same. Outside, the temperature was climbing, it had been in the low nineties for the last few days and was expected to rise further. Rain was predicted and had been for some time but nothing came. Michael found it amusing to be eating Christmas dinner on a day like this, but it was tradition, probably going back to colonial times, interesting he thought.

Gilbert had taken the car and had gone to a neighbouring station the night before to deliver, as he always did, some of the pig he had killed in return for beef steak to be eaten over the festivities. It had been a custom at this time of year for local station owners to gather at one station or another to for a few beers and to talk 'farm talk'. It was a ritual not to be missed. At twelve thirty, Gilbert returned and out came the presents. Everyone was seated on the veranda, either drinking cold beer or local wine from the Yorke Peninsula. Michael handed out his presents, firstly to Hettie, then to the girls. Gilbert held up his work boots and looked at their soles.

"A damned good pair of lightweight boots" he mumbled, as he tried them on.

Silvester ripped off the red Christmas paper and opened the little package. He hesitated, then cautiously slipped out of the silver cloth pouch a pair of Ray Ban aviator glasses. He stood and, taking three steps, extended his hand and slapped Michael on the shoulder.

"I wasn't expecting that," he said smiling, "thank you, thank you Michael." In return, Silvester handed Michael a book.

"This is where you will end up." His smile said it all, "it's about passenger planes of the future. You might find it interesting."

Rebecca and Patience were looking at the silver chains Michael had given them. He knew the presents were the same, but he did not want to favour one over the other, so getting them a similar gift was the best he could do. He opened the present Rebecca had given him; it was a four year diary, taking him up to the year 1953. He glanced her way and she smiled back.

"My God, where will we all be in four years' time?" asked Gilbert.

"I don't want to know, " Hettie replied, pinning her new brooch to the pink blouse Gilbert had given her the previous Christmas.

"Thank you for your present, Michael," the girls spoke as one. From Hettie and Gilbert, Michael received a Parker fountain pen along with writing paper and envelopes.

"Now you have no excuse for not writing to your mother," Hettie's prompting carried some weight, so Michael took notice.

At six o'clock everyone sat down and ate their Christmas meal, starting with prawns and crayfish and ending with Christmas pudding with custard and in-between, a belly full of pork, roast potatoes and everything that makes up the traditional Christmas dinner. Michael found it hard going, even with a number of cold beers he felt uncomfortably hot. In the end, he managed to finish what was put in front of him, minus a portion of pumpkin. For the rest of the afternoon the men spent time discussing work related subjects, including safety measures and the implication of new chemicals that would be introduced in the coming months. Gilbert told stories of his childhood on the station; his children had heard them all before so it was for Michael's benefit, they were retold. They sounded like hard times, especially for the women who had to make do with very little. Similar to tales he had heard before back home in Wales. The girls were in the kitchen cleaning up and listening to the Fred Alen show on radio, stopping every now and again to top up their glasses with a local red wine.

"What time will you be leaving in the morning?" Silvester asked his father.

"Before dawn. Eric's expecting me at ten, I'll load as much phosphate as the Ute can carry, it should last us until our delivery arrives."

23

It was Christmas Day 1949. Michael looked at Hettie sitting quietly at the kitchen table. Pain has a way of showing itself in many ways, no one saw the depths of her loneliness or heard her pitiful sobs. No, she had spared her family that. They had to bear their father's death as best they could. In the immediate aftermath of Gilbert's death, they had shared grief and sorrow, but there came a time when, as Hettie had put it, the pigs had to be fed and the cow had to be milked. This was not to draw a line under their bereavement, or to diminish the devastation that this event had caused. Hettie had quietly made a vow to herself, to God and anyone else who was listening, that enough was enough, and after three months of grieving she was going to lead by example.

It had been a terrible year. Gilbert's passing had taken its toll on everyone and now, two days from the anniversary of his death, the atmosphere at Delta Downs was sombre, yet not morbid. Hettie would not have it that way. Michael was surprised at how she had coped; she was an exceptional lady. The first three months had been the worst. Then slowly, with her children by her side, work on the station gradually got back to, somewhere near, normal. Michael, as well as feeling obliged to stay on, wanted to help out for as long as they needed him.

The day after Boxing Day the previous year, Gilbert had travelled to a neighbour's station to pick up some bags of phosphate and was expected to be back by mid-afternoon. It was early morning with a temperature in the high nineties when he set off and although rain was expected and had been for a couple of days, none had arrived. Four hours after Gilbert had left, Tim came into the house saying that he could see smoke on the northeast horizon and heading west. Bush fires were something that happened now and again and was a thing station owners had to contend with, but there had not been a big one in the area for a number of years. An hour later, the smoke could still be seen moving west. Silvester was getting a little concerned about its direction. If it had not turned in an hour's time, he was going up to have a look.

"You're not going up to have a look," Hettie said, giving him a stare that would have defied the devil and neither are you, her gaze shifting to Michael. Silvester paced the veranda looking to the horizon.

"Do you think Dad will stay at Eric's place?" Rebecca was beside herself with worry.

"He would be wise to," said Tim. "I wouldn't risk it; he knows better than most how quickly these fires can race and change direction." Another hour had passed and there were reports now, coming over the radio, of the fire on the peninsula and at the same time a plane was spotted flying over the area. At that moment, Patience came rushing out of the house.

"The phone is down!" she cried, "the phone is out, it's dead and Dad is out there, Jesus Christ, I hope he's not on that bloody road." Hettie was on edge, wringing her hands. She hesitated, not knowing what to do.

"Go then!" she shouted, there was fear and anxiety in her voice and she was on the verge of tears.

"Go on, Silvester. Go see if you can find him." Silvester didn't need her to ask again, he was off, with his mother's voice ringing in his ears and Michael hot on his heels.

"Follow the road, Michael," he shouted, "I'll fly to Eric's place," were Silvester's last words before Michael strapped himself in the Tiger Moth.

Michael planned to stay up as long as he could. He headed into the wind, fifty yards behind Silvester and rose into the air like he had done hundreds of times before. But this time it was different, this time he was not looking for his next spraying run, but to follow the road from Delta Downs to as far as needed. The fire was on the twenty five mile stretch of natural bush, some 30 miles up the road from Delta Downs. It wasn't a large area as bushfires go, but it was enough and every minute that Michael was in the air the fire was bearing down on the road that Gilbert was traveling on. Michael had never seen a bush fire but had been told about them. 'Megafires' could generate their own weather by creating a draft supplying the fire with additional oxygen, burning whatever was in its path at a faster rate. The heat generated in these bushfires was such that it hardly needed a naked flame to ignite eucalyptus trees. The oil in their leaves was flammable and if all conditions were in place, dry undergrowth, wind and a source that could ignite it, then leaves would simply burst into flame. Fires could be started in various ways, other than by people, or by lightning strikes.

Michael had a range of some 300 miles before his fuel ran out and if he didn't get back home by then, he would land in a field somewhere. He followed the road as Silvester had told him to do. After peeling away from Michael, Silvester headed for Eric's place. In the distance Michael saw the smoke, the billowing black plumes rising lazily into the sky. He eased the nose of the plane up, gaining another 100 feet. With the fire now only minutes in front of him, he glanced at the road as he flew parallel with it. He had left the virgin bush a few miles behind, it was still intact, but in front he could see the fire rage. He pulled back, flying now behind the fire but still parallel to it. He reckoned that within fifteen minutes the fire, in parts, would be across the road that he had now lost sight of. The trees were crowning with fire as the flames raced across their tops, leaping from tree to tree aided by the updraught created by the heat of the inferno. This, in turn, sent burning embers high into the air that fell to earth well in advance of the fire, igniting fresh kindling, spreading the flames forward wherever the wind took them.

The fire now had a 25 mile front and at all points the road was bridged. Michael could see kangaroos scatter before the flames, running in all directions seeking a way out. A few would make it but most would perish, dying in their hundreds, outrun by the speed of the fire. Koalas did not stand a chance and simply perished in the trees or on the ground, along with everything else that lived there.

Michael flew on and met the road on the other side. There was no sign of anything. If Gilbert had attempted to outrun the fire he would have failed. Michael turned, as he was using up both time and fuel. It had been, he feared, a futile exercise. Gilbert's only chance was to have stayed at his neighbour's place, or he could have got clear of the fire earlier on, but he did not have time. Michael thought it strange that he didn't see anything of Silvester. All kinds of thoughts were going through his head, and he was glad to see Silvester's Tiger Moth on the strip when he got back.

The inquest into Gilbert Thomson's death read like fiction. Written in black and white, it was something not to be believed but this was not fiction. The emergency services had found his body at 9am the following morning, half an hour before Silvester and Michael had arrived on the scene. His Ute was burned out and his body lay covered with a hessian sheet alongside that of a big kangaroo. Silvester was prevented from seeing his father's body. A fireman had told him that if he did not want nightmares for the rest of his life, it was best not to look. The official report surmised that Gilbert had hit the kangaroo as it fled the fire. The impact had sent his vehicle off the road and, because of the weight of the load he was carrying, he was unable to get back on the track. Gilbert had another 15 miles to go before he would have been clear of the fire. That would have taken him another twenty minutes, but the fire was running faster than that. So, it was unlikely he would have made it anyway. Two days later, the rains came.

Without Gilbert, work on the station was hard going for everyone. Especially for Hettie. In a lot of respects, she took over the day to day running of the station. Gilbert had a habit of not doing his books, writing invoices or paying others on time, saying that it was all in his head. It was a nightmare for Hettie, but in a few weeks she had everything squared up. For six months they were also without Patience as she had moved to Tiger's place, 18 miles away. Tiger's father had been poorly for some time and with Patience expecting a child, Hettie had suggested she move to his place. Patience begged her mother, saying that she wanted to stay at least until the baby was born, but Hettie wouldn't have any of it. They settled on Patience coming back at weekends.

A lot had happened in the twenty months since Michael had been at Delta Downs, apart from Gilbert›s death and Patience moving to her husband's home, another lady had moved in. Lorraine was the girl that Silvester had met in Adelaide the Christmas before. Michael remembered it well as four weeks later Silvester went back to Adelaide, this time on his own. He didn't say a lot, in fact he said very little to indicate that he was fond of this city girl, but as the weeks went on, even with the loss of his father, he could not stay away from her. It soon became clear that he had found the girl he was looking for. At first his mother was concerned that being a 'city girl' Lorraine would not be able to become a 'country girl', that the call of the city would be too much for her to resist. But Hettie was wrong and from the moment Silvester brought her home, Lorraine didn't want to return to the city.

The household on Christmas Day 1949 consisted of Silvester, Lorraine, Rebecca, Patience, her husband, Tiger, Hettie, Tim and Michael. Michael's relationship with Rebecca was getting to the point where, in his mind, he was undecided whether to stay or move on. Other matters arose at Delta Downs that needed serious thought. Earlier in December Hettie had been approached by a company that wanted to buy both Tiger Moths and everything in connection with the spraying business. The family had sat around the kitchen table to discuss the proposition. Michael had been invited on the grounds that it would also affect him, but he had declined, saying that this was a family matter.

It was no surprise that this conservation would, at some point, take place, although it happened a lot sooner than anticipated. The company had given the family until the first week in January to reach a decision. There would be no haggling over their figure once an inspection had been done and that figure would be with them within the next two weeks. The two men, Hettie and her sons, walked past as Michael stood on the veranda.

"They don't need me there." Rebecca said, as she slid her arm through Michael's, both watching the group walk to the shed and beyond to where the planes stood. "I don't know," she said. "It seems everything has fallen apart since Dad died, and it's no good Tim saying, 'she'll be right', all the time, she bloody well won't be right. When those planes go, I'll still be here and when you go, I'll still be here! Sometimes I think, sod it, I'm off too, but I have nowhere to go." Michael felt her arm go tense as she spoke of the future.

"I think I'll go to Adelaide and pinch someone's spot on Rundle St. and make a living that way. Tell me Michael, who am I going to meet, stuck out here in the bush like the bloody Sheila that I am? The blokes I meet here I don't fancy, I don't know why, I just don't …" Michael stood in silence not knowing what she would say next but he expected more. "Jesus Michael, I would have a naughty with you any time you wanted, with no strings." Her words were rushed and incoherent. "I'm not a piece of china, I won't break, or hold you to ransom."

Without saying a word Michael grabbed her hand and led her from the veranda and around to the back of the house where they ran to the hay barn. And there, out of sheer frustration and a craving for each other, they fell onto lose hay. This was lust on both sides, with no preliminary courtesy or thoughts of consent, none were needed. In moments clothes were discarded and the hurried act of physical need overtook them. Like moths to a flame, they were consumed by an urgency that neither had any intention of drawing back from.

With mixed emotions, the Thomson family sat down on Christmas Day to a meal that was littered with memories, happy ones, and ones that, in two days' time, would bring back the pain of that fateful day. Michael now knew his future for the next four months, after that he wasn't sure.

Hettie and the rest of her family had discussed the long term direction of Delta Downs and decided that the crop spraying side of their business should be sold off and with the income from that no longer coming in, they would increase the number of sheep on the station to a figure that would sustain and, hopefully, surpass the income they would lose.

Michael was asked his opinion on the suggested decision, he agreed and put in a suggestion himself.

"It seems the company wants to move your business wholesale to another site. My question is why? Why would they want to do that when you're the only crop spraying business within 100 miles of the next one? And… even if they buy that one out, you're well suited here as a central base for the area. They've already stated that they would keep Silvester on as a pilot. So, I suggest you put it to them that for a moderate rent, they could use Delta Downs as, like I said, a central base for this area." Michael first looked at Hettie, then at Silvester and Tim. Rebecca raised her eyebrows and smiled. Hettie glanced at Silvester, he shrugged and nodded, giving a grin of approval.

"I think it's a good idea," said Hettie. "Not only because, in the long run, they'll be saving money, but it will, as you say Michael, be an added income for us. I'll put forward your suggestion and we'll see what happens." Everyone agreed.to Hettie's proposal.

24

On Monday the 25th of April 1950 the Delta Downs crop spraying service ceased trading. By the 30th J SMITH & SON would be operating from the Delta Downs station for a period, until a new facility was built on the land at the turn off to the station. It seemed that the suggestion of a base in the vicinity of Delta Downs was advantageous to the company and as Silvester was now in their employ, they would have the peninsula covered.

The period up until the takeover was, for Michael, a little like waiting to scramble for your Spitfire during the war; you knew what to do and how things should work out, but it was not over until your wheels were back on the ground, or in Hettie's case the cheque was in the bank.

Michael's relationship with Rebecca had settled into one of acceptance. She knew he would leave and understood that this would happen. She also knew that a broken heart wasn't too far away. Their lovemaking was discreet when discretion was called for, which was most of the time. They had their moments and made the most of it. Rebecca was a passionate lady and as Michael was her first lover, she wanted lasting memories of him to keep. For Michael, this was how he expected their relationship to end. He thought a lot of Rebecca but had made up his mind. The time, the place and everything about their relationship, as nice as it was, did not seem right. She was an attractive woman and one day she would find another love, of this, he was sure.

On the 17th April 1950, Michael flew out of Ned Miller's crop spraying base 8 miles from Narracoorte, a small town 200 miles south of Adelaide and a twenty minute trip west to the Victorian border. His accommodation was two rooms in a lodging house in the town. It was sparsely furnished, with pictures of the Australian bush hanging on the walls and a bed that had probably rested more bodies than the cemetery he could see from his bedroom window. Although it was old and dated, the room had an unusual but comforting feel about it.

Silvester had driven Michael to Adelaide, where he had stayed the night. It was every bit as hard saying goodbye to this man as it was to anyone Michael had ever said goodbye to. Would he ever see him again? He didn't know, but he would always remember him. Silvester was a likeable and thoughtful man and Michael owed a lot to him. So far his Australian adventure, as Michael called it, was all down to Silvester. Michael had learned a lot and seen a lot. Every day had been an experience since he had left home. He wondered if Silvester had foreseen his future. He remembered that the sound of a passenger plane flying overhead when they were last in Adelaide had caused them both to look up. Silvester had commented,

"I could see you in one of those, Michael."

"As a passenger?"

"As a pilot, Michael."

"Think of all those places I could visit." Michael answered back and they both laughed. That year, Silvester's Christmas present had been 'A Book of Modern Day Passenger Aircraft'. The more Michael thought about it, the more he liked the idea. He would look into it.

The following day, Michael bought a car and called in at Adelaide's Qantas head office. Sometime later, he came away with all the information he needed for the transition of his pilot's licence to one of a commercial licence needed to fly passenger aircraft. With this paperwork in a brand new briefcase and visions of himself flying a Lockheed DC- 4, Michael set off to Narracoorte. He knew it wasn't going to be easy, but he also knew he would get a licence in the end.

His departure from Delta Downs had all been rather sad. Surprisingly, Rebecca had kept her composure and, with a dignified hug, had wished him good luck and Godspeed, then stayed to wave him off. Hettie had said her goodbyes and as she did she had given Michael an envelope, saying that it was a little something for the idea of getting J SMITH & SON to rent some ground from her. Tim, rather shyly, had shaken Michael's hand and smiling had said,

"Good on ya mate and hooroo". As Michael bid his farewell. Hettie came to the window of the Ute and told him to keep in touch and that if he ever needed anything, to let her know.

Rebecca had turned and, with a lost heart, walked to the rear of the house and to the barn beyond. She was numb. Slowly opening the barn door, she paused and stared inside. The disturbed hay that had been witness to mutual trysts over the past three months, lay unaware of what was happening. She smiled, feeling surprisingly calm and then closed the door. She walked back to where she had seen Michael wave his last farewell. The clouds of dust Silvester had left behind had already drifted through the gum trees that were close by, with some of it settling back on the road from where it had risen.

"Goodbye Michael," she said to an empty road, then turned to face her own future.

The transition of Michael's pilot's licence was proving to be a headache. His crop spraying would be a steady five day week flying all over the south of the state, or the stations that they were contracted to spray. In reality, the crop spraying business had become very competitive, with the bigger companies undercutting the independents. Ned Miller, the owner, or director as he tells people he is, was a real character. He was in his early forties, a father of five and had a flying history that defied belief. A local man, he had sunk all his money into this venture. He had been in the business for just over twelve months, but prior to that had been connected with various aviation projects. Ned had a reputation for being shrewd and calculating but his word could be trusted. Michael had been in contact with Ned by phone before leaving Delta Downs, courtesy of a friend of a friend of Gilbert's who had been in school with Ned in Mount Gambier, a town 50 miles from Millicent. From the beginning Michael was up front about his future intentions, believing that being honest about it would not backfire on him later. A curious smile came over Ned's face when Michael revealed his intentions of becoming a commercial airline pilot. Ned then changed the subject and mentioned the air crash in Western Australia the previous night.

"It's a sad business," he said, Michael gave him a curious look.

"That plane coming down in WA last night. I did hear something about a plane crash, it was a night flight, wasn't it? It was on the radio's morning news, but I missed most of it, well pretty much all of it." Michael stopped.

"A Douglas DC-4, flying out of Guilford airport, on its way to Sydney.

"Is it right, everyone was killed?"

"It seems so, apart from one. I spoke to a mate of mine from Perth, he works at the airport." Ned stopped talking and lit a cigarette that was hanging unlit in the corner of his mouth. I was on the phone to him an hour ago and he tells me they found a bloke wandering about with his clothes on fire. The ambulance men had to carry him on a stretcher for three miles in the bush. He was taken to hospital still conscious, poor bastard."

"What time did all this happen?" Michael asked, biting his lip. Ned shrugged.

"They left Perth at a quarter to ten last night and 46 miles out, they came down in a thick wooded area 8 miles from York. It seems that the captain, two co-pilots and two hostesses, along with twenty four passengers lost their lives. A sobering thought, Michael, a sobering thought."

Michael made a mental note of the date, the 27th April, a date he would remember.

"And you still want to go flying?" Ned smiled and raised his hands in the air.

"It's all I know, Ned. I just can't stop wanting to be an airline pilot because of a plane crash. Jesus, I'm lucky I've lived as long as I have. A lot more will die in future plane crashes, I'm sure, but that's not going to stop them from flying, is it?"

"You're right and at the moment I think we have, maybe ten years before you won't see a passenger plane in the sky with propellers on it. Jet planes are the future. Planes with propellers will be used for joy rides and crop spraying." Ned gestured with his hand. "Take a seat, Michael," he said, "I'm going to tell you a story." Michael sat at Ned's office desk and with a hint of a smile, Ned sat opposite.

Michael wondered if Ned was about to tell him that his services were not needed anymore, since he had told him about his future career plans and to stop wasting both their time, but he didn't, he just lit a cigarette and started talking.

"In January three years ago, I was in Sydney kicking my heels. I'd been laid off, having just flown some prize merino sheep from one end of the state to another. You must remember that after the war, there were a lot of pilots around, many looking for something to do. Most were glad to be on the ground but there were just as many who missed the flying and I was one. I don't know what it was like in England, but over here If you had a plane that could fly, you could make some money, and if you didn't have one, you could get a job with someone who did." Michael sat listening to this guy in front of him who had transported bloody sheep.!

"They made money out of flying sheep around?" Michael was thinking of the cost.

"It just wasn't sheep they were taking, Michael. If you wanted something to go to Melbourne, Adelaide or anywhere fast and had the money to get it there, there would be plenty of pilots who would take it."

"What planes would you be flying, Ned?" Hardly believing what he was hearing. Ned smiled again.

"Ex RAAF planes, transporters and bombers these were going under the hammer for next to nothing. Jesus, Michael, it was a free for all. It would only take two or three pilots to get together to buy one, then they could set themselves up as a transport company, it was happening all the time. These companies …" Ned paused. "Do you fancy a cup of coffee Michael? I've a throat like a wombat with a sore bum." Michael chuckled to himself.

"I haven't heard it put like that before," he said.

"Me neither," replied Ned, before taking a drink and sitting down. "Now where was I? Yes, these companies were situated in every city and in every state. Immigrants from Europe and the UK were the prize, since the Australian Government had opened its door to them after the war."

"But the planes, Ned, what planes were being used? It's a bloody long way from Cardiff to Melbourne, the pilots must have hedge hopped all the way here."

"Curtiss Commandos, Lockheed Hudson's, the Italian S M 95s and a load more. If they could get ten people in it, they would fly it. Some planes would carry thirty to forty people, maybe more. Then, as word got around, more and more airlines from all over the place, including some from here back home, wanted a piece of the action." Ned reached for a cigarette, offering one to Michael, who declined. He took a heavy drag, the smoke leaving his nostrils like the vapour trails of a jet plane he had seen. "Of course, the Government officials were pulling their hair out as the shipping companies were snowed under with the numbers of Europeans waiting to be shipped out. Those who could afford the airfare, were jumping the queue by flying in. Qantas Empire Airways and BOAC were the official carriers of migrants but they were overwhelmed with numbers, and this allowed these charter companies to go in to meet the demand. The problem was that the Australian Department of Civil Aviation were making things difficult for the charter lines. Some would be told to offload their cargo of immigrants, because in the business, that's what they were, a paying cargo. These people would be collected the following day and put on flights with TAA or another 'approved' Aussie airline. So, what did these charter lines do? Fly back to Europe for more passengers and be Aussie bound again. Because of the ADCA's actions some charterers started to dump their passengers in places like Singapore, Rangoon or Calcutta, leaving the problem to someone else to, eventually, carry them on to Australia."

Michael had heard that chartered flights were bringing in migrants from Europe, but what he was hearing now was in the realms of fantasy. So, he just sat and listened, digesting every word. Ned stubbed his cigarette in an overflowing ashtray and immediately lighting another and sat back in his chair.

"Now a little side story to all this. It was in November, I think, last year. I was co-pilot in a Curtiss Commando. We had thirty eight Greek Cypriots on board and flew into Sydney to refuel on our way to Brisbane when a guy from the ADCA came aboard. He didn't say much, fuck all to me, but he wanted a word with the captain. These are arrogant people, Michael. I can understand the Government's concern about safety and they had to deal with a lot of shifty people who didn't give a shit about the rules and regulations, but…anyway, it turns out that this ADCA guy wanted to go on a jolly with his lady friend to Brisbane for a few days and he just wanted to hitch a ride. The captain explained to him that his paperwork for the flight had to be in order, including a full crew and passenger list. The captain, John Stains, I think his name was, had good reason to think he was being set up. Sometimes the ADCA would try to catch charter companies out with falsified documents, and no doubt it happened. Jesus, going through customs was bad enough, they'd often offload everyone and go through the plane, looking for contraband which would delay the flight by hours.

The upshot of this little episode was that this ADCA guy was legit, so his name got listed on the flight manifest as the co-pilot and his lady friend as the hostess. So, for the next few hours I sat on the bloody floor of the plane, spending my time trying to converse with these Greek Cypriots and our new hostess and co-pilot." Ned stopped talking and looked at his watch, lit another cigarette and smiled. He seemed to be enjoying reminiscing about not so long ago. "It was an exciting time, Michael; I made a lot of contacts within the ADCA while I was involved in this immigration business. Now, this smart ass' co-pilot', I got to know quite well on the flight to Brisbane. He turned out to be an ok kind of guy, just doing his job, so he said, but it seemed everyone was on the take and he was no exception. For a few pounds, he could be persuaded to wave you through custom, as long as you weren't taking the piss. The names of the easily persuaded were passed around from one airport to another, so we all knew the score. I knew a lot of shit about a lot of guys and if I'd have spilled the beans, a lot of them would've been looking for another job, but I didn't and wouldn't. Besides, these guys could come in handy someday."

Ned lit another cigarette, inhaled deeply then continued talking. "Things are a lot different now. Toward the end of last year the ADCA were cancelling the contracts of a lot of the charter companies, except for some approved, foreign and Aussie ones, but the bubble had burst and that was the end of what was called the 'Migrant Caper'. The ADCA have now tightened up on all pilot's licences and do a rigorous inspection and aviation checks on all planes. Of course, it will all change again when jet passenger liners come along, but planes with propellers will be around for a good few years yet. Anyway, by then you'll have moved on, Michael. God knows what kind of things will be in the air in twenty years from now. I wish you well and I'll help you all I can. Like I said, I've got contacts, who have contacts. They might be able to help hurry things along for you, possibly saving you months in the process of getting a licence."

Ned stubbed out his cigarette and lit another, crushing the now empty packet and throwing it into a bin. Then, with a curious look he asked Michael a question. "Michael," his voice slow and hesitant, "Are you sure you want this? I mean to go on and fly passenger planes?" He was straight faced as he asked. Michael, now standing, was a little confused about the question and thought for a moment.

"The only thing I've ever doubted, Ned, was my own ability to fix a Rolls-Royce Merlin engine that came out of a Hurricane, or at least know where the problem was. As for the decisions I've made in my life since then… all have been the right ones at the time and, so far, I've no regrets. So, in answer to your question, yes, I do want to carry on flying.

"Now I have a question for you." Michael was smiling, as Ned reached for the door. He turned.

"Fire away" he said, raising his hands as if in surrender.

"What reason did you have in asking me that question?" Ned tilted his head.

"I've known a lot of pilots, some good and some I'll never know how they lived to see the end of the war." He opened the door and stepped out. Michael followed as Ned continued talking. "Most of these men thought they could jump out of the cockpit of a Spitfire or some other fighter plane and into the captain's seat of a passenger aircraft, then fly away with the same mentality they had with a 109 up their backside. Now these people are not to be confused with the pilots of a Lancaster, Wellington, or heavy bombers who, along with the rest of their crew, had another three engines to contend with, unlike a fighter plane with just one. Fighter pilots don't automatically make good pilots of passenger planes and for those who don't, there are no jobs out there for them. Thankfully those guys have by now, and with relief, put their past and memories behind them and retired from the world of flying."

Three months later, Michael was on his way to getting his commercial licence. It had taken many hours of study and many trips to the flight training centre in Adelaide. As to the cost. Half his savings had gone and it was Ned who, through giving him leeway in his working schedule, while still paying him a wage was able to fly when he could, mostly weekends and days when he was free. It would take him, probably, another three months to complete a Civilian Aviation Course and be granted his co-pilot's licence. By that time, Michael would have got his three hundred hours of flight time needed, as the authorities had considered time already spent in the air. From there, all being well, he would either go to Melbourne or Sydney to take up a position with Qantas, or any airline that would employ him. On the 24th September 1951, aged thirty, Michael caught a plane to Sydney.

25

Sam read Michael's letter and placed it back on the shiny, ebony surface of the baby grand, where Grace always places the house mail.

"And how is Michael?" Grace asked. Sam grinned.

"He's just flown into Sydney; well, he had when he wrote this."

"Has he got his pilot's licence then?"

"From what I can make out, he has a co-pilots licence and it's a time and hours thing to become a captain' He's done well for himself. Here, have a read." Sam passed Michael's letter to Grace.

"I wonder when we'll see him again?" and without stopping she asked Sam how far it is from Brisbane to Sydney?

"I was wondering about that myself…and the distance from Brisbane to Sydney? I don't have a clue. Are you thinking what I'm thinking?" Sam looked at Grace and she raised her head.

"It would be nice if they were to meet," she said smiling.

"You're talking about Billie?"

"Yes, he knows she's in Australia and has done so for a long time but, as yet, has only acknowledged that Brisbane is a long way from Adelaide. The truth is, they wouldn't know each other if they were to say hello in the street. Their only connection with each other is us."

"How old is Billie now?" asked Grace, folding her daughter's cardigan and placing it over the back of a chair.

"Twenty nine," said Sam, reaching to pick up the cardigan after it had slid off the chair Grace had placed it on.

"Good Lord, she'll be thirty next year. That makes me feel old."

"Me too." Sam fleetingly remembering his first vision of Billie in the railway carriage on his way to Liverpool docks.

"When is your mother due back?"

"Anytime now. It's a long walk to the cemetery," Grace replied.

"I can't believe it's been five years since your father died," he paused, "I don't like her walking all that way. If she'd waited till I got home I would've given her a lift."

"I told her that, but she said she'd prefer to walk. I suppose it gave her time to think." Grace thought about the five years without her father and the pang of the lost life of Richard came to mind.

"It seems like I've been here for a lot longer than I actually have." Grace sighed as she thought of her time in America. Of the friends she had made, being able to live a life she could only have dreamed of and the feeling of being reborn the moment she had set foot on the streets of New York. She often thought of her father and her time living in the Admiral Rodney a walk away from the docks in Liverpool. She looked at Sam, she adored him, the young man of yesterday, who had stolen her heart.

They both heard the front door open and the shuffling of feet. Sarah poked her head around the door into the lounge.

"I've bought some groceries; I'll pop them in the kitchen. When are the kids home?" she asked, Grace looked at the timepiece hanging on the wall.

"In half an hour or so. Henry won't be here for tea; he's gone with Martin Harper to see a basketball game."

The Pryce family of 226 Hudson Street, Manhattan had settled into a routine and, like every other growing family in New York, their monthly calendar of events looked very much like the month before. The children, all except Henry, were in high school. Sarah at fourteen, had been learning to play the piano and could now hold an audience while playing classical music and popular songs that were played on the radio. Mary, was of average intelligence, excelled in sport, especially swimming where she held the fastest time for various lengths in her age group.

As for Jimmy, he was an extrovert in the making, always confident, sociable, liked the company of his friends and would go off and try anything. Sam and Grace still saw their friends, Joe and Pageant and Curtis and Isabelle, and often went to each other's homes for meals and social gatherings. But, like most young families, it was the children that took up most of their spare time, fetching, carrying and, in general, being a pain in the ass as Sam would say. Henry had left school at fifteen to work in his father's business but would often wag school long before that. Working alongside Sam was all he ever wanted to do. Sam's company had been steady for a number of years and the profits had been sunk into his Property Holdings. Sam had eight properties, that he rented out. Curtis was his advisor in all matters concerning his acquisition of properties and in the process had acquired two himself.

Sam had never forgotten Michael, and the two wrote to one another at least twice a year. To begin with Sam didn't know why he was so concerned about Michael's welfare, but as he got older, he realised that apart from his own father's relationship with Michael's father, it was his name. Michael … the very reason he was in America. Michael Gill was the Irishman whose letter Margret Doyle had given when on his leaving America all those years ago. The very letter Sam had handed back to her on their first meeting.

As for Billie? A little like Michael, Sam had seen her from the age of six grow to be the woman she had become. She had told him about her experience at Pearl Harbour and her fears of going to Europe. She would sometimes write him sad letters, all the time telling him not to repeat her words to her mother and father for fear of them worrying about her. Sam never betrayed that trust, not even telling Grace, although she may have read them, but she didn't say. He remembered with fondness the bond Billie had with Willena and he loved her for that. She would write whenever the need arose and he would write back, reassuring her that he would always be there for her. And now she was in Australia, doing a job she loved. Sam didn't know what path Billie would eventually walk in life, but if there was any way he could make that path easier for her, then he would.

26

Jim stood in the rain, looking straight ahead, seeing nothing. The mourners had gone, which left just the three of them. Three of them on the side of a hill… as it used to be, as it should be. Jack had been here a long time. Bill, just that morning… How long would Jim stay? Until he was cold. But he was already cold. "Not as cold as those two," he thought. Yet the thought was not as odd as it sounded, in fact his war time buddies would have appreciated the comment.

"Fuck it", he said under his breath "Bill was fifty, fucking six years old. Shit." Bill had fallen down the stairs at his home a week ago and broken his neck.

"Fallen down the bloody stairs, Jesus. Bill has fallen from greater heights than the bloody stairs at his house." But he was dead when Megan got to him. She'd been in the garden…it was two o'clock in the afternoon, she'd been out for over an hour, so God knows how long Bill had been at the foot of the stairs. Megan didn't hear a thing. She had been singing The Old Rugged Cross or some such hymn, so wouldn't have heard anything anyway. Jim shivered, then standing rigid, he glanced around. Rain dripped off the end of his nose. "Things in a graveyard never look right when disturbed by a new hole in the ground," he thought. Fresh flowers sticking out of a metal frame covered in moss with a little note attached didn't do a lot for the overall scene either." Dead ones," he thought, flowers that had been lying on the ground for months, their petals withered, the earth having soaked up the colours that had once defined them.

Jim noticed some ivy clinging to a few headstones, ones whose chiselled inscription were illegible due to the elements. All added to the aura of the place. He noticed Tommy Spencer's shovel, or as he would call it, his 'grave digger's shovel', sticking out of the top of the mound of earth that would be shovelled back into the hole Bill's body was in. Jim smiled, grave diggers shovel. "It has a curious and intriguing ring to it, don't you think, Jim?" Tommy Spencer had once said. His shovel had been, by way of association, introduced to a dozen or more people buried here at the cemetery.

Jim glanced at Jack's headstone. There was only himself left now of the three of them that had gone to Egypt in the Great War. Jim acknowledged Jack's presence, by touching the cold slab of granite that marked his existence on earth and then with a nod, he walked away.

Megan was devastated at the death of her husband. To find him quite dead at the bottom of the stairs was something she was unprepared for. Bill's untimely demise had somewhat tempered her joy of discovering, two days later, that her daughter had given birth to a fourth grandchild. At the time, if she were totally honest, Megan didn't give two hoots about a new life. Bill had been her reason for living. That mantle, her reason for living would now be passed on to her children and grandchildren.

At the funeral service, Bill's mother and father had sat in the same pew as Megan. Mrs Jones, which is what Megan had always called her mother in law, sat stone faced, not a tear in her eye. She had already shed her tears for Bill, with just as many falling when he was alive, especially while he was away at war. At one moment during the proceedings, she reached for Megan's hand and gave it a gentle squeeze, as if to say, everything is going to be fine. Mrs Jones remembered that Sunday afternoon when Megan, then a sixteen year old, first walked side by side to her home. The joy she felt then would always remain a joy, even now.

Michael heard of his father's death by way of telegram sent by his sister, Sally, the day after his passing. At first, Michael didn't understand. He didn't want to understand. He wanted to know more and his immediate reaction was to catch a plane home.

"I have to go, Ricky I have to go home." Ricky Danton, a pilot of two years for Qantas Empire, was someone Michael had flown with as co- pilot on a few occasions. He was staying the night at Michael's place before flying out to Melbourne the following day. For two hours Michael paced the floor of his flat.

The realisation that he would not see his father again burned deep in Michael's conscience. Never again to hear his voice or see his face. Michael sat at his kitchen table staring at the wall opposite. His mind full of thoughts, thinking of words his father had spoken, deeds he had done, his first recollection of him and his last. Other people's stories of him as man and boy, all this tumbling over and over in his mind, wave after wave. And what was he left with? In truth, he could still see and hear his father and he would carry his image and his words for as long as he breathed.

Two days later Michael had decided not to return home for his father's funeral. He had been in contact with his mother and she, having resigned herself to the thought of her son coming home then having to leave again, filled her with despair. But, she did make Michael promise that he would come as soon as was possible. She told him that he would be in her thoughts and prayers on the day of his father's internment. On that last day of his father's existence above ground, Michael felt privileged to have known the man about to be lowered into it.

Michael, acting as co-pilot in a Lockheed Constellation, was cruising at three hundred and 45 miles an hour, at thirty thousand feet. Below him was the Nullarbor Plain, an expanse of flat semi-arid scrub land stretching over two states totalling a distance of seven hundred and forty 6 miles. His destination, Perth, a total flight of 1,324 miles. He thought of his father a number of times on that trip, nothing specific, just his image and his smile and that was all he needed.

In the new year of 1951 Michael had acquired his mandatory miles and had passed numerous exams and training courses to become a captain and by June that year he had swapped seats and was now sitting to the left of the co-pilot, making regular flights across Australia, as well as flying into New Zealand, New Guinea and Hong Kong. Passenger fares were expensive, but for the rich and famous it was an exciting time, with new destinations coming available every few months. It was also an exciting time for Michael. A new job, a proper job and altogether a new experience. Everyone he had met were strangers. With a lot of pilots and co-pilots being ex-forces, a mix of Australian, British, a few Americans, New Zealanders and anyone from anywhere who had done what Michael had done in making the transition from his RAF pilot's licence to one that was internationally accepted. Many countries had their own air lines and were expanding to meet the demands of a globetrotting public. The expansion in cargo transport ran parallel with the expansion of passenger flights, with new destinations coming all the time. Yet a new era in passenger travel was also underway, with established airlines leading the way and others close behind. It seemed that in the, not too distant future, jet passenger and cargo planes would rule the airways.

27

Megan read Michael's letter that was posted in Bombay. She noticed the stamp. It had a picture of a flaming torch, like the ones held by torch bearers at the Olympic Games. Only this stamp was for the 1st Asian Games that had taken place in New Delhi the previous month. It was the third such letter Megan had received from Michael in the past few months, each one with a different stamp from a different country. The first was from Singapore, then one from New Zealand. Megan looked at the stamps and thought how far Michael had come since leaving home to him now flying aeroplanes all over the world.

Since Bill's death, Megan had thrown herself into doing out-work for Phillips Cycle Factory in Newtown, the company that both her daughters worked for. Once a week, a lorry called and dropped off four dozen cycle rims, hubs, bundles of spokes and nipple screws at Megan's home. And a week later, they came back to pick up the wheels, spoked and ready to be finished off in the factory. It took Megan about twenty minutes to complete one wheel. It was piece work, so the more she did, the more she got paid. The driver brought her pay for the previous week's work when dropping off the next batch. The outwork helped Megan's finances. She had no rent to pay, but her old age pension was a few years away.

Megan visited her friends for company. She had sat with Bill's mother in church, ever since Bill had first left home, but sometimes she found Jessie's company hard to deal with. Megan acknowledged the reason why, but God forbid she should stop her visits. Jessie was her mother-in-law, her children's grandmother. There were times when Megan came away from the house in tears, but who else was there to listen to Jessie's tales of Bill, her only child. She told Megan how, during the war, she would go into his room and open one of his drawers to smell his clothes. Of course, his clothes went with him when he married Megan, so it was a surprise when Jessie asked if Megan could give her an unwashed shirt of his to put in his old bedroom. At first Megan thought it odd, but now, nearly twelve months later, she understood.

Jessie had photographs of Michael set up on her sideboard and mantelpiece. The one Megan liked most was one of Bill in Egypt, standing with Jack with a pyramid in the background. She often found that it was the little things that upset her the most, like Bill's letters to his mother. Jessie had them bound in a blue ribbon, like Megan had on her letters from Bill. Megan went home that day and changed the colour of her ribbon; she didn't want his letters to her bound in the same colour ribbon as his letters to his mother. Megan knew it was a silly thing to do, but Bill's letters were unique to her and that went as far as the ribbon they were tied up in.

On Saturday afternoons Sam's father was hardly ever home when Megan called. She sometimes caught him in his shed. He would smile and always ask about Michael. Megan liked the thought that he was pleased that his son was in contact with Michael, putting the family ties that existed between them on a more permanent basis. Apart from his enquiries after Michael, Jim didn't say a lot, he just pottered about in his shed, forever sharpening his sickle or gutting rabbits to sell to the dealer on his weekly round.

Violet had got used to Sam not being there and after a number of years she realised that he would never come back to live at home again. She was content to receive a letter every few months, mostly in Grace's handwriting, but sometimes her grandchildren would put pen to paper and that was always a nice surprise.

Bill's death had a profound effect on Jim, Sam's father. Megan remembered him standing in the rain at the cemetery. Of the three of them, he was the only one left and as she had passed through the stone arch of the cemetery, she looked back and saw this man, a hero to her husband, standing vigil at his friend's grave. Megan had often wondered what he was thinking at that very moment, but she would never ask. Violet had told Megan that since Bill's funeral Jim had become more like he used to be, more sociable and talkative. It was a subtle change but a change, nonetheless. Maybe after all this time and with the passing of the Second World War, he had come to terms with what had happened in Egypt, thirty six years earlier. Somehow, Bill's passing had created an interest in the living for Jim. For a number of years after the Great War, Jim had sought solace in his visits to the vicar of Montgomery. They would meet in a field and talk about anything under the sun. And now? Anything under the sun was still a good subject to talk about.

Leaving their home, Megan considered what Violet had said about Jim. She hadn't noticed any difference in him, as he always greeted her with a smile whenever they met. Not thinking too much about it, she walked home, wishing Michael would let her know when he would be coming for a visit.

Billie had heard of Michael getting his captaincy and, again, wondered if she would ever meet him. Letters from her Uncle Sam would always include news from his home in Wales and although she had never met any of his family, she knew a lot about them. She was saddened to hear of the death of Michael's father, yet having been engaged in the world of life and death for so long, for her own sanity, Billie knew better than to get too involved. She had become accustomed to switching herself off from the trauma; she had been there and had seen it all. Walking through a hospital ward with a dead baby in your arms, then going off for a ham sandwich and a cup of tea in the canteen while listening to the girls discussing their evenings activities, was not easy. You needed to be able to carry on, in effect, as though nothing had happened.

Well things did happen, devastating things, mostly to other people."

"It takes a long time for people in our profession to be able to switch off, but once you can do it, your mind belongs to you again," said Billie.

"I could never get used to that," answered a girl, as Billie tried to explain her experience facing trauma situations to a group of trainee nurses.

"And you are right," said Billie. "It is something that's hard to get used to, but you will learn to accept and manage the feeling of despair and sadness that comes with the job. And if you can't handle it..." Billie paused, looking at the six girls in front of her. "Maybe nursing isn't your vocation."

"But surely there's another side to nursing, that doesn't involve the, how, can I put it," she stammered, "the blood and guts bit. I'm looking for the... you fix them and I'll take care of them, kind of nursing." The girl was flustered and unsure of how to explain her thinking. Billie smiled and nodded her head.

"You're quite right Janet and your question is valid, but even that side of the nursing can be heart breaking. Some patients you may get to know very well and for no other reason than they are nice people. Then one day you come on duty and they're not there and you will never see them again. That can also be hard because, like you said Janet, they come to you having been put back together by other people and all you have to do is nurse them back to health. Well, I'd take umbrage at those who would say, 'all you have to do', because those five words are an insult to those who look after the sick. To be honest, that is exactly what nursing is, to care for the sick and, in a nutshell, that's what your profession is all about."

Billie still lived in the nurse's quarters that she had first moved into. She had no reason to move on and her friend and neighbour, Tessa, still made her carrot cake, a big favourite of hers. Billie had been working at the hospital for four years and had been home only once in that time.

Twelve months earlier, her parents and brother had paid a three week visit to Australia. Billie had taken them, via a Greyhound bus, to see the Great Barrier Reef on the northeast coast. They had stayed in the town of Mackay for five nights. Their lodgings were just a stone's throw from the palm tree lined beach where they spent most of their time in a tranquil dream. They saw the reef from a glass bottomed boat. The pinnacle branches of coloured coral and fish like rainbows swimming in the warm, clear, Pacific Ocean. It was a wondrous sight. Billie's mother, not the most adventurous person, was amazed and could not get enough of the sights unfolding before her. The whole experience was, in her own words, immensely enjoyable.

While on holiday, Billie and her mother got to know each other again, this time as adults. Accepting the differing points of view, they may have had. Pageant did not altogether approve of her daughter's liking of alcohol, or rather the amount she consumed, even though she herself enjoyed a glass or two of champagne. Billie, on the other hand, found that a few drinks on her nights off was, as she would say, therapeutic in relieving the work-related stress and pressure that she and her colleagues experienced. In other words, she liked a few, even to the point of getting a little tipsy, as it would take her into a world other than the corridors and wards of buildings that people would rather not visit. Billie thought of trying to explain it this way, but she knew her mother to be a rather fussy individual, inflexible in standards of conduct. Billie, at this point in her life, knew when to stay quiet. After all, mother knows best.

As for Billie's brother, they had absolutely nothing in common except being sired by the same father and shared the same mother. Like other eighteen year old lads, basketball, American football, and surfing were his predominant interests. Alan was a student at Columbia University in New York, studying Quantum Mechanics, whatever that was. Billie tried to engage him in conversation regarding his chosen subject.

"I don't know enough about it to give you a meaningful answer," he replied and the conversation ended there. Altogether they got on reasonably well, Alan enjoyed snorkelling and spear fishing but, most of the time, did his own thing. A week later, the family holiday ended with a tearful farewell at Brisbane airport and, for a moment, Billie felt a little guilty for feeling guilty about not wanting to go back with them. She knew though that if she went home it wouldn't be long before she would want to leave again. The subject of Billie not having a gentleman friend had been mentioned but only once and thanks to her father's presence, the subject was dropped. Billie let it be known that she had many gentlemen friends, adding, as she winked at her father, that some of those were her present lovers. Billie's mother, noticing that she was the subject of the comment, smiled and let it pass over her head. No more was said.

In the departure lounge at Brisbane airport Billie looked at the Fijian air hostesses. They were young, smartly dressed and no doubt prepared for any eventuality. Her parents and brother joined the queue of about forty people to board. Billie noticed two pilots walk to the passenger plane parked on the apron outside the terminal. At the top of the boarding steps Billie›s parents turned and waved. She waved back, wondering when she would see them again. Their flight was with Fiji Airways on the 1728 mile trip to Fiji, from there would catch a Boeing 377 to Hawaii, where they would spend two days sightseeing before flying on to Los Angeles, a longer trip, some 2,470 miles. The last leg of their journey was a flight across America to New York. Billie was surprised that her mother was up to it all as she had never really been much out of New York since she had arrived from England when Billie was six. As for the cost of it all, Billie dreaded to think. Her father, by all accounts, had sold some oil shares on Curtis's advice and had wanted to take Pageant somewhere far away from New York. More to Billie's surprise, thankfully, her mother had actually seemed to enjoy the whole experience.

28

Back at work, Billie thought more about Michael Jones after seeing the pilots boarding her parent's plane. She wondered what her chances were of ever meeting him. "Slim indeed," she thought. The thing was, she wasn't sure where he now lived. Her Uncle Sam had mentioned that he had left Adelaide some time ago, so, by now, he could be anywhere. She had wondered if he ever flew into Brisbane. Maybe she would write to her Uncle Sam and enquire as to Michael's whereabouts.

At the time Billie was thinking of Michael, he was on his way to Bali taking, amongst other passengers, a delegation of New South Wales businessmen on a trade mission. Since the 1949 independence of Indonesia and the recognition of such by the Australian Government, diplomatic relations between the two countries had been stable and such missions were not uncommon. The Japanese had left the island six years earlier after occupying it during the Second World War. That time was now well and truly behind them.

The plane landed in Bali to refuel, before taking off again for Hong Kong. Michael handed the controls to his co-pilot for this second leg of the journey which would take them 2,123 miles, with a flight time of just over six hours. Michael and the crew stayed twenty four hours in Hong Kong before boarding the same plane home via Darwin and Melbourne. Michael liked Hong Kong, even flying into Kai Tak Airport was interesting as the runway jutted right out into the sea. He liked to sit outside the cafes and 'people watch', which he enjoyed wherever he went. He rode the funicular Peak Tram on Hong Kong Island and from the top, gazed out over the harbour and wondered about the lives of the fishermen in their little sampans far below.

The staff accommodation that Qantas had in Hong Kong was sparse but acceptable and after he had made provisions for his flight the following morning, Michael retired to bed. He had made the acquaintance of the crew that had just flown in with him, but there were two new hostesses that would be joining them on their flight to Darwin. He found it interesting to meet other employees as each had a story to tell. One of the two new hostesses had his mother's name, Megan. She was a pretty girl, weren't they all? She was originally from Geraldton in Western Australia and had been with Qantas for nine months. She now lived in Melbourne with another girl who also roamed the skies. Megan's story was a sad one. Twelve months before she took her first flight, both her parents lost their lives in a road accident. She, at the time, worked at a bank in Geraldton but had left soon after. She couldn't see her way while living with the memory; everything around her reminded her of the happy life she had lived before. Her three elder brothers tried to keep her there, saying that, in time, she would come to terms with what had happened. But in the end, it was to no avail. They suggested she move to Cottesloe, a suburb of Perth, to live with her aunt who had suggested the same thing. Megan was there for a few months when she noticed an advertisement in the West Australian newspaper regarding Qantas hiring air stewardesses for their airline. She applied, passed the interview and started her formal training almost immediately. Nine months later, Megan was sitting on a balcony in Hong Kong talking to a pilot with a story of his own.

At six thirty in the morning, Michael was up and soon after, he and the rest of the crew boarded a Qantas Constellation. Within a half hour, they were on their way to Darwin.

Darwin, in the Northern Territory, was a place Michael had been to on a number of occasions. He had heard of the Japanese bombing of the town during the war but not much more than that. The man sitting next to him in the cockpit was about to enlighten him on the subject.

"There isn't a lot to tell really. Darwin had a population of around seven and a half thousand people and eleven years ago, on the 19th of February 1942, the Japanese attacked the town."

Michael's co- pilot, Terry Trevor, looked through the cockpit window at the landscape below. Every time he did this, be it in another ten minutes, or in an hour and ten minutes, the landscape was the same. It was never ending, the mulga bush, spinifex, hummock grasses and other arid plants of the plains stretched for mile after mile on this 1,940 mile stretch to Melbourne. Terry, a thirty five year old New Zealander, had flown a Lancaster Bomber during the war, making many raids over Germany. He continued his story.

"The pre-war population of Darwin was, as I have said, but quite a number of those people were evacuated some weeks before the bombing. Anyway, at nine forty five on the morning of the 19th some two hundred and forty Japanese planes flew in and bombed the shit out of the place, sinking what ships there were in the harbour and destroying what planes were at the airfield. The raid lasted about a half hour, then they were gone. An hour later they were back, this time with just over fifty planes and gave the place another smacked arse for another twenty minutes. The official figure shows that two hundred and thirty six were killed, but that depends on which official figure you want to believe."

"Was there no warning?"

"Apparently not. The sirens went off as the first bombs landed, or not much before." Terry leaned over and again, looked out of the window.

"You know, Michael it never ceases to amaze me, all that land down there and it›s good for sod all. And there's a lot of it."

"And that's it?" Michael asked. "The bombing of Darwin?"

"Pretty much," Terry replied. "I think they came back a few times after that, but it all came to an end four and a half months later when the yanks sank a few of the Japs aircraft carriers in the battle of midway. The very ones that were used to ferry the planes that bombed Darwin, or so I've been told." At that moment, Megan popped her head around the door of the cockpit.

"Anyone for coffee?" she said with a smile. A while after their coffee and cream biscuits, Michael made an announcement to the passengers regarding their descent, mentioning they would be landing at Melbourne airport in approximately fifteen minutes.

Michael took control of the flights to Sydney and Brisbane, both only short runs and a total of no more than three hours in the air. The seats vacated by passengers who had disembarked in Melbourne were taken up with new people whose final destination for the day was the sunshine state of Queensland. The weather in Brisbane, in the late afternoon, was clear and warm. A manifest of all passengers and crew on board was always on hand for the outward bound flight, not that a lot was done with it, but it was handy to know who was seated where. Sometimes a passenger, or passengers would be acquainted with the pilot, or some other member of the crew and always asked to see the cockpit. This request was usually, and within reason, granted to anyone ensuring good public relations and enhancing the company's image.

The DC-4 rose into a clear blue sky, banked starboard and levelled off. Michael switched on the PA system and announced his name and that of his co-pilot, along with relevant facts about the plane and the flight. He wished his passengers a happy flight before switching off. The flight to Brisbane was more than three quarters of the way through when the connecting door into the cockpit opened and Megan came in, her face ashen and her speech quick and to the point.

"We have a situation in the aisle Captain Jones. A passenger has collapsed, with a suspected cardiac arrest. At the moment a male passenger is attending."

"Is he a medical professional?" asked Michael, his voice calm and precise. Go back and ask him how serious the situation is, we can't divert; the nearest airport is the one we're going to." Less than a minute later Megan was back.

"A young lady has taken over and the gentleman is now assisting her. She is a nurse and the elderly female passenger has, indeed, had a cardiac arrest. Her condition is stable at the moment. I think you'd better come and assess the situation for yourself, Captain." Michael transferred control of the plane to his co-pilot and stood and followed Megan out of the door, closing it behind him. Megan stepped into the gally. Michael passed her and walked to where a lady with her back to him was kneeling beside an elderly woman applying CPR. The patient was lying on her back with her head toward the rear of the plane. The gentleman assisting stood to one side.

"Come on lady, let me know you're there," said the nurse, as she forcibly pressed down on the chest of the prone form lying in the aisle. "Don't you dare die on me." She leaned forward and performed mouth to mouth resuscitation.

"Is there anything you need?" Michael asked.

"A glass of water for me and a gin and tonic for the lady," came the reply. The nurse then signalled for the man standing to take over, and as she got up, he took her place.

"That's a glass of water and a gin and tonic?" Michael said with surprise.

"That's right, the water's for me, and the gin and tonic is for the lady. Actually, make that two gin and tonics. I don't know how long we'll be here, and my gentleman friend may need one as well. I'll have time to drink the water and if she doesn't make it, I'll have her gin and tonic. Just make sure there's an ambulance ready at the airport when we arrive. She's in a bad way and may not survive. I don't want people gawping at her, so if you could give us as much privacy as you can, I'd appreciate it." The nurse turned, looked up and smiled.

"Yes miss," Michael said, he was lost for words. He turned to Megan. "Give her whatever she asks for and bring me the manifest please."

Michael then made his way back to the cockpit. "Jesus, Terry, that's some lady back there. Where the hell did, she come from? She certainly has something about her, very professional, not sure about the gin and tonic though."

"Will the old lady make it?" Terry asked.

"I don't know if she will, Terry. Now who the hell is she?" Michael said, still thinking about what had just happened.

"Get in touch with Brisbane and tell them to have an ambulance ready to meet the plane. We'll be there in fifteen minutes," Michael got back into his seat and made another announcement, asking all passengers to remain in their seats after landing to allow medical personnel on board and the evacuation of a passenger that had been taken ill.

The elderly lady was still receiving CPR as they came into land. By the time the plane had come to a stop, she had regained a steady but weak heartbeat. She was transferred to the waiting ambulance within minutes. Because of flight commitments. Michael did not make it back to see the passenger being taken off the plane, and after he had negotiated his way down the aisle through disembarking passengers, the young nurse and her patient were gone. Michael stood outside on the boarding steps to see the ambulance disappear around the airport's terminal building and disappear. In his hand was the planes manifest of passengers. Seat A 32, Miss Billie Fleming.

Michael had Miss Fleming's personal effects brought to him in the airport terminal after debriefing his crew. The names and addresses of the three passengers involved in the incident were on the list that Michael held. The gentleman assisting Billie was a retired veterinarian, a Mr Anthony Gwilt, who admitted to Megan that he knew more about animals than he knew about people but was happy to help out. The elderly woman was Mrs Margaret Willison, the grandmother of a local businessman who happened to be at the airport to meet her. Then there was Billie Fleming, an American nurse who had worked at the Woman's Hospital in Brisbane for a number of years. Michael was surprised at how quickly this information was gathered, but there it was, all in a matter of an hour and a half.

It was a proud moment for Michael to announce to his crew that he knew of Miss Fleming and that she knew of him, not that they had ever met. Out of courtesy, Miss Fleming and Mr Gwilt would both be contacted by the airline regarding this incident and thanked for their prompt action. Michael decided he would contact Miss Fleming personally as soon as possible.

Michael rang the Woman's Hospital and enquired as to Mrs Willison's condition and if they knew the whereabouts of the nurse who had accompanied her in the ambulance, a nurse by the name of Billie Fleming. Michael mentioned that he was the pilot of the Qantas aeroplane that she had flown in on and he would like to contact her as he was in possession of her luggage. Michael was asked to wait for a few moments, then he was told that Mrs Willison was stable, and that Nurse Fleming was still in the hospital. If he could ring back in ten minutes, he would be able to speak to her.

"Hello, this is Billie Fleming, speaking. I believe you're the Pilot of the Qantas aeroplane that I was a passenger on? I gather you have my luggage. I was about to go back for it but, as you know, I had other things on my mind.

"Hello Miss Fleming. Yes, this is the pilot of the flight you were on." Billie then again spoke.

"The ambulance men said that there was no need for me to go with them, but as they were taking the lady to my hospital, I insisted I accompany her." There was a slight pause, then Michael answered.

"Firstly, I would like to thank you for your assistance regarding the incident that occurred on your flight. My name at this moment is not important." He hesitated, "As you gather, I am in possession of your suitcase and I hope you don't mind, but I was wondering if it would be possible to meet you. More importantly, I've something to say that you may want to hear, something I would like to tell you in person. I know we've never met, except on the plane, and we may never meet again, but I can't stress enough that it's in both our interest that we see each other as soon as possible. We can meet wherever you want. Is there a cafe near the hospital?"

Billie thought his insistence that they should meet was rather strange but went along with his suggestion; at least she wouldn't have to go back to the airport for her luggage.

"Evan's caff on Butterfield Street, just up from the main entrance to the hospital. It's a fifteen minute taxi ride from the airport. I'll be there in a half an hour, if that's convenient?"

"Yes, that will be fine. Till then, goodbye."

29

There were more people than usual in the Upper House on that particular Friday night. The topic of conversation was the death of King George V1 that morning. Some of the old-timers raised their pints at his passing, others discussed the inevitable process of Princess Elizabeth being their new Queen.

Locals privately and openly talked of the King›s death like they would have had a popular figure in their village died. David, the village blacksmith, wondered how long it would be before there was a coronation, saying that at the age of twenty five, Princess Elizabeth was very young to take on such responsibility. The debate on this event of the 6th of February 1952 went on for days.

On the 2nd of June the following year, a television receiver, the only one in the village, stood on a low table in the bakery, where rows of seats had been placed in front of it. Excited children and villagers watched the Coronation of Queen Elizabeth II on this marvel of modern science. Days before, Edmund Hillary and his companion,

Tenzing Norgay, had ascended Mount Everest, the highest mountain on earth, this being all part of the celebrations.

Megan stood in the bakery with Jessie, her mother in law, and watched the pageantry on a snowy nine inch screen. A village party had followed, and a memorable day was had by everyone.

Jessie Jones had never recovered from her son's death and with her husband Albert, suffering from dementia, she now lived a rather lonely life. If not for Megan, and the congregation she met at church, she would see few people. In contrast, Megan, now filled her life with her four grandchildren who visited most weekends. Her youngest son, Dan, still lived at home. His lady friend was a farmer's daughter who wanted a big wedding. The date was set for the 18th of September, some twelve weeks away. For selfish reasons, Megan was feeling a little apprehensive about the wedding. It would be the day her last child moved out of the family home and she knew that, on the day, her thoughts would be of Bill, Michael and of the many years before. Most Sundays on her way to church, Megan called at Bill's grave to say 'hello'. It wasn't a morbid encounter but one of gratitude. Sometimes she would talk to him over the stone wall that was the boundary to the cemetery, other times she didn't. But like men who would doff their cap on meeting a friend, when standing by Bill's grave she would gently touch his headstone.

Her house, now empty of her children, was now witness to the sound of her grandchildren's laughter and their cries for attention. For Megan, that was worth everything. Her life had come full circle. Although she felt she had a lot more living to do. Who was going to tell her grandchildren of her life? The life of Megan Jones? She felt they needed to know who they were and the legacy she would leave behind, hopefully, to be remembered.

Megan was disappointed that Michael had not been home for so long, even for a visit. She knew that he was trying to better himself, but it had been six years since she had last seen him. His saving grace was that he wrote on a regular basis, so she knew exactly what he was about. His last letter from two months earlier had been posted in Singapore. Affixed to it was a ten cent stamp with the portrait of the Queen and below that, the words Singapore Malaysia. She wondered how much longer she would have to wait before seeing him.

Sam and his accountant casually went through his yearly accounts, his company's income against its outgoings, wages, rents received, maintenance to all his properties, payments to government departments and tax due. The business had been on a marginal rise for a number of years with an annual increase in return of between five and ten percent. Sam's wealth was estimated at around seven hundred and thirty thousand dollars. He sat back.

"If I wanted to spend a bit of money, how much could I take without causing too much of a bother?"

"How much were you thinking of spending and on what?" Herbert looked at Sam and smiled.

"I don't know, I haven't been home for a few years now and I've been toying with the idea of taking the family for a trip. It's the kids really, I want them to know where their father and mother came from. They're of an age now where I think they need to see that part of them that will always be me, and their mother of course."

"Will you be taking the dog?"

"We don't have one."

"I know, but if you had one, would you take it?"

Sam smiled, "Probably."

"And when were you thinking of taking this trip?"

"Anytime really. If not this year, then next."

"By ship?"

"Ship takes too long." Herbert leaned forward.

"Now you're talking real money."

"I know."

"Have you discussed it with Grace?"

"No, I haven't, well not in so many words."

"And how many words does it take to tell her."

"Not many." Sam gave a forced smile.

"As for the cost. I'll look into it for you."

30

Billie sat at a table outside the café. She had declined a coffee saying to the waitress that she was waiting for a friend. She had hesitated over the word 'friend' but then thought no more of it. Turning in her chair, she looked at her reflection in the cafe window. She wanted to know how she looked. Billie was not a vain person, but being presentable at all times was an insistence of her mother's and, in that respect, she was right. Billie was still in her travelling clothes. She had been about to go home and change when she got word over the tannoy to go to the hospital's front desk.

Billie›s travelling companion, a work colleague, had picked up Billie's small suitcase and taken a taxi back to the complex where they both lived. The plane's captain was bringing along her on-board holdall. Billie sat not knowing what to expect, she had not registered the captain's name when it was announced at the start of the flight. She had heard the public address and the captain speaking but that was it. As polite as it was to introduce yourself as the flight captain, their names were hardly ever going to make an impact on your life. She looked at her watch, then glanced up. At some distance she could see a pilot's uniform coming toward her and inside it, the man who had spoken to her while she was on her knees in the aisle of his plane. He was quite tall and carried a holdall that was presumably hers.

"Miss Fleming?" Billie stood.

"I believe this is yours? Please have a seat," he gestured. Michael placed the suitcase at Billie's feet. She sat and he sat opposite. Billie smiled but said nothing.

"Thank you for agreeing to meet me. Firstly, I would like to apologise for being evasive on the telephone but I had reason to be." He stopped and a broad smile lit up his face.

"How is your Uncle Sam these days?"

Billie was taken aback and with her eyes wide open she stammered. "How, how do you know my Uncle Sam?"

"I'm Michael." That's all he said.

Billie sat, unable to move, before an intake of breath and a gasp of recognition.

"Michael, Michael... from Wales, is it really you? I had no idea." Tears came to Billie's eyes as the realisation of who he was came in waves.

"Uncle Sam is your relation too?"

"Kind of," answered Michael.

"My God this is not how I thought I would meet you, but I am so glad, so glad that I have."

"Would you like a coffee, Billie?"

"Not before I give you a hug." Billie blurted. They both stood and it seemed the most natural thing in the world that they held each other and for a moment, just that moment, Billie felt a fleeting sense of joy. Michael felt her warmth and her excitement at seeing him. As they sat down, he looked at her with eyes that spoke volumes.

"I need something stronger than coffee," she said, still not believing what had just happened.

Two hours and three strong coffees later, they were still talking. Billie was floating on clouds that had no number and Michael could not believe he was in the company of a woman whose confidence and vibrant personality hit him like nothing else had ever done. They talked briefly of their parents, their life before Australia and their love of seeing the world through different eyes. They asked questions of their experiences, sometimes crossing paths, like in London during the war, when they had both frequented the Elephant and Castle pub. She told him of the man she had met, the one that had died on the beach during the D Day Landings. In Italy when Billie recalled the Spitfires doing barrel rolls above their heads, with the nurses rushing out from the hospital tents to wave at the pilots.

"Was it you, Michael, who flew above us?"

"Perhaps it was, my friends and I did that now and again," Michael answered.

"I'd like to think it was us," Michael answered … "As to say it wasn't, could be a lie."

Billie told Michael about being at Pearl Harbour and the day General Patton had walked through her ward.

"Can I see you again, Billie?" The question came from nowhere, Michael was surprised he had even asked it.

"I would love to see you again, Michael."

"Tonight?" he asked, "I fly out tomorrow morning." Billie smiled and looked at her watch.

"Do you know what time it is?"

"I don't really care. How far away do you live?"

"A five minute walk," Billie answered.

"Can I meet you here in two and a half hours? I'll pick you up. No, on second thoughts I'll walk you home now and pick you up from there, if that's ok?"

Michael just had time to shower and change before stuffing some notes into his trousers pocket and walking out of the door. He caught a taxi and as he rode to meet Billie he pondered on the events of the last few hours. He hadn't felt like this for a very long time if he had ever felt like this at all. He didn't want to think too much, he was tired, aching and his mind was in turmoil, but he had to see her, even for a few hours.

The following morning Michael flew out of Brisbane airport. He put aside his thoughts to concentrate on the job in hand. At thirty thousand feet, he relaxed enough to think of the night before. Billie filled his senses, he could not stop smiling and was mistakenly conscious of being looked at, thinking that everyone could see the change in him. He tried to deny himself the feeling of not being in control. How could he let this happen? Up until yesterday, he knew who he was, nothing he did, or very little of what he did, was influenced by others and now he felt vulnerable, but it was a vulnerability that excited him.

Billie lay awake, usually it was thought of work that meant she couldn't sleep, a patient who had said a last farewell, stepping up to an operating table the following morning, or getting out of sync through being on night duty. There were many reasons to look at the ceiling, wishing sleep would come. But tonight, work was the last thing Billie thought about. She kept repeating his name over and over. She thought of her Uncle Sam and chuckled to herself, thinking that he was not really an uncle to her and no relation to Sam either, but a dear friend to both families. She replayed the afternoon and evening in her mind. Michael's impeccable manners, his choice of words and the way he talked about her and not about himself, much like Sam, he was like that too. Michael was unassuming and all together a nice man. He had a dry sense of humour. He had asked her if the two gin and tonics had been enough while administering CPR to the woman on the plane. Billie had replied that she had considered asking the stewardess for the rest of the bottle but had second thoughts. Perhaps it wouldn't have been such a good look, getting off the plane while attending to a critically ill patient and with a bottle of gin in her hand.

Michael and Billie's parting was reminiscent of a romantic novel. He had held her hand, looked into her eyes for longer than was necessary, then closing them had bent his head, kissed the side of her neck, immediately taking in the scent of the perfume she wore.

"I would like to see you again, if that's alright with you?" he had said. Billie smiled.

"I would like that, there's so much to talk about."

"How can I reach you?"

"Just ring reception the number you rang before, they're very good at taking messages." Billie opened her handbag and wrote her address on a notepad and handed it to Michael.

"Here you go." She beamed, the smile that she'd worn since meeting Michael in the cafe having not yet left her face.

"Thank you for these last few hours, Michael. I still can't believe that I' have met you. I must write to Uncle Sam and let him know." She paused, "How can I get in touch with you?"

"I'll work something out." That was when he held her hand and kissed it, his parting words.

"Au revoir, Billie. It's so nice to have met you."

Michael landed in Sydney then flew to Los Angeles. He disembarked, leaving the Constellation passenger plane on the tarmac. He had flown there via Fiji, Canton Island and Hawaii. From there he really wasn't interested in where the plane went. He had two days before flying back, enough time to think. He and four of his crew took a cab to their Qantas accommodation, where he unpacked his suitcase and had a shower before getting himself a beer out of the refrigerator and sitting down.

Michael's fellow crew members did the same but they seemed to be more enthusiastic about being in Los Angeles than he was. Although he had never been there before and was looking forward to exploring the city, his thoughts of Billie were constant and he was anxious to speak to her again. He looked at a clock that stood on a shelf in the lounge, it had an advert for Qantas airways on its face. Michael adjusted his watch to seventeen hours behind Brisbane. There was a pay phone in the hall, but he decided to send a telegram instead as the cost to ring Australia was extortionate. In any case, he would be back in Sydney in three days' time. At ten o'clock that morning, he found a mail office and sent a telegram to Billie's address.

'Dearest Billie STOP In Los Angeles All Is Well STOP Looking Forward To Seeing You STOP Will Ring In Three Days STOP Affectionately Yours Michael STOP'

He wasn't sure how to end his message, did affectionately yours, sound too presumptuous? Perhaps regards would have been a better word, but that would have sounded too formal. He still wasn't sure as he handed the message form over the counter.

In three days, Michael rang Billie from Sydney. The following day they were having a meal together in a Brisbane city restaurant, both having decided on a prawn cocktail to start and a beef wellington for the main course. There wasn't an awkward moment.

"This is a little like old times." Billie said before savouring the crusty pastry of her meal.

"Old times?" Michael raised his eyebrows and smiled.

"Billie," he hesitated, "do you think we could make this moment old times? I mean, in years to come, do you think we could look back on this as being old times?" Billie laid her fork down and taking a sip of wine, looked at Michael and thought for a moment.

"For that to happen, Mr Jones, it seems to me that we would have to spend a lot of time together." Then unflustered, she smiled.

"Would that be a problem for you?" Michael tilted his head, not taking his eyes off the lady sitting opposite.

"Not at all, the only problem that I can see is the matter of 466 miles," Billie replied.

"Presuming we intend to see each on a regular basis, I think 466 miles between Brisbane and Sydney will be nothing more than an irritation to be worked around. That's if we both feel that this is what we want."

There! Michael had made the point of wanting a relationship, and the ball was in Billie's court. For a moment Billie was silent, not that she needed time to make a decision. She had made that decision as they sat together at Evans Caff the week before. No, her silence was to confirm that, in her own mind she was at a crossroads. She knew with certainty what she wanted to do and who she wanted to do it with.

"Michael, do you think we could make a go of it? I mean for us to be together. Where do we go from here?" Across a half-eaten meal of beef wellington, Michael reached for Billie's hand.

"I was hoping you'd ask that. I've been thinking. How would you like to come to Wales with me? I know it'd be all rather sudden, but it's been a long time since I've seen my family and my brother's getting married in a couple of months. Would you like to come with me?" For a moment Billie couldn't take in what Michael was asking her, but she was prepared to put all her trust in him. Then not thinking any more about it and with no hesitation, she answered.

"Michael, I'd love to go to Wales with you. Tell me what I must do, the dates and how long we'll be away. I'll have to let my parents know. I'm due some holiday but will still have to make arrangements at work." With laughing eyes, she exclaimed. "Good Lord, Michael we haven't shared a bed yet and here I am agreeing to go on holiday with a man I hardly know. Actually, that isn't altogether true, is it?"

"No, it isn't and if I don't treat you right, I'm certain Uncle Sam would have something to say about it. I promise I'll be on my very best behaviour at all times." Billie's eyes widened and a smile spread across her face.

"At all times? Wouldn't that be a little dull?" As she spoke, she reached for Michael's hand.

"Whatever you desire, I'm all yours, Billie."

"Are you really?"

"Really, what?"

"All mine?"

"Every bit of me."

31

Joe and Pageant had rung Sam the day before he had received Billie's first letter. They had told him about Billie and Michael, Sam was overjoyed that the two had finally met. Billie's second letter was more of a surprise. Immediately Sam contacted his accountant enquiring as to his flights to London.

The following weekend Billie and Michael met spending Friday, Saturday and Sunday together. On the Friday morning Michael had hired a car and picked Billie up. She had told Tessa about meeting Michael and about the subsequent rendezvous since, not omitting a single thing. Billie was like a child who had waited all year for her Christmas present, only to discover that her Christmas present was more than she had ever hoped for. Tessa was her confidant, her unconditional friend, one whose advice was taken on board, but not necessarily acted upon. In most cases, Billie was going to do what Billie was going to do. For whatever reason, her trust in Michael was absolute. At nine thirty, she was ready to leave. She had taken other shifts at the hospital, so as to have three days to do as she pleased. As she went through the door, she shouted to Tessa.

"Don't wait up for me."

"Lucky girl," Tessa shouted back.

Michael met her with a kiss on the cheek, before opening the car door.

"You look inviting."

"It's how I intended to look," she laughed. "And what have you in mind?"

"Never mind what I have in mind, what would you like to do today."

"Can we go shopping? I need a few things for our trip."

They parked in a side road. At ten thirty the city was quiet and they walked hand in hand down Rundle Street. This was a new feeling for Billie, a lovely feeling, holding hands and looking as though they had been together for a long time. They walked and talked, sat on wooden benches and browsed shop windows. The weather was kind, with a warm breeze that blew through the city streets like an invited guest. They sat outside a cafe; Michael went to order coffee and Billie watched him through the window. He was dressed in grey trousers a white open necked shirt and a dark blue summer jacket. She wondered how on earth he was still single. He must have had previous lovers; it was ridiculous to think otherwise. What was it about him to walk away from past relationships, or for women to walk away from him? There was nothing to indicate a failing of any sort on his part. Nothing to dissuade her from continuing the relationship. Was he too good to be true?

Surely her Uncle Sam would have mentioned something if, indeed, there was anything amiss. If Michael's intention was just to bed her, he could have done that without asking her to go with him to his home in Wales. She shook her head. No, she wanted to believe he had waited for her. Then she had a scary feeling, she was falling head over heels in love with this man and it frightened her.

The morning passed into the afternoon. Billie bought two dresses and two cardigans, some makeup and perfume, three pairs of nylon stockings and two pairs of shoes. She had bought underwear the previous week as it would not have seemed right for Michael to have been with her for that, a step too far in most people's eyes. Mid-afternoon, they went to the cinema. The Barefoot Contessa, as they both agreed, was not a film to rave about. Humphrey Bogart played a part that was out of character, but Ava Gardner, as beautiful as ever, was cast in a role that suited her. The best part of it all, was that they had held hands for the entire one hundred and thirty minutes that the film had lasted. As early evening came, Billie began to feel anxious about how this day would end. She didn't want to go home but she was reluctant to say anything, so she waited and waited for Michael to suggest that they go to a hotel.

"Do you want to go home, Billie?" Michael asked in a whisper.

"Not unless you want to take me," she whispered back.

"Then can I suggest we find ourselves a hotel? We will have separate rooms of course."

"Of course, Michael, but won't that be terribly expensive? I mean two rooms. We're meant to be saving up to go on holiday?"

"You're right, Billie, maybe I should sleep in the hotel and you can sleep in the car." They both laughed as Michael steered her in the direction of the nearest hotel.

Michael booked a room at The Royal Albert Hotel, for two nights, telling the front of house that they would be bringing their luggage later. He had booked in as Mr and Mrs Michael Jones. Billie immediately thought of… "what was his name?" The man she had spent a few hours with, in a hotel room in London. Then she fleetingly thought of the Piccadilly Commandos, the street girls who were so much fun. And now, for the hell of it, she imagined herself as one of them, how exciting.

How does one explain the overindulgence of something pleasurable? The word decadent came to mind as Billie threw open the blinds to their third floor hotel room. She had about her a white sheet that had been discarded from the bed during a night of passion. It was nine thirty, the sun's rays fell on the bed as Michael stirred. His hair was as unruly as hers and they didn't have a comb between them.

"I can't go out looking like this."

"No, I think you'd better put some clothes on. The sheet looks very good on you, but it's perhaps a little too daring for the street."

Billie put on the clothes she had worn the night before, but not until after a game of hide and seek. It was another two hours before they finally left the hotel. Michael picked up his car and drove to Billie's unit. There she changed and packed a few things. Michael then drove to his place to do the same. The events of the previous night had set a precedent for future activities. The anticipation was eagerly awaited by both.

This arrangement was repeated once more, and apart from the odd meetings of a few hours' duration, their correspondence was by telephone.

Michael had notified his mother of his trip home, stating that he was bringing a lady friend with him but that she was not to be alarmed; he was a big boy now and the lady in question was not a complete stranger.

Sam had also made all necessary arrangements and would be in London a day after Michael. There had been some adjustment in who was travelling with him. Sam's eldest son, Henry had decided not to come, preferring to stay and keep the workshop open as first proposed. Instead, the business would be closed for one week only, to give the boys a holiday. Sarah and Mary had also decided not to come, saying that they would appreciate it more in a few years' time and that, in any case, they had their nan to run the household and were old enough to look after themselves. Sam and Grace were disappointed that at this stage the girls didn't want to go, but they were adamant. Jimmy was the only one who was enthusiastic about the trip. At thirteen years of age, world travel was preferable to school.

At first, Joe and Pageant were a little apprehensive about Billie's relationship with Michael, but Sam had vouched for Michael's integrity and reassured them that Billie's welfare was Michael's main priority. They had come to terms with the fact that their daughter had finally found a man that was a little more than a friend. Pageant was also quite pleased that her potential son-in-law held a position of prominence as an airline pilot, and to that end, there was no question of his suitability. The journey for Sam and Grace would take fifteen hours, flying to Gander in Newfoundland, then across the North Atlantic to Shannon Airport and on to London Heathrow.

Michael, and Billie would be sitting together on the four day journey, it was one he had never flown before, so in a professional capacity, it would be an interesting flight. Their plane tickets were both free. Michaels for obvious reasons and Billie had been notified that due to her prompt action in assisting, by way of medical intervention, a paying passenger of the airline, her fare for this trip would be waived. The captain's written report of the incident had been a significant factor in the airline's decision.

On the morning of the 11th of September, Michael and Billie, boarded the Boeing Stratocruiser 377 to London via Darwin, Singapore, Calcutta, Karachi, Cairo, Castel Bent and Rome. The flight time would be fifty eight hours over four days. The whole trip was an eye opener for Billie. The flights were luxurious, with a party atmosphere. Drinks were free and the food was as good as any restaurant. Passengers had dressed as if they were going to the theatre but it was all very relaxing. Michael was contracted to fly one leg of the journey, but other than that it was, as Billie would say, a breeze. They landed as fresh as when they had boarded the plane, with Billie dressed like a model who had just stepped from a Paris catwalk.

32

Michael and Billie spent their first night in London. They had chosen to stay somewhere they had both been to before, The Elephant and Castle in Kensington. The hotel wasn't up to much, but it was a place they both remembered. In the bar they bought drinks, hugged, and for no reason, Billie started to cry.

"I can't believe this is all happening," she sobbed. "In a million years I could never have imagined being here again. It brings back so many memories, some sad but mostly happy memories of my friends. They were with me through a time I'll never forget." Michael suggested that they get some fresh air, leaving their drinks on the bar. The barmaid placing them to one side. Standing on the pavement, Michael handed Billie a handkerchief and as she dried her tears, she smiled.

"Do you know Michael, the very spot we're standing is a spot I've stood before with my dear friends... and the Piccadilly Commandos." They both laughed.

"I remember them too."

"Oh Michael, I'm so happy and I have you to thank for that."

"No Billie, we have each other to thank for being here." They stood with people passing like silent ghosts, all with their own concerns. Billie and Michael's presence on the pavement was a mere inconvenience. When they returned to the hotel, the barmaid smiled and moved their drinks forward. The couple's love making that night was unhurried, unlike the frenzied encounters of not so many weeks ago. They rose early the following morning and, with bags packed, caught a cab to Euston station. Boarded the eight thirty train to Shrewsbury and arriving three hours later. After a light meal and a coffee at the station, Michael hired a car and they set off for the Welsh border. The trip to Michael's home in Llandyssil was 27 miles, around forty five minutes away.

They crossed the border from England into Wales at the village of Middletown, then travelled on to Trewern and the town of Welshpool. Billie was enthralled by the rolling hills of the countryside saying how green and vibrant the landscape was, in comparison to the barren pastures of Australia. Turning left off the main road they drove over the River Severn, a river Michael told Billie that he and his friends used to swim in when he they were kids. They turned right and then left under Montgomery station bridge. They were now just five minutes away from Llandyssil. Billie found the narrow, twisting roads a little scary but laughed them off as an experience not to be forgotten.

On the outskirts of the village, they drove up a steep incline. On their left was the cemetery and just beyond that on the right was Michael's home. The stone built cottage stood back from the road, they passed it going another thirty yards and pulled into a small layby. Billie leaned over and gave Michael a peck on the cheek and got out of the car. They left their baggage for now and walked back towards the picket fence that Michael had painted many times before. For a moment Michael stood and looked at the home where he had spent his childhood. He felt a tightening in his chest as he reached for Billie's hand. Michael swung open the garden gate and they stepped onto the gravel path leading to the porch. In ten steps they had reached the front door. Squeezing Billie's hand, Michael reached for the brass horseshoe that hung from the door and knocked.

Megan had woken early that morning. According to Michael's telegram, that lay on the kitchen table he would be home that day. Although it said to expect him on Wednesday 15th September, no specific time was stated. All in all, it had been a busy two weeks, what with the wedding and Michael coming home.

The wedding arrangements had been taken care of, mainly by Nancy, the bride's mother. The couple were to be married in the village church, then the wedding party would gather at the Upper House pub to socialise and have a few drinks before the wedding reception. Like most of the farming community thereabouts, the wedding reception would take place at the bride's family home. A reception for forty guests had been prepared. They would be seated to dine and rise to toast the well-being of the bride and groom. Various modes of transport had been arranged for guests to travel to and from the bride's family home. Some guests, no doubt, would be spending the night in hay barns.

Having guests from Australia and America attending her daughter's wedding would be a big plus for Nancy's family. Taking their image in the locality a rung higher than it already was, almost into the realms of the gentry, well at least in Nancy's mind. Notwithstanding the prestige that having a Qantas airline pilot as a relative, through marriage, would bring. She had contacted the County Times about the forthcoming wedding, so it should read well in the newspapers. She was a little up-herself, Megan privately thought, but she was all right and clearly thought the world of her son.

The sleeping arrangements of Michael and Billie were of particular concern to Megan. She really couldn't give a fig about who Michael was bringing home with him, even if she was a jezebel, at least he would be home. Billie couldn't possibly sleep with Michael under the same roof, Megan smiled to herself, whatever would people say? The house had been cleaned and swept within an inch of its life. Dirty and clean dishes had all been washed and put away again. Now all Megan could do was to wait. The knock at the door startled her. She took a deep breath. For a moment she hesitated, then gathering herself, went to open it. Michael stood in front of her, his smile melting her heart as he reached and lifted her clear off the ground and swung her around. Megan's muffled sobs were lost in their meeting; incoherent words spilling from her lips were leaving her breathless. She was a nervous wreck as she ushered them both inside, giving Michael another hug, before letting him go.

"Mum, I would like to introduce you to Billie, my lady friend." Billie stood and held out her hand.

"Billie, this is my mother."

"I am so pleased to meet you Mrs Jones, Michael has told me all about you."

"You must be something special." Megan said, still not believing her son was home.

"Please come and sit down, the kettle has been on the boil for most of the morning. Can I get you a both a cup of tea?"

"That would be lovely, thank you."

"Milk and sugar?" Megan asked.

For the next hour they laughed, talked and cried. Sometimes it was all a little too much for Megan, especially when she spoke of Michael's father. Seeing Megan in distress prompted Billie to suggest that she take a walk in the garden so that the two could talk in private. But through her tears, Megan had insisted Billie stay, saying that as she was her son's love and had every right to hear of his father's passing. Perhaps Michael could take Billie to the cemetery to introduce her to his father? A little later Michael did what his mother had suggested.

Across the road from Michael's family home, a five foot high stone boundary wall encircled the souls that were buried within. Thirty yards further down, the entrance to the cemetery had a stone arch and a pair of low gates, wide enough to accommodate the passing of a coffin and its bearers with a foot on each side to spare. As Michael and Billie entered, crows gave flight from between the gravestones, dispersing in various directions; some flying high and landing in horse chestnut trees and others on the ruins of the old church, long abandoned since a new one had been built many years before. One crow rose but three feet, settling on a large leaning tombstone, its black head turning with eyes that burned into those who dared to trespass upon their dominion.

Fresh dahlias and gypsophila lay on the grave where Michael's mother had told him he would find his father. He stood with Billie side by side, the fingers of their hands threading through each other's. For a few moments there was no need for words.

"Hello, Mr Jones, I'm Billie. Very pleased to meet you. Michael's told me so much about you and I think we will get on just fine. So, I have been wondering … would you mind terribly if I were to call you Bill? I know it may seem improper to do so, but I'd like that…now I'll leave you in the company of your son as he has a lot to say." Michael glanced at Billie and as he squeezed her hand, she let go, turned and without looking back, walked through the stone arch, out onto the road and out of sight.

Michael spent half an hour talking to his father, telling him how much he was admired and loved and of the man, his father … who had done and seen so much.

He talked of his time in the war stopping every now and again to ask his father questions about his time in his war. It didn't matter that he got no answer, just to ask the question was satisfying enough. He told him of his life in Australia and his love for the lady who'd just introduced herself. He talked of his mother, his sisters and brother, the wedding, Sam, Joe and Pageant and the deep sadness that parting always brings.

Later that afternoon Sam, Grace and Jimmy arrived in the village, stopping outside Sam's family home, a fifteen minute walk from Megan's house.

It had been a number of years since Sam had been home, the last time when he married Grace. It was an emotional greeting. His mother Violet failed in holding back tears that involuntarily flowed down her cheeks. Eventually she ushered them from the doorstep and into the house, where she opened a cupboard door to retrieve an expensive bottle of red wine, a prize she had won in a Christmas raffle the previous year. Emotions were still high as Jim, Sam's father, beckoned young Jimmy, taking him to see his ferrets. He explained how they were used to catch meadow beef, referring to rabbits, two of which were hanging up on his outside shed door. Jimmy told his grandfather the only rabbits he had ever seen were in cages and that they were white.

Two hours later, a black Austin drove past Megan's home and parked behind Michael's car. As Michael looked through the window he called to Billie,

"I think you'd better open the front door." Billie looked confused but did not question Michael's request.

On opening the door, she squealed with delight not believing her eyes. There at the end of the garden path stood her parents and brother.

"My God, my God, Michael didn't tell me." For a moment she froze then ran up the path and into the arms of Joe and Pageant. She didn't have enough arms to hold them both and held them as much out of joy as she did for fear of falling. Michael and Megan watched from the doorway. Everyone except Billie knew that they were coming, they had travelled on the same flight as Sam and Grace, spending a few hours in Shrewsbury, before travelling the last few miles. As well as coming to meet Michael and his family, Joe and Pageant would be visiting relatives in the midlands who they had not seen since first emigrating to America over twenty years earlier. They wouldn't be going to the wedding but were to spend the next two nights at Michael's home before travelling to Birmingham early on Saturday morning.

Billie was overjoyed to see her family and Michael, having never met them, soon fell into their pattern of talk. It soon felt like he'd known them for a long time, no doubt Sam's description of them in his letters had something to do with that. Pageant had liked Michael immediately, before he'd even spoken a word. He was tall, dark and handsome, someone she would have chosen herself for a son-in-law. For years she had worried about her daughter. There had been a big change in her character when she came home from Hawaii. She became distant, and somehow distracted, on a different level. Pageant had often wanted to ask what had happened there but didn't. The only truth she could find was what she had read in the newspapers. It was all a long time ago now and the moment had passed but still she wondered. Joe had no fears for Billie's future. He knew that whatever happened from now on, his daughter would be with someone who would look after her.

Before the day had ended, the gathering of the clan was almost complete when Sam and Grace, along with his parents and Jimmy called by. But there were two people missing. Early that day Michael had taken Billie in the car to meet someone special. He had told her stories of his grandparents, Jessie and Albert, and of how his mother, at the age of fifteen had become acquainted with them. Michael had written to his grandmother to tell of his impending visit and as old as she was, her mind was sharp and she wanted above all else to meet Michael's lady. Albert suffered from dementia and didn't know who anyone was, but he still talked with great clarity of days long past. Later, Michael brought his grandparents to Megan's, drinking tea, eating cake and talking of how things used to be. Jessie and Megan spoke of Sam and Michael when they were children, embarrassing both with talk of the mischievous things that each of them got up to. For Sam and Michael, it was a memorable gathering and for everyone else, an insight into the lives of two boys, although years apart in age, who through their own endeavours, became men.

A little later Michael and Billie took his grandparents' home. Albert wouldn't be attending the wedding, so Jessie had arranged for someone from the village to look after him for the few hours she would be away. She told Billie she would not have missed the wedding for the world. That first night Michael stayed with his grandmother, it had been a long day, but he wasn't tired. Maybe travelling time had something to do with that.

For the next two days Michael and Billie spent some time with his brother, sisters and their families, so more introductions were called for. The night before the big day, Sam, Joe, Michael and Billie went to the pub for a drink. They hadn't been in long when Michael's Uncle David, the local blacksmith, walked through the door. The drinks flowed. Many locals had heard of Sam and Michael's homecoming and took the chance to greet them. Handshakes and questions came one after the other. There was talk of old times and of the future, of Michael's flying and Billie's experiences nursing after the D-Day Landings. People wanted to know all about New York and the way of life there. One local said that they had an aunty living in Brooklyn, Michael smiled and told the lady that a lot of people lived in Brooklyn.

At closing time, the family walked to their allocated homes and lay in their allocated beds. Billie accompanied her father to Megan's, Michael to his Gran's and Sam to his parents' home. By the time Michael had left his Gran's and arrived home the following morning, Joe Pageant and Alan had already left.

"Good morning, Michael, I hope you slept well? Have you had breakfast?" his mother reached up and stroked his face giving, him a quick peck on the cheek.

"Yes, to both questions. I slept like the proverbial log and have had two boiled eggs and soldiers that Gran put on the table for me." Michael asked about Joe and Pageant's departure, saying that he was sorry to have missed them.

"Billie was up early to see them off … They seem like a lovely couple. As it was still early, I told Billie to go back to bed," Megan glanced at a clock that hung on the kitchen wall.

"My goodness, that was an hour ago. Go up and see what she wants for breakfast." Michael climbed the stairs and knocked on Billie's bedroom door.

"Is that you Michael? Come in." On opening the door, he found Billie still in bed.

"How did you sleep?" He asked with a smile and in a manner that suggested she may well have had just a little too much to drink the night before.

"I slept really well, but another couple of hours in here would be fine, if you'd care to join me."

"As tempting as the offer is, I'm afraid you must get up. We have to be at the church at eleven thirty."

"I know," she said, flinging the blankets to one side and stepping onto a blue rug at the side of her bed. She had little on and looked very inviting.

"Haven't we got time to…?"

"No, we haven't," said Michael, as she moved provocatively toward him. She bit her bottom lip and wrinkled her nose as he gave her a kiss and walked out of the room.

There were nudges and whispers as the Jones family walked into church. It seemed that the entire village had turned out to see the bride, with most gathered outside. Michael looked around, all the pretty young, single ladies were dressed in their finest clothes, but none looked as fine as the lady sitting next to him.

For Billie, it was an experience unlike any other. She had been to weddings before, but never in the company of a man that loved her. This was where her Uncle Sam and Aunt Grace were married and Michael's parents. Megan had told her about the wedding ring she wore, given to her not by Michael's father, but by Michael Gill, the Irish man whose name was passed on to the man by her side. It was Megan's story that brought a lump to Billie's throat and a tear to her eye as she watched a new bride walk down the aisle; she so wished that it was her.

Meanwhile, back at the farm, preparations were being made to receive the guests that would be arriving. There was a hum of expectancy as the last piece of cutlery was being placed and the flowers arranged according to Nancy's instructions. Outside, the local Young Farmers Club members had been set to work putting up banners congratulating the happy couple and painting much the same on the road leading to the farm. They were dressed in white dairy coats and had formed an arch outside the church, ready to hold long handled hay pickles above the heads of the bride and groom as they walked through clouds of confetti.

After the speeches and toasts, the reading of telegrams and the general banter associated with weddings, the invited guests mingled, complimenting each other on whatever reason they needed complimenting on. Michael and Billie went outside. In the farmyard, young men were sitting on bales of hay drinking cider, talking about which bridesmaid they would like to know better. Old men, drinking stout and whisky, were discussing the price of cattle in the previous Monday's market, and older women sat, supping port and sherry, talking of, amongst other things, the death of Mary Thomas who had passed away suddenly the previous week.

As they looked at the surrounding landscape of fields and woods, Billie pointed.

"What is that?" Michael followed her pointed finger."

"Montgomery town hill."

"And the thing stuck on the top of it?"

"The Monument. It's dedicated to men of the town and surrounding villages who died in the First and Second World War. I'll take you there before we leave, but before that, we'll drive to the coast." Billie smiled.

"Can I have you all to myself?"

"For the whole day." Michael said, giving her a tap on the bum.

In the early evening and with all gratitude and thanks expressed to all concerned, Michael took home his gran and mother. Albert was at home being looked after by a neighbour who had told Jessie to enjoy herself and not to hurry back. After dropping Jessie off, Michael and his mother walked on. Michael told her of his plan to take Billie to Aberystwyth the following day.

"That's nice," she said, "and while you're about it, why don't you stay the night? Goodness knows you two haven't spent much time together since you've been home…"

"Mum, if you don't go to heaven, I'll have something to say about it."

"Well, you're young, and spending time together in the kitchen is not quite the same thing is it." She smiled. "I have been there with your father," she paused, "haven't I?"

Billie was up early. Megan could see the bounce in this lady that had stolen her son's heart. "If I were to die tomorrow," she thought, "I'd be quite content."

"Mrs Jones you really are something. I don't know how to thank you. I love your son more than I can say."

"Then that makes two of us." They talked until Michael arrived, and, unashamedly, Billie kissed Megan on the brow as they said their goodbyes.

"You're an angel."

"Not yet, I still have things to do."

33

It started to rain as Michael drove along the seafront town of Aberystwyth. Stopping outside The Pier Hotel, he helped Billie get out of the car. The rain was intermittent, but they still got wet as they rushed across the road to the railings that fronted the sea. There were few people on the promenade as Billie held the cold iron railing and looked out beyond the crashing waves, breathing in the salted air and savouring the moment.

"Is Ireland just across the water, Michael?"

"Yes, about 160 miles or so."

"A lot of Americans came from Ireland."

"A long time ago, Billie. Now come on, we're getting soaked."

In the hotel lobby they shook themselves and carried their cases to the reception desk. On the second floor, in a room that looked over the sea they made love, then went for a shower. Soon after, the rain stopped, and the sun came out. The temperature had risen to make it a pleasant day. They walked the full length of the promenade, had an ice cream on the pier, even spent a shilling in the arcade, rolling pennies in the hope of winning a teddy bear. With no luck, Michael bought one.

"Well worth the money," he thought.

They walked miles through the town, visiting the castle and climbing Constitution Hill, eating fish and chips and in general, enjoying each other's company.

"By the way, what name did you book us under when you signed the register?" Billie giggled as she raised herself on one elbow as they lay on the bed, fully clothed, as she posed the question.

"Mr and Mrs Jones," Michael said with a smile, "what else?"

After a night of disbanded bed sheets, pillow fights, scattered clothes and acts of mutual consent, they fell asleep in each other's arms, not getting up until the morning light and Michael's watch telling them to do so. They left Aberystwyth and headed for home. Two miles from the village of Abermule, Michael suggested they call at the garage for petrol. On the garage forecourt, Michael got out of the car just as a young lad approached.

"Could you fill her up please?" Michael paused. "Is Walter here?" The lad took a curious look at the stranger.

"He's inside," he said, nodding toward the open doors of the garage. Michael beckoned Billie. As they walked in a man in blue overalls with his head under the bonnet of a Morris Minor looked up.

"Good God, is that you Michael?" With a wide smile and an oily rag, Walter reached out, and shook Michael's hand. "I heard you were home. It's grand to see you again after all this time."

"It's grand to see you too, Walter. You're right, it has been a very long time."

"And this must be the American lady you›ve brought over? I've heard all about you," he said smiling. He looked at his hand.

"I won't shake yours, but I'm pleased to meet you."

"Hello Mr Corfield, pleased to meet you too. Is this where you once worked, Michael?" Billie asked.

"It is," Michael answered.

Walter offered them a cup of tea and they talked for a while. As Michael paid for the petrol, Walter picked up a half inch spanner and handed it to him.

"Take it as a keepsake, Michael; It' will remind you where you come from." Michael was taken back by Walters thinking and, shaking his head, he thanked him for the gesture. As Michael drove home, he pondered, accepting the fact that he would likely never see Walter again.

After an early lunch Megan had been for a walk to see Jessie and had just got home when Michael and Billie arrived. They told her about their visit to the coast and that they had called at Abermule garage to see Walter.

"So, what have you in mind for this afternoon?" Megan asked, clearing the kitchen table.

"We'll visit the graveyard again. I'd like to introduce Billie to the people who had once walked the roads and fields of the area. Then a long walk to the town hill. I want to show her Montgomeryshire from a vantage point that's as good as any."

For the second time they walked under the stone arch of the cemetery and once again with their squawking, the crows rose into the air. Pausing by his father's grave Michael said 'hello'. Close by was the headstone of Michael Gill. He had explained to Billie the significance of this man to his family, and felt it was meaningful for her to see where he and the rest were buried. He showed her the graves of Jack and Mavis and of other locals who Michael had mentioned were all part of his childhood at one time or another. He spread his arms encompassing the whole cemetery, explaining that in such a place, all of these people were important; they were all once wheels within wheels of this small community.

After saying their farewells to the inhabitants of the cemetery, they carried on up the lane, climbing the steep, winding track that was hardly wide enough to take a horse and cart. Once on flatter ground they bore left, through a gate and onto open ground. From here, they walked across fields, following sheep tracks through gorse bushes and grassland. All the time their objective was getting closer. At last, they stood in the shadow of the monument… both looking onto the floor of the Severn Valley below. They gazed in silence.

Michael read out the names of those who had died in both wars from a list on the sides the monument. He knew of some from the first war, and a great number who had fought in the second. It was a poignant moment for both of them, especially for Michael as his father would have fought, laughed and probably cried with some of the men named. Turning to Billie, he ushered her to sit on the plinth of the monument and reached into his pocket. He brought out a small box, opened it and took out a ring. Billie gasped and began to cry as Michael held her hand and slipped the silver band onto her ring finger. Through her tears she saw, set in sterling, an Australian black opal.

"Yes, yes, yes." Billie screamed as she flung her arms around him.

"I will marry you."

"I haven't asked you yet, and I… I haven't asked your father either."

"You're not marrying him, Michael," Billie squealed as Michael lifted her and swung her around. After a few moments, Michael took a deep breath.

"I'm going to say a few things and I don't want you to interrupt me."

Billie nodded.

"I'd like us to be married in Brisbane and, for the time being, I think we should live there close to your work; I can easily get a transfer. As for the rest of our lives, we can live it as fast or as slow as we like. The world is ours, Billie, and whatever cards we're dealt, we will make it through and love each other until hell freezes over."

Billie looked her man in the eyes.

"I have nothing to add to that."

THE END

www.ingramcontent.com/pod-product-compliance
Lightning Source LLC
Chambersburg PA
CBHW071401200726
48294CB00002B/268

9 781805 414766